Still Breathing?

By August Smith

1969.

The tyres threw mud and gravel at me as they sped off into the night. I watched the tail lights disappear then it was total blackness. I could only feel my two children as they whimpered and clung to me, their hopeless mother who had taken them from hell to a murkier hell. I would heave this stone around in my heart all my life.

Darkness thickened and congealed around us on the moor. How could I gather the shards of my soul together and continue after what I had just done? I was lost in the dark with no way out.

The rain was soaking us again. I had no clue as to where I was. I felt sodden grass and dead bracken through my worn shoes, it was all around like quicksand sucking at my feet. I was sinking into forlorn hopelessness and pulling my innocent children down with me. The life I had run away from seemed luxury compared to this. Strain sat on my shoulders like a sack of wet cement. But I could never go back.

I was frantically working on keened instinct, this was the start of my fragile hunted freedom. I knew I would never be completely free. I tensed every fighting muscle for this is what I was doing. Battling for my children's future.

I stood afraid and erect like a struck match. The baby clung to me for warmth and security I could not give. I felt stabbed by the discipline of listening for danger in the dark. Gradually, my eyes adjusted to the blackness and I saw a little of my surroundings. There were sheep staring at me in surprise, their curious baas frightening Sarah as one, two then many noisily made their way towards us. I took a few sodden steps at them and they wobbled into little runs to safety, losing interest now they knew I was not the shepherd with food. They put their heavy heads down to nibble in the task that was their life. A dull light started to show in what I supposed must be the east. The sun was coming up although it was hidden by milky grey clouds, thick and heavy with water. Sarah, not yet two, wanted a wee, she was hungry, drenched and desolate. I had a packet of Farley's Rusks in the bags but had to find them first. I peered around. The grey dawn was showing me high hills all dotted with sheep and vast, climbing lines of dry stone walls. I was quite high up myself, the land fell away steeply. That is where I saw our bags, at the bottom of the hill, where they had been callously thrown. One was gaping open spewing its impoverished contents across reeds and dung.

I wedged Ben between two tussocks of thick grass so he wouldn't roll downhill. Sadistic east winds fluffed our hair and slapped our cheeks.

'Stay here Sarah, look after our baby whilst mammy gets our stuff.' She wasn't happy but nodded, her maternal instinct already showing as it did in all females no matter how young. She sat beside Ben and sucked at her old teddy-bear's ear, for once not the wettest thing we had.

I teetered and slid towards our only possessions. It was slippery as my feet involuntarily gathered momentum jogging me faster and faster towards the bin bags. My teeth clanked and my brain rattled inside my skull. I had no control of my legs as they thumped repeatedly downhill. It was almost a relief when I caught my thigh on a jagged rock and fell hitting my head on a series of outcrops with sharp edges. Momentarily stunned, I realised I was rolling out of control, banging and crashing, my arms flaying, my mouth filled with sheep dung and the metallic taste of blood. I stopped much further down than the bags. The light was almost full now as I looked up to where my children waited. I thanked God I was not knocked out. My shoulder hurt as I pushed myself up, blood trickled from both knees and my hands were scratched and torn. I had nettle stings on nettle stings. It was only the power of being a mother that pushed me on to stumble up and along towards saving our pitiful possessions.

The land was steep, each unsure step pulling at my calf muscles, the pain seared through me from everywhere. My whole body sang with agony but I had to surge through it to get to the top. I heaved myself gradually up, grabbing onto the very rocks that had attacked me. I found a blue Babygro and two towelling nappies lying in dung and dead thistles. I pushed them under my jumper before gathering up the bags in one hand using the other to grab onto anything I could find. I lay down for a moment hugging my bundles to me and let the tears come as my chest heaved and shuddered. I had to get this stuff up before Sarah saw how weak I was. The rain had eased but all around me was soaked through. With strength I did not know I had I pushed on, quickened by lusty baby cries and big black crows cawing raucously and flapping great wings seeming to land where my children were.

I'd heard of rooks and crows picking the eyes from lambs, Ben was so tiny, he had no defence. The sloshing gallop of my own blood in my strained ears, my breath rasping, tearing my throat pushed my sore body upwards. I felt like I'd been tipped out of a sack.

Panic clawed at my empty stomach and raging brain. I imagined Ben eyeless and sightless as he screamed on with more and more urgency. Sarah squealed.

The determination of all mothers through the ages swamped into my blood to quicken my fumbling efforts into what I was afraid to find. Each step slipped on wet mud or grass, each grip onto thick sedge or heather cut into my hands but I ignored it all. My progress was painfully slow, each time I looked up I saw large black wings swooping. My ears filled with louder and louder raucous cawing. A slick of terror tore through every cell.

At last my head was above the edge of the hill and I was able to toss the bags to safety. My brain was zig zagging like a frightened rabbit. A monumental pull on tussocks of sharp needled sedges flopped me to the top. Four big crows flew away from my children and I saw Sarah's terrified eyes widen with relief.

'Nasty birds tried to eat Ben mammy!' She cried.

I dashed towards him and saw teddy Humph lying upside down on top of him.

'I throwed Humph at big birds mammy.' She was frozen in her fear. Ben was wailing but unhurt. I drew him close, the wet was through to his skin. He stank to high heavens. I rifled clumsily through the bin bags. Using a clean nappy to dry him and clean his bottom, I struggled with his flaying arms and screaming as the cold hit his naked body. When he had a dry Babygro and dry nappy I snuggled him in to breast feed and warm him. Sarah watched wide eyed. I felt like my brain had been swivelled one way and my body another. I had to shut my eyes against the pain of pulled muscles, cuts and bashes. The only heat I felt was from my nettle rashes now bumping up and stinging like mad.

'Me want chucky egg now mammy.' My heart melted as I looked at her scared yet accepting face. How could I have done this to her? Taken away her home and her favourite breakfast. 'I have rusks for you darling. You love those don't you?'

I rifled for the box, the corners were crumpled in and bits of dead bracken stuck to the wet cardboard. I handed her the big round baby biscuit. Only four left. She took it and put it to her mouth.

'Too hard mammy, me want milk in Tommy Tippee cup.' I delved to the bottom of our scant belongings, the cup was there but it was empty.

'We will get water soon.'

She looked around. 'No taps mammy, no sinks.'

My eyes scoured the dull hills and sheep and I strained my ears. There was a slight tinkle to my right. 'Let's find some magic water, maybe fairies will be drinking there.'

She had to walk, her little legs in damp tights protruding from her wet red coat, her small hands blue and stiff as they gripped her rusk and cup. She followed me as I hugged the baby close with one arm and heaved at the plastic bags with the other. I had to look down to avoid the rock outcrops and holes. She fell many times. My useless arms full and aching with the baby and our belongings. My bruised body was stiffening with injury. Cold alarm slammed into my chest.

'Ups a daisy! Show me how big you are! Good girl!'

Her sucked biscuit hit the ground many times as we made slow progress toward the water noise but I could do nothing about it.

We reached a gushing stream tumbling over rocks, I knew it would be fresh because of the rain. Gripping the baby, I held the pink plastic cup under the stream of fresh water trying not to tumble. I passed it to Sarah.

'It funny water mammy, me want from tap at Sarah's house. Me want Sarah's house.' She began to cry and it broke my heart. What had I done? My children were soaked and cold, one of them was hungry, we had nowhere to go and I was bone weary. I could never go back, I would be hiding from what I had done for the rest of my life.

I eased the sobbing body of my first child towards me, smudging my sticky blood onto her coat. 'Shush, we will frighten the fairies away. They need a drink too and have to leave their little houses in the roots of trees to find better things. Maybe they need a new house, just like you.' She calmed as she thought about this and took a sip.

'Me like fairy water. Me want to see fairies.'

'We must watch quietly then, and drink it all up.' My cuts and scratches stung as I tried to clean them in the running stream. I had never been so cold and miserable.

When she had finished I popped the tiny bits of rusk she had left into my own mouth then dipped the baby cup again and gulped two cups down hoping it would be enough to keep my milk flowing. I filled it again, pressed the lid down and told Sarah to carry it which she did carefully putting it to Humph's cross stitch mouth every now and then. The squelching of moss through my thin shoes and the crack of twigs seemed so loud. I feared the whole world would hear that and the banging in my chest. They would all know what crime I had committed.

When we stood up I looked about. Maybe I should stick to this half made road and walk to Harrogate. The road wound and snaked, no cars had come by. It was just us and the sheep.

I trudged on for hours under a pall of clouds stopping to rest or change the aching baby carrying arm with the bin bag dragging arm. The rain was light now and clung to my thin coat. Our fair hair looked like it had a net of dew. We made a game of shaking the diamonds away and Sarah seemed happy for a while. My feet squelched and slipped. My hands grew stiff trying to hold on to my babies, my bin bags, my life. The twisted knot in my stomach grew heavier and more gnarled.

We drank our fairy water and refilled the cup at the many streams. It was beautiful here, despite the mist and wet, grey sock sky. I did not know such a place existed. I had never been out of Newcastle or the woods my dad had worked in. Exhaustion sank into my bones so that I had to lie down and try to get a little sleep. It was impossible with wet ground, a squirming baby and a tired, cold toddler. My adrenaline levels were so high that my heart beat furiously as my mind raced. We had to press on. The hours dragged with our trudge, Sarah ate another rusk and I the soggy remains. Misery dragged at my feet and it was becoming harder and harder to think of inspiring things to say to the now fractious Sarah. I promised her glimpses of bunnies, soft grey doves and fairy homes. We saw none of these but she still believed we would. I told her that the sheep had babies in their tummies and soon we would see tiny lambs drinking milk just like Ben. She looked at my chest and I could see she was wondering how the lambs would get there. I did not have the energy to explain any more. There was a tiny gap in the clouds and the sun came out for about six minutes. It brought cheer to my sore heart and Sarah sang 'The sun has got his hat on. Hip hip hip hooray.' I joined in thankful we could see further for a bit. The sparkles lit the rain on bilberry bushes, thickly covering acres of moorland. I had collected cans of these in autumn for my mum to make bilberry pie. I would come home with black fingers and mouth, so full of fruit and an aching back from bending to these low bushes. Now in late March they were bare. My tummy rumbled. Digestive juices arrived with nothing to digest making an acid feeling in my gut.

I looked down the hill. The sun reflected and highlighted some tumbling building but it was too far to make it out. With new vigour I stepped closer towards the cream stone. I did not know what it was but it might give us shelter. Black clouds swallowed a sun too weak to fight back. The wind strengthened, tearing at our clothes, we had to breathe in snatched gulps.

I was sodden with wind lashed despondency.

When my feet would not carry my sore and bleeding limbs another yard I looked up to see piles of half fallen stones. This seemed to have been some abbey.

There was no roof, the ecclesiastical arches that once held doors and windows were empty. The wind blew through the long forgotten ghostly assembly of master crafted stonework. There was no shelter here but I could walk no further. I looked about for a solid bit of wall that we could at least take a bit of relief from the wind and the rain which I could see was racing in with it. There had been peace here, I could feel it. Now I only brought anguish and desolation to add to the history of centuries. Sarah and I climbed across piles of fallen stones so heavy I wondered if they had killed some-one as they tumbled. I ushered Sarah around trying to look cheerful as I dragged myself and Ben into a corner. It would have done but it was in the teeth of the wind. We would have darted out if we had the energy but instead we just shuffled. Sarah disappeared for a moment, I could not keep the fear from my voice.

'Sarah!'

She called back but it sounded muffled yet had an echo.

'Here mammy. Sarah in dirty old house.' I turned towards the noise and rushed as hard as my exhaustion would allow me. Ben jiggled in my arms and my cut hands were numbed into a skeletal grip around the bags as they banged around my knees. She was down some sort of underground place. I felt calmness as the damp smell hit my nostrils. Looking up I saw the long gone majesty from the vaulted ceiling. It was dull in here but not dark. The reason was a tumbled down chimney opening, the fireplace long ago unused but it gave the place some light.

'Sarah? Where are you pet?' I tried to keep panic from my voice. She appeared round a bend I would not have known was there. My eyes adjusted to what she could see.

'Mammy, puppies live here, they showed me.' She said excitedly.

I felt like there was some-one there so I put my fingers to my lips. Then said a tense and quiet 'Hello?' There was no reply but there was a feeling.

'Is anyone here?' My voice came out cracked. There was only the wind. I was so exhausted that I had to tell myself it was only the wind, only the wind. But I wasn't sure.

'No darling, no puppies live here, but maybe we can.'

'Sarah sawed them mammy. They runned away.' She was beaming so I said no more, grateful for anything that gave her hope.

Here it was cold but dry, the wind was just a noise and for that alone I was grateful. The ground was dusty soil, I had to move stones about, at least the ones I could lift, to make a flat surface to lie on. I did not know how much longer my muscles would hold me up.

I peeled the wet clothes off a protesting Sarah, rubbing her shivering body roughly with a dry nappy to get her circulation going. When she was glowing in her rosebud sprigged winceyette nighty and dry socks, I rubbed my hair with the damp terry towelling. In my rush to escape I had not brought anything for myself. I had a duck shaped toilet bag with Sarah's toothbrush and paste and her crocodile shaped pink comb. We would just have to share. I spread my drenched coat over rocks and hoped it would dry. My thin dress was damp and stained but only wet around the neck and the front bit where my coat parted. I unwrapped Ben, peeling him like a revolving apple. He was dry apart from his nappy so I fumbled as I changed then swaddled him. I kissed his plump cheek trying to make him feel loved. The blanket I had wrapped him in was just wet on the outside surface so I gave it a good shake then hung it on the highest upright stone.

'Mammy, it is too light for Sarah's nighty. Me want dungarees and coat on.'

'Come here,' I murmured as I pulled her close. 'I will tell you of all the creatures who sleep during the day because they have been busy through the night, just like we have.'

She did not seem impressed so I tickled Humph's tummy and said. 'Starting with bears.' It began to darken again with heavy rainclouds, the bend in our shelter cutting out the wet. Terror sat in my stomach like a stone but I had to pretend.

Absorbed in stories of striped badgers, pretty mice and jewel eyed tigers, she fell asleep. My daughter had inherited my love of animals but I could never allow her to have a pet after her white rabbit, Thumper who we kept in the hutch in our yard had scratched Ed as he yanked it off her in anger. The rabbit's long claws had scratched his arm and he had wrung its neck viciously there and then, tossing it into the dustbin with only foul swearing for its eulogy.

I could not move my puny warmth away from my babies. I felt like I had been ripped to shreds. I watched the bit of sky from the chimney as it darkened into dusk. Sarah was lost in deep dreams of exhaustion.

I tried to follow her but I was buzzing with guilt and fear as I sifted the night sounds for danger. I was afraid of the deep part of the cellar where the rats had run to, anything could be in there. Anything. Fear hung around me like a cloud covering the horizon of my life, but I could not allow it to affect my children. The wind howled fresh fat rain into the mouth of the cellar. There was scratting and tiny running sounds. I prayed it was mice not rats. I remembered flea ridden rats caught in special traps in the grain-stores and hay-sheds of the farm I played around when I was young. Their bared teeth were yellow and long, their thick tails snakelike and bitten. They carried diseases and would bite my babies. And there was that feeling. It hung there, somewhere in these stones.

When it was light I would flush them all out with a stick, for now I had to stay on watch. My mind felt like a mush of cold mashed potatoes. I had put myself in a cold sphere of solitude. I covered myself and my night time terrors in my damp coat. My spirit writhed; did I have the strength? I was far too scared to sleep. I was chilled and forlorn, looking at bleakness as I listened to the sleepy breathing of the tiny bodies beside me. I had brought them into the world with nothing to give them. I owned only one thing.

My famished soul.

My mind whirled and kept going back to last night and what I had done. It all played out like some horrible film I could not escape from.

Even God knew that I had the right to kill him. Especially that night.

I had held my poor weapon above my head. The frying pan was so heavy but it was all I had. Could I crash it down on his head as it lolled in his drink induced stupor? He was a thief who was stealing and destroying my soul. My brain flared with the memories of his cruelty making my wrists ache as much as my mind, forcing me to relive the reasons I had to bang his rotten brains out.

As the side of my face was slammed into the cold floor tiles I felt his knee ram into my chest. I tried to focus my wet eyes onto the bottom of the avocado coloured kitchen units but all I could see was the missing wet crust, sucked clean of its butter. My toddler's tea four hours ago. The rough hands grasped my throat and squeezed. It hurt, but it meant I was still alive.

My two babies were in the next room, one snoozing off his breast milk and the other sitting on the floor, her chubby hands determinedly tearing up a mail order catalogue page by page just to hear the rip. This is who I had to fight for.

I saw nothing but red as I struggled for breath. I grabbed him and heaved to try to get him off me. He loved that. A reason to push his thumbs harder into the soft flesh, a justification for the purple marks I would have to hide for a week. He glared into my eyes where he knew I could never hide anything. I shut them tight, screwing them in a bid to hide my desperate thoughts. Even when he hit me making my teeth rattle. He mustn't know about the plan. He must never find out.

Of course, as always, I deserved this attack. I had dared to complain that he had taken our food money and spent it on drink. It would be days of eating rice boiled in packet soup or chips from the sack of potatoes I had dragged up the hill from the farm. It made an even heavier load in the old pushchair squashed between the two babies. But it could never be as heavy as the load in my mind.

I needed to have my head in the sun once more and to do that I had to rid my world of this man. The same man whose hands put a ring on my finger before lunch and choked the hope and life out of me before supper. If I ran away my babies and I would have no home, no little beds and no roof to keep out the rain. He would hunt me down and kill me, he told me many times, his lip cruelly curled, his face pushed into mine as he gripped me roughly. His woman. His property. His to do with as he wished.

How could I do it? I was weak and immature, I knew nothing of the world yet I had to fight my husband....but not in the way that he knew how to fight. I had to find a new way. A way he would know nothing about.

How had I turned from a nature loving little girl running in woodland collecting wild flowers and day dreaming by babbling brooks to this? This was now me, twenty years old with two babies and a violent and cruel husband who resented us all. This was vibrant Newcastle and the swinging 1960s, but it was all lost to me. I was a victim, pushed down into murk and despair but I did not intend to stay that way. How could I gather the strength?

I had to get out yet he held me prisoner with threats of murder. I had to stay alive to protect my babies from him, the other parent responsible for their being. The one who made our lives a cold hell.

'Still breathing?' That was always the signal that his resentful, manic attack on me was finished. The word was not wrapped in caring concern but in mad eyed pleasure that once again he had stopped squeezing just before I passed out. His children needed a mother, so I was allowed to get up, clean up the mess of broken dishes and cold food he had slung across the room at me when I had dared to ask why he was so late.

'Get a scarf on that scrawny neck of yours! I don't want to see your disgrace!' He grunted as he sat at the table and flicked open his racing paper meaning he expected me to re-cook another meal for him before I could put my babies to bed. Everything about him was brutal. The short cut light brown hair, the weasel moustache he tried to grow to hide his thin mean lips. He tried to make up for his lack of height by making sure his muscles showed. His hard marble like brown eyes were always looking for things to explode about.

As always, I had to pour his beer from the bottle with shaking hands and tearful gulps. He was already full of lager, I could tell. He was two hours late for his supper, the meal he insisted was ready the moment he appeared in the door beery and vindictive. I had become more and more creative making cheap meals when he took more and more money from my purse to drink on the way home from the building site where he worked as a joiner.

I used to ask him in the early days to come straight home, to ease my burden of looking after two babies.

'Isn't a working man entitled to a drink after a day's work?' He would sneer. 'Why are you always nagging?' That was on a good day before his look turned from annoyance to malice.

'You'll never find another man to put up with you like I do! Look at you, ugly and scarred, stupid and unable to get on in life. You are a crap mother, always moaning!'

Now I had no nerve to ask anything. Now I was soaked in shame and misery. Now was when I had to find courage. But from where?

I left him drinking and eating to take the babies one by one up the stairs to bathe and settle them for the night. Thank God they were too little to understand. But they would one day. I could not bear that for them.

I lay throbbing with pain beside my twenty two month old daughter Sarah so she could play with my hair as I breast fed Ben, at five months old already showing signs of distress. I traced his curved cheek and gazed into his wide trusting eyes. His tiny velvet fingers squeezed gently in and out at the top of my full breast. He looked so like my mother my heart burst. There was no way I could let him take after his father. What had I birthed them into?

As my mind spun around looking for the way out of my fearful misery that persistent thought came to me again. There is a reason you are alive, there is some-one, somewhere that you have to save. I went into that lulled state, a sort of meditation where I could remember just a tiny bit of before I was born. The beauty, the peace…the vibrant colours and blanketing love. Even when I was little I had this memory of being sent here into my life for a reason, I had some-one to save but who? I thought everyone felt this and when I found out they didn't I kept it to myself. I developed a passion for saving animals as soon as my tiny hands were big enough to cradle thumb size baby field mouse bodies. I braved the prickles of abandoned hedgehogs, the smell of fox cubs and the claws of hurt cats. It was not some wild eyed tabby who was responsible for the inch long white scar above my top lip, but that is what I told every-one, just in case they coaxed the awful truth out of me. I always cared for injured birds or fallen fledglings. It was as if I was practicing for something. We had lived in the tiny bungalow in the country then. Mum was alive and cooking whilst dad, in his job as a forester came home with bronzed back and ever bigger muscles, then with injured mammals when he saw my concern for those in need. They had their one special child when mum was forty and dad forty five. It was a shock when I popped out but mum only lasted until I was fifteen. Her insides were never the same said dad, after a late baby, so when she died I felt it was my fault. My very being grew her death. He had a heart attack after that, his grief caused him so much anxiety. He did his best and loved me but now all the years of outdoor work in north eastern winds and frosts crippled his hands with arthritis and bent his once strong back. If he knew what my husband did to me he would try to give him a good hiding, the same he gave to poachers and log thieves. But that was when he was strong. Now Ed would seriously hurt him, he would have no compunction. In fact he would add it to his image of himself as indestructible. I was thumped out of my reverie as Ed slumped onto the bed beside me, elbowing me along so that I had to carry the children to their own room. I worked slowly, sodden and heavy within the deep sea of my wretchedness.

'Come in for a second!' My head turned as I awkwardly pushed the double pushchair out through the gate of the tatty terrace house that had become my prison. It was Jane, the round cheeked grandmother from next door. The person I tried to keep my screams low for as she sat on the other side of my kitchen wall in the warm loving home she shared with her eighty year old husband of sixty years. I pulled the pushchair into her yard, and she let me leave the door open in the cold March wind so I could watch from her kitchen as she held my hand.

'How are you pet?' I knew she must hear the banging and screaming, the filthy insults and the sudden silence that we never mentioned. It hung between us like a wet grey blanket yet we could not make it real by giving it words. The warmth of her smile was food to my starving soul. I wanted to stay in her pleasing atmosphere of mind forever.

'Fine'. I pulled the worn and bobbled scarf further up my neck as if I were cold, I knew she knew. Eighty years of life could never affect the knowingness between women. I was involved in some secret war that I had no words to describe and was too ashamed to anyway.

'I am here for you Rose.' She smiled, comfortable as a fat hen as she squeezed my fingers. How envious I was of her peace, the love she received and was allowed to give. She had a bloom of contentment on her red cheeks and soft white hair that waved out from beneath her knitted hat. I would never have that bloom. I knew she was a loving soul but she was also an old lady, weak in body and knowledge of the horribleness of some lives.

'You are getting too thin Rose. Where has that pretty smile gone? You need a haircut.' I pushed dry fingers through what used to be my mother's pride and joy, blond curls that bounced and shone under her silver backed brush. Now lank and poor, it was the least of my worries.

She followed me out as I took up the handle of the pushchair with my sleeping baby. From her paper-skinned hand she pushed a half crown into the mitten of my little girl. 'For sweeties when you get to the shops.' She knew and I knew that it would be spent on fresh fruit to supplement the cheap white bread which was all I could afford to buy today. My children had to be fed properly.

'And try to get that twinkle back into those beautiful turquoise eyes!' she called as she waved. 'You deserve to be happy.'

It was Saturday morning and Ed had been out 'seeing a friend about work' which meant he'd be drinking until 2pm and would roll home careless and drunk and wanting a fight. The knot in my stomach tightened as I tottered, trying to hold back the pushchair, down the hill with the pub he was in at the bottom. I walked quicker and quicker so as to lessen the chance that he would see me walk past the window and come out to pull my purse from my pocket and take my last pound to keep drinking.

In the small square of red, blue and white bedding plants the council called a park, I perched on a graffiti ruined bench. Sarah sucked on her orange and ate the grapes that her half a crown bought her. I had to spend it all on her as Ed had taken her money several times, asking 'Has that old bag next door given you money for sweeties Sarah?' At first she had shown it to him proudly not knowing that his next action was to grab it from her tiny fist and rush off to pay for beer that would have him rolling home and nasty. I ate what she left in the hope that some goodness would get back to baby Ben. He woke and I covered my breast with my scarf to feed him hoping no one would accuse me of being indecent. His socks had dropped off, he often only had one on. I watched through my lonely sadness, Sarah pretending to feed Humphrey her adored blond teddy bear, holding him close to her chest. She so wanted to be like me. Please God, never let her be. Everything was down that steep hill from our place, which meant that everything had to be pushed up it too. Just like my life.

When the children were settled again. I shoved off for the leg testing time up the hill to the house that was my miserable jail. It was nice to feel the early spring sun on my legs as I rushed passed the pub windows trying not to see the men or let them see me. I had few clothes to choose from, only the miniskirts and tops I had bought for my office job, when I had been free without knowing what freedom meant.

The depression grew as I neared the terraces of houses where I hated living. The high walls of the yards with paint peeled doors and little coal holes were ugly, like my heart was becoming. I settled the babies on rugs on the floor and cooked the tiny bits of meat and veg as quickly as I could to mash and get into their needy bodies before he came home. I prayed to God that they were not sick.

The door cracked open and as I looked up my head was forced back by a blow from a clenched fist. Both children cried and I ran to them but he pulled me away.

'You filthy whore! How do you think it makes me feel when everyone in the pub rushes to the window to see your legs?'

He threw me to the wall and his fist flew into my chin crashing the side of my head into plaster. 'Parading yourself in front of all the men I drink with. You slut!'

I tried to avoid the rapier thrust of his tongue. I felt mortally wounded and weakened.

'But I was just pushing the babies up the hill.' My impulse to shout my innocence was squashed by exhaustion. I had to become disconnected from this.

'Flashing your legs and making me a laughing stock, you filthy shit.'

'Do you think I was happy when some-one shouted, 'Phoar, I could give that one'...about my wife? Whore!' He blanketed me in a look of pure disgust. 'I am going to start locking you in the house when I go to work!' He watched my look of fear and enjoyed it.

My daughter screamed louder, the baby whimpered. Again I tried to reach them but he twisted my arm behind my back. He grabbed my hair and pulled my head backwards. All I could think of was not letting the children see this so they would think it was normal. Then suddenly he let go and I fell in a heap on the floor, banging my knee against the table leg. I crawled towards them and encircled them in my bruised arms. My spirits fell into a deeper abyss than I had thought existed.

I came downstairs when the children were asleep, Sarah had sucked on Humphrey's ear as she always did when she was upset. I could see he had calmed down to somewhere near reasonable. I had to speak, try to show him that this was a life I would not tolerate.

'I cannot bear this. You must be kinder or I will have to leave.' My words were dangerous I knew but I had to give him the chance to change. I trembled with my terrified daring.

'Oh you want to be dead do you?'

'You wouldn't…the children…and you would go to jail.'

'You know that my best mate Terry is a copper in Carlisle Police force, he knows how to make charges disappear. He has done it before for me. And he knows how to find people who go off and can't be found. So you'd have two of us on your tail if you left. We'd never give up. I would search to the ends of the world to give you what a deserting wife deserved.'

As always, the threat of Terry tore through me like rusty nails. Could he find out what I did when I was eleven? The police were called then, but I was only a child. I wish I had never told Ed how I had got this scar on my lip. This feeling of dread doubled, turning my already heaving stomach to mush.

He looked at me then. 'It would be your fault if I have to kill you. You push me past what any reasonable man can stand. Nagging! Nagging! Nagging! It is all you do!' I tried to hide the shaking but he saw it and was pleased. I started to walk away into the kitchen. His horrid words crunched on.

'If a man who works all week wants a drink and smoke, he is entitled to without a nag. You do not deserve those children.' I flung round, he knew he had hit a nerve. His lips curled in the pleasure of hurting me as he continued. 'Ben is my son, I will not be robbed of the pleasure of taking him to the pub when he is older and teaching him how to be a real man.'

He looked me up and down in disgust.

'My mam will look after them. They'd be better off without you.'

I thought of his mother drinking cooking sherry and smoking as she asked me to wash her hair in the kitchen sink. The feel of the sticky old Tupperware tumbler she gave me to rinse out the washing up liquid that brought the three week old dirt streaming down from her head to the dishes below. The sweat and grease smells joined the overflowing ash trays she had stolen from the pub, and the never emptied cat litter trays. She will never get my precious babies. Never.

He slammed the door after shaking my purse onto the kitchen bench. Thank goodness I had spent it all to feed my children. He stayed out until eleven.

My mind tumbled as much as my sore body as I lay next to his unconscious beer soaked being. I was not living, just hoping to live. Only I held the key but would I have the courage to turn it? How had I got here? To this hell on Earth.

'Do you Rose, take this man Edward…?

'Well no actually! I don't want him. I know he is not what I want in a husband but I am too ashamed of my pregnancy to stay single.' That is the reply I wanted to give the priest as I stood in my home-made dress in the December cold church.

But I said 'I do.' Even though I didn't. I hoped my fears were unjustified, after all he was such a precise and creative carpenter producing tip top work in houses and shops. He would at least always have some-one paying for his good work. He had made and fitted a wonderful melamine kitchen in the latest shade of avocado green, into the house we had bought from the son of an old lady who had died in the bedroom we would sleep in. He had also moved the bathroom upstairs from downstairs. He had high standards and I took hope in that fact. Surely he would be a good father to the mite who was growing in secret inside me. I had only a hint of his selfishness then.

So it was as my husband said; my fault….all my fault.

I stiffened as he pushed clumsily off the bed nude as a worm, stumbled to the wardrobe, opened the door and urinated into the corner where my pitiful few clothes were. He had done this before. I waited until he sank once more into alcohol oblivion before I got up, went down for the bucket and disinfectant to begin the 2 am clean. The second that month.

I could not stand the cold winds of my life. At this moment I had nowhere to go. No money and no job. It would be hard. I imagined my life as a long winding river snaking through the ages of a woman. I was only twenty miles along. The really hard bit, rocky and crashing with whirlpools and falls would be awful for five or six miles and then I would sail free for the rest of my life, perhaps another sixty years. The terrifying rapids had to be braved. It would be worth it. Right now I was stuck in the soul sucking mud on an unfriendly, threatening riverbank but I would have to find the strength to push off, handle the sharp rocks and crashing waters before the sun and calm could sail us away. How would I get the strength?

In the early days, I rang the police twice, they wouldn't come. Their reply made me even more alone. 'You are married to him, if he kills you we can do something…not until.' Did they put the phone down and think about a woman in need of protection, of what fist might be slamming into her now? Or did they stir more sugar into their tea and look at the clock trying to move it on until home-time.

There was a lull of a few days before the next explosion of threats and violence. I could see that Sarah was growing hungry so I emptied the twin tub washing machine into the sink, the baby clothes were all on the line. The pump stalled and I had to jiggle the big machine to start it again. One caster was loose causing me to struggle when I had to push it back into its place beneath the kitchen bench.

I had hidden a ten shilling note between the tea box and its inner packet, confident that my hiding place for the means to feed my children would not be discovered. I settled the baby into the pushchair and held the hand of my toddler.

'We are off to the corner shop to buy some eggs for our tea. This was enough to excite Sarah who loved the ritual of making soldiers for her chucky egg. I stopped at the kitchen cupboard to retrieve the ten shilling note but it was gone. I tore the cardboard apart in frantic searching hope. He had worked it out. It would be in the till of the pub by now. I cried.

'No, he has taken our food money and drunk it.' I shouted through my frustration. I saw Sarah's lips quiver at my distress so I sniffed back the tears to cheer her up. I emptied my purse on the bench. Just enough to buy a loaf but no eggs. Lost in a stupor of hopelessness I dashed across the road to the corner shop and stood in the small queue that had to wait until the tiny, bespectacled shopkeeper had gossiped with each customer until he knew it all. I listened for a while as the talk went from the weather to why the council might give permission to build on the school playing fields. This was his pet fury.

Sarah was impatient, she began pulling at her blonde hair which bent and flicked as mine once did, so I picked up a cheap cut loaf. 'Could I just pay for this please?' I said pushing in front of the lady with arms folded for the duration.

'Eggs mummy. We want eggs for our tea.'

'No darling. Not today!'

'But you promised.' She pushed Humph's ear into her mouth.

'Do you want eggs or not.' Snapped the shop keeper, angry that his full flow speech of enjoyable indignation had been interrupted.

'No, thank you.' I picked my toddler up to take her away but she turned her face to this shop keeper and said. 'My daddy stealed our food money and drinked it.'

I felt my face crumple with shame and misery. I grabbed the bread and turned to dash with the pushchair through the suddenly staring customers. I could not bear the looks of pity and interest that they had seen a life worse than theirs laid bare.

As I got back to my horrible little yard with the cracked concrete the sky darkened. When I'd settled the children indoors and given Sarah some toast, I noticed the rain getting heavier then dashed out to grab their little tops and pants from the washing line. Upstairs, after I hung the damp washing on the cord above the bath I looked out of the window to see Ed, bent against the wet, striding up the road. He looked up at me and I attempted a smile and a little wave of welcome that I did not feel. He scowled and crashed into the yard. I ran downstairs just as he flung the door open. His wet coat pressed to me as he grabbed me by the hair. 'You love seeing me struggling in the rain don't you? Watching me coming in tired from a hard day's work while you are cosy and warm doing nothing here all day' He twisted my head so that he was breathing beery fumes into my mouth. 'Watching for me so you could get your fancy man out of the back door were you?'

'No…I was hanging the washing…you are early.' I hated my whimpering voice.

He let me go then and hung his coat on the door hook. My hair roots stung, my jumper was wet and clinging.

'Aye well, I am early 'cos I got paid off. Hit the foreman when he put me on the worst shuttering job. Thought he could do what he liked with me, but I showed

him…bloody nose is what he is taking home tonight.'
This was the third time he had assaulted a boss. My eyes
closed in hopelessness.

He plonked his angry body on a chair at the table. 'I want
tea….and a sandwich.'

I filled the kettle and took out the bread I had just bought.
Looking in the cupboard, there was no jam or sandwich
spread…nothing except a small scraping of butter with
black toast crumbs clinging to it. I spread this between
two slices and gave it to him. He bit in immediately,
chewed then spit onto the floor before peeling open the
slices.

'What the bloody hell is this?' he stood up and flung the
food into my face. 'There's nowt in the bloody middle!'

'I…everything has run out!'

'Well the bastard shop in only yards away. Too bloody
lazy to go that far to feed your man properly!' He yelled,
his face wide eyed and threatening. My mind was thick
with words that would not form properly.

'I went, but I had no money, you had taken it.'

I would pay for that sentence.

'Ah you mean your secret hoard. The money you hid from
me in the tea so you could buy yourself lipstick and
perfume to tempt other men with! Aye I took that.'

I thought of the drawer upstairs. All that was in was a tiny stub of Rimmel pale pink lipstick I had bought three years before when I was working, and an empty bottle that once held 'Joy de Vivre' cologne. I kept them both to remind me of a time when I was only responsible for myself. I often removed the lid from the bottle and tried to breathe in the fading smell of femininity and freedom.

'It was to feed our children!' I was brave but knew his fists would knock that out of me. He pushed back the chair and towered over me. 'Are you saying that I do not provide for my family?'

'You spend too much on drink. Sarah needs shoes and the baby is growing out of his Babygros.'

'You sod. You nasty piece of work. I go out all day banging hammers to feed a lazy stay at home wife and two ungrateful brats and you begrudge me a drink after work!'

Full backhand. Grabbed by clothes. Thrown to floor. I was used to it. This sequence was my life. I had to bear it or run. I lay on the floor, sore and apparently accepting. He was strong and I was weak.

He looked down at me, pushed his hand into his pocket and took out his severance pay. He peeled one five pound note off the role and threw it on top of me.

'There! Buy some food you lazy bitch! And make it last the week! I want none of your stupid excuses or empty sandwiches.'

Sarah tried to sink further into her cushion on the floor and sucked harder on the wet ear of her bear as her eyes widened taking it all in with a wisdom beyond her few miserable months on earth.

He honestly thought that he had a good marriage except that his wife nagged.

I was skinned to the bone with misery and hopelessness, my body hardly able to take the desolation it was asked to take.

I couldn't sleep, so charged with anxious despair that the muscles around my heart gripped into violent pain. I could not draw a deep breath. The steel band tightened around my chest. Surely this was a heart attack! But I was so young, I had been so fit, but two babies very close and now this hideous life. Maybe I would die and get out of it that way. But even that was denied to me. I had to stay alive for the two little souls I had brought into this world. I wish I had not.

I was still alive when Ed flung back the covers and went to the bathroom. He did not speak to me as he ate the cornflakes I laid out for him. He ignored Sarah who was messily spooning Rice Krispies into her mouth with great concentration. I thought of other fathers who would do anything to bring joy into the lives of their precious children. Why couldn't I have married one of those? After he slammed the door behind him I flung myself onto the floor in waves of sobbing.

'Mummy, noooo.' I heard the pitiful wail of insecurity in my little girl's voice.

'Mummy is just tired darling. Come on. We can go out and sing our songs all the way!'

Pushed further into distress than I could bear, I was operating in a fuzz of desperation. I dressed Sarah who studied my face in a struggle of childish misapprehension. What did she know of the world? Only that I was her protector and I was disappearing behind a steel door of hopelessness. I fed the baby and changed his nappy, slinging the dirty one into a bucket of water to soak.

I folded the money he had thrown at me last night.

At the park Sarah ate two apples I sliced for her. She had begged for them when I bought the carrots, onions, cabbage and barley for the soup of boiled bacon bones that would last us four days if I made dumplings, rice or potatoes to stretch it. As long as I did not eat much myself. I slumped onto the cold bench and wondered where I would gather the strength from to ever get up again.

'Are you OK, you do not look well?' A soft voice came from Pam, a lady I often saw as we pushed our toddlers on the swings. She wore a pretty lipstick and her dark hair shone with conditioner and health. Today she was with her husband who was swinging her two year old back and forth as she squealed with joy. He lifted her onto his broad shoulders where she clung to his crisp curls as he trotted around singing 'Horsey, horsey don't you stop. Just let your hooves go clippity-clop.' I felt sick with envy when he came over and hugged her close.

'Hello, you must be Rose! I'm Keith, Pam has told me all about you.' He tried to hide it but there was pity in his gaze. I realised then that I had become a wretched thing to be pitied. Where had my youth and love of life gone?

Keith eased his darling child to the ground then ran after her towards the sandpit.

'I'm just tired Pam. Didn't sleep last night.' She squeezed out an understanding smile, but I saw her eyes move to the bruise on my cheek. The tinny chimes of the ice cream van broke into our closeness and Sarah bounced up and down, 'Ice Cream! Ice Cream! Me want ice cream.'

I knew the money I had must last the week and so had to refuse her. She wailed and turned away from me. I saw Keith put his hand into his pocket as he sauntered with his daughter to the van. He returned with five loaded cones gripped like a bunch of robust flowers. His wife delicately relieved him of some of his burden before he handed one to a beaming Sarah and one to me. It had been so long since I'd had a treat I hardly knew where to lick.

'I reckon your baby is too little for one of these!' Keith said slurping and wiping his daughter's face. They giggled in some family closeness I could only dream of.

My heart ached with grief for what I would never have. I had been downtrodden so long that I had forgotten what kindness in a man was.

I watched the family leave hand in hand and I could have wept.

In the Co-op. I spent all the money on food trying to work out what would last the week. It was the only way not to have the money taken. Not to have any.

With aching heart I bundled a now tired Sarah in beside her tiny brother and set off for the uphill struggle to my hideous home.

Hands chafing on the worn handle of the old pushchair, I sank further down than I knew any human could. I felt dizzy as I slogged along, the babies seemed heavier in their slumber as they curled around my bags of cheap shopping. I had to force one foot in front of the other to try to make it home. Inside I cried with despair.

Suddenly I was above myself looking down. I could see the crown of my head and my bent back as I heaved my load ever onwards. Was I dead? How could I be watching myself?

I was shocked to see what others must see. A thin girl soaked in misery. It was time to get myself and my babies out. The part that was out of myself said, 'Look at yourself! You are worth more than this! Do something.'

I had to take the hand of my wishes, no matter how hard it clenched.

I felt more ill than I had ever felt before when I returned to my shaking body. Miraculously, it still plodded onwards. As I turned the corner the red telephone box was in front of me. Keeping the door open to watch my children and allow some of the urine smell out, I shuffled through the yellowing phone book to find the doctors number.

The receptionist must have heard something in my voice as I begged for an early appointment because she put me through to the doctor.

'I have to come now.' My voice sounded strange even to me.

'You can't it is the anti-natal evening.'

'I have to…please.'

There was a pause then, 'OK, can you make 7pm?'

I prayed that Ed would be in from his new job on the Leech building site before then and by some miracle he was.

'Can you watch the babies whilst I go to the doctors?'

He was not pleased. 'There is nothing wrong with you! You should be ashamed of wasting his time.'

'Do you have any bus fare you can give me?'

'Now you are taking the piss! You can bloody well walk and take those two with you. I am off out!' I looked at his back as he opened the door. My whole life was scrunched up by this one mistake. Him.

So I started off, sickly and weak, for the three mile push up the hill to the next village to see Doctor Green. He took one look at me and sat me down. Ben clung to my bosom and Sarah clung to my legs. My angst poured out to him. He looked up from his notes, gold rimmed glasses sliding down his straight nose so that concerned old eyes could see into me. 'Have you ever considered suicide Mrs. Tomlinson?'

He looked deeper into me and I knew that I had to say yes, even though I would never take myself from the children.

'I am going to make an appointment for a psychiatrist to visit you at home.'

'No! My husband will never allow it!' My terror had me on my feet. Sarah whimpered.

'Do not worry, what time will he be out?'

An appointment was made for Monday, in ten days, at 11am.

My stomach played up all the weekend before the appointment. What if he found out? What if he stayed off work.....what if he knew what I had to say.....what if he came home in the middle of it and beat up the psychiatrist?

Jane agreed to have the children and had a rug laid out in front of the fire with her music boxes and china dogs for Sarah to play with. She loved the cuddle she was getting when I put Ben into her arms. She smelled of lavender soap and the ginger biscuits she had just taken out of the oven. They were shaped into teddies. I had an hour.

Dr. Spencer-Smith was tall and official looking as his eyes swept my home before he sat down at my table. I was so glad I had polished and swept. He had a kind tilt to his head which made me answer his every question with tearful honesty. His copious notes flew from his expensive fountain pen. He blew on the ink of the last page then shut the big black book with a thump.

'Right Mrs. Thomlinson. You do not need a psychiatrist. You need rid of your husband.'

The relief and joy I got from that statement. Clear and knowing. Confirmation that I was not what Ed made me out to be, but I was still me hidden beneath the pain and stress. I glimpsed a silver tint on the black clouds of my life.

The next day a letter came from my dad saying he had fallen in his greenhouse and cut his head. I felt I had to catch the bus to see him and hoped Ed would be in a decent mood when he came home. I scrabbled in the box of Omo washing powder where I had hidden my last half crown of the week. Gritty white granules pushed down into my finger nails and the detergent irritated my skin. I washed my hands and then, making sure no-one was about, went out to the little hole in Jane's brick wall where I hid the coin for my bus fare behind a cement dusted cobweb.

'I need to check on my dad. Can you stay in tonight and watch the children?'

He looked annoyed, then pulled the evening paper out of his haversack to rustle onto the TV page.

'Well there is football on tonight, so you are lucky. But don't make a habit of it.'

I was pitifully pleased, and he used this to his advantage bossing me about and making me do all things to please him, so I was going to be late for the bus.

I winded the baby after his good evening feed and made sure Sarah ate well. She hugged Humph close and I noticed how threadbare the wet ear was. He watched as he mopped gravy from his plate with folded bread. 'That bear is a disgrace! It belongs in the bin.' He said thoughtlessly. I noticed that Sarah turned away from him and hugged Humph even tighter.

'Can you put the children to bed please?'

'I don't see why I have to do your work so you can go out gallivanting till all hours.'

I struggled to put my bitterness back in its cage. He was just hoping for something to start a fight so he could stop me visiting dad so I just smiled a smile I did not feel.

'I won't be all hours, the last bus is 10pm.'

'Go on then, get out. See that useless father of yours. Do not give him my regards!'

I had to run as the bus was just leaving but the driver saw me in his rear mirror and waited. I rubbed the cobwebs from my coin before handing it to the conductor.

It felt strange going out without my babies. My hands seemed empty as they hung by my side. Usually I would take them with me but not at night, they needed their sleep.

Dad smiled when he opened the door and then looked embarrassed.

'Hello Chicken. It is lovely to see you.' he kissed and hugged me too hard, just as he always did, only a bit weaker. How I wished I could tell him of my horrors, but he was too delicate. He had enjoyed a good marriage and was proud that he thought I was well set up with a man, home and family. His strong Christian beliefs made him totally against divorce. It would break his heart to know how awful my life had become. I never asked him to the house as he would detect the depressing pall that hung over everything there, I brought the children to him once a week. It was a struggle as the old pushchair was too big for the bus but he always met me and helped carry one of the babies to his home where we were all spoilt and for a few hours I could pretend to be happy.

We went through the kitchen and there, in his old fashioned living room was a lady sitting with a cup and saucer and a half eaten biscuit. I smelled Helena Rubenstein Apple Blossom.

Dad flustered. 'This is Maureen Forsyth. She drove me to the hospital when I fell, waited and brought me back. I am taking her to the pub to thank her.'

My surprise came out with my voice. 'Hello Maureen, nice to meet you.' She had an open smile and I could see a clean white bra strap slipping down her arm as she lifted her cardigan over her shoulder. Her hair was only just starting to grey and her mouth was soft and kind. Her cheeks glowed with some Co-op chemist's cosmetics.

'I will go then.' She stood up and smoothed her pencil skirt.

'No Maureen. Please don't change your plans. I only came to see if dad was all right and I can see he is.' Dad blushed.

'Well we will stay in now. Want some tea?' Dad smiled in relief that I seemed to like Maureen.

'No way dad, I only popped in for a minute. You go. Enjoy yourself.'

I went out for the 8pm bus. The clocks had just gone forward an hour and it was almost April. The light was just fading. As I waited I thought of mum and how she would be pleased if dad found some-one else to love him like she had. He'd been on his own too long.

I dashed down the dirty terraced street lit by the few tall lights that still worked. The loneliness of a moaning wind sped me on.

As I walked into the house it was quiet. Too quiet. There was no-one there.

I panicked, where had he taken the babies in the dark?

The fire was banked up, making me look over when it made a sudden noise as the coal caved in sending sparks up the chimney and flames to devour newly fallen cinders. There was a note on the mantle-piece next to the one photo of us on our wedding day. I would have to burn that. I looked at the note.

'10.30pm, just popped out for cigarettes.'

I looked at the clock, it was only 8.30.

In panic, I ran upstairs to the children's room. They were there, lying in bed with their clothes on, jam smeared mouths open in sleep. Sarah's face was tear streaked. Humph was nowhere to be seen.

He had left them on their own, with a blazing fire, the doors unlocked and no one to protect them. I sweated in an acid mix of fear and relief. He could not be trusted even to take care of his children for a few hours. This was the ultimate betrayal. Lower than the violence, the theft of my self-esteem, the lack of care whether we ate or not. This is how selfish he was.

This was it. The night I would make my move.

My mind raced as I sweated in the chair next to the now dying fire. How could he? What sort of man would do this? How could I escape? I had no money, no job and nowhere to go. I only knew that I had to get us out, into the rest of our lives in safety.

I wondered what could have made a man like Ed behave in such a way that he destroyed everything in his path. He could have had love from a wife who would take care of him and respect from his children as they grew. I had asked him once in the early days as he had broken down in tears when he saw my black eye and swollen lips. I had thought it had been a breakthrough because he saw the damage he had done, at least physically. He told me that he missed his father, a man I had never met. I had melted a bit then but wondered if it was like father like son and feared for Ben. I remember the story Ed's mother had told me on my first visit to her house for tea when Ed and I had been seeing each other for a month. Like all young men of his age her husband had been called to fight for his country. She had missed him terribly and not even known where he was. One night when she had gone to the picture house to watch a Kirk Douglas movie she had the surprise of her life. Whilst watching the newsreel that always preceded the big film, there was grainy black and white film of the men piling into boats at Dunkirk in a dangerous attempt to reach the shores of Britain. Her eyes had focussed on one man who held himself like her Pete, he even walked like her Pete but it was too swift a glimpse for her to be sure. Her stomach slumped, she had not heard from him for months but neither had she received the dreaded telegram that was the very moment a wife knew she was a widow. She had found it hard to concentrate on the film star she had fancied so much and was glad when it was over. As the people clapped then stood for the National Anthem she decided not to join them as they filed out to make a queue at the chip shop. Instead she had waited until the owner who she knew doubled as the projectionist, came out and started to push all the red velvet seats up in preparation for the cleaner in the morning. She watched him rhythmically bang each seat backwards, clack, clack, clack. It stopped and she turned to see if he had noticed her sitting alone where she had been all evening but he had found a chocolate from a discarded box of Milk Tray. He rubbed it on his waist coat before popping it in his mouth with a gentle 'Mmm,' of appreciation. She laughed then and stood up giving him a fright out of his dreamy occupation.

'I saw you Jimmy Richley!'

He blushed then but she had known him from childhood and he was a good man so she said. 'Was there not one left for me in that box?'

'What you doing here, trying to hide until the next showing so you don't have to pay?'

'Cheeky!' she had called as she walked nearer then told him about what she thought she had seen. He got her to sit down whilst he messed around in the back to replay the newsreel. He told her to raise her arm when the bit she thought she had seen her husband was on. He could see her from the square hole in the wall from where the light shone onto the screen. Nervously, she had sat on the edge of her seat until her arm went up so suddenly she scared herself. The film froze and there in front of her stood the husband she had not seen for two years. She almost fainted from excitement and was sad when the film began to move again. Jimmy told her that the film would melt if he left one bit with the hot light shining on it too long. But she was so thrilled she hugged him and promised him a full box of Milk Tray when they came off ration.

It was not until six months later when her Pete had returned home that she learned he had been wounded at Dunkirk minutes after that film had been taken. He died of those injuries fifteen years later when the baby they had made shortly after his home-coming was only a teenager. This was Ed. Rose could not help wishing that they had not bothered to conceive the person who tonight had proved he deserved everything she was about to give him.

It was 11pm when the back door cracked open. Ed staggered in drunk and past fighting, he was in a stupor as he flopped into the easy chair and his eyes rolled backward into his head.

Not caring what happened I shouted at him. 'How dare you leave the babies on their own?'

He opened one eye. 'I only popped out five minutes ago...' He slurred the lie as his eye shut. '...a man's entitled...'

I was so angry that he had put our children at risk I wanted to scream at him and shake him into sense but he remained semi-conscious and uncaring. His breathing slowed as he sunk into alcoholic oblivion. I felt tainted and worthless in this stagnant silence.

I could kill him now and end my misery. I went to the kitchen searching for a weapon, a tool to change my life. I held each of the knives but I could not use them, the blood would never come out of the carpet we still hadn't paid for. Frantically opening drawers and cupboards, I caught my breath as I noticed Humph's legs sticking out of the waste bin. He was half covered by Ed's crumpled newspaper. Blazing fury energised my mind. I picked up the heavy frying pan taking it to stand in front of his disgusting, unconscious body. I practiced a few swings. Where do I hit to kill him? I twisted the pan back and forth as I considered his temples? Between his eyes? A full swing to the side of his lolling head. What if he woke? He would use the pan on me. Terror tore at my brain, I might never get the chance again. A precipice yawned at my feet.

I held the pan, finding a way to get maximum strength into my swing. I would go to jail. My children would have no mother. They would go into care. I would be a murderess forever. This was not in me. I was not this person. I was a carer not a killer. The police would hunt me down. But I knew that if I left him alive, he would hunt me down and kill me. This was my one chance. I had to grab it.

He stirred.

Chapter two

The children complained as I took them out into the cold
night, woken suddenly from their beds, not knowing what
was happening. I could not get the pushchair onto the bus
and so had to leave it. I stopped only to pull Humph,
Sarah's teddy, from the bin. But as I reached the concrete

bus stop, I knew. The last bus had gone. The streets were deserted. I had to get as far away as possible. I could only walk lugging Ben with one arm, dragging a scared toddler and bin bags of stuff with the other. I set off for the nearest big road not caring where it led.

A cold wind from the Pennines kept waking Ben or maybe it was the jiggling and constant stopping I had to do to try to explain to an exhausted child that mammy couldn't carry her, not tonight. At last she seemed to accept that her feet would hurt as she fell into the same sort of trudge as me. She hitched Humph onto her hip mimicking the way I was holding the baby. The tears ran down my cheeks in gratitude that she seemed old beyond her years.

I had been stop-starting for about an hour when Sarah sat down. Her cold hand slid from mine. We were nowhere near a main road yet. 'Sleepybyes mummy, sleepybys.' She sucked at Humph's ear. I knew she could not go on. I found a piece of soft looking grass, moved away an old beer bottle then I laid the bin bags down and her on top, taking off my coat to cover her.

The keening wind passed right through my jumper to my aching bones. I crouched over my offspring wondering at their innocent sleep. If they knew I was dragging them into uncertain hopelessness, what would they feel? But they didn't. They trusted me and would follow me where ever I went. I had become reckless with misery.

The gusts blew rain in from the west, annoying splatters at first and then heavy big drops mixed with hail.

Two cars passed. One slowed down and seemed to decide that I was a tramp or somehow dangerous, then sped off. The next stopped and two men strained to look out of the slightly open window, I smelled drink and cigarettes. I told them I was waiting for my father.

The baby was wailing into the night, his little heart breaking. But I could never return. Ever.

My back was drenched as I used my body to shield the small, sleeping bodies. I was dog tired and shivering. I thought of my bed made with clean sheets that morning then shifted my position but placed my palm and wrists on fresh vigorous nettles. The rash stung and burned. Was there anything further to make death seem a good option?

I felt then saw a white van whiz past. My head raised as it stopped suddenly then noisily reversed. Rain trickled into my eyes from my wet hair. It was a woman this time. I grabbed my children close and they protested at being woken.

'What on earth are you doing there? Have you had an accident?' She got out and began picking up my bags. When she studied the babies she bustled with us all. 'Get into the dry. I have the heater on.' Miserably, I lifted Ben and a protesting Sarah onto the front seat. The woman tossed my bin bags into the back of the van.

I could have cried then. This little human kindness was like a light in my tomb of misery.

She wiped rain from her eyebrows. Her black hair was like a short back and sides my dad got once a month. I saw a home-made tattoo on her wrist as she changed gear and set the van in motion again. The van smelled a bit of BO and a smoky smell I couldn't place.

She turned to look at me. 'It is 2am, what are you doing out in this weather?'

I could say nothing. My mouth was sealed by shame, worry and fear. She looked down at Sarah, who snuggled up to me and sucked on her bear's ear. 'Are you in trouble?'

I could see that she was reading the sorrow and desolation clattered across my face. I felt accosted by her eyes.

The breath-sucking heat was thawing me so I rearranged the baby bundle on my lap. I could still not reply.

'Well, where are you going then?' Her head shook impatiently. I noticed light lines around her eyes, she must be about 45.

'Where are you going?' I managed to croak.

'Harrogate. I've come down from Craster with the best kippers in the world. Those posh Harrogate hotels like to serve their kippers fresh. Six o'clock deliveries, I make one every Friday morning. I'm Maeve by the way.'

'Harrogate? That is where I am going too.'

'Really?' she squinted. She knew I was lying but said nothing.

She drove on, looking at me every so often, trying to work out what she had picked up. The rain hammered on the windscreen. Wipers swishing and juddering. Exhaustion slammed into me so that I closed my eyes. They opened when the van jerked. We seemed to drive over something.

'Just a rabbit, love to hit them, they are so stupid.' She laughed. 'I ran over eight one night…haha, could do it tonight if you are up for a bit of revving and swerving. What do you say?'

This offended my very soul, lift or no lift I had to speak out.

'No thanks, they deserve the life given to them as much as you do. And they are not stupid. They are very clever at being rabbits. Just not in possession of all the facts when it comes to traffic and big wheels, that is all.' I sounded unnecessarily sharp and regretted it.

'Well each to his own. It is sport you know, killing animals. Don't you like sport?'

'Killing animals with a gun or car is not fair sport…it is cowardly.'

'Ha, pheasants then. You can't object to them stupid birds. They are bred to kill.'

I looked at her, 'Just because a bird has a small brain does not make it stupid. Birds have their own unique way of sensing this world. There are birds who can fly home even when dropped off thousands of miles away. Some use stones or sticks as tools, they grieve and die of broken hearts. Do you want to cause this pain in another creature?'

Maeve sniffed and dragged a tattooed arm across her nose. 'Bloody hell, I have a right one here.' I stayed quiet, pushing my wet hair back, she noticed an almost healed jagged cut in my hairline.

'I bet a man did that to you eh?'

I fussed with the blanket around the baby and he stirred. He'd be hungry.

'Bloody men. They're all bastards! Love using their fists.' She looked at the road through the swishing wipers. 'I was married once.' She thrust her arm at me. 'I kicked the shit out of the little coward when he started on me one night. That is why I have this.'

She pushed her fist near my eyes, bitten nails gripped to her palm so that I could read the ink on her wrist. It said. 'Female Freedom'.

'Given up on the spineless toads.' She looked over at my crumpled face. 'I guess you have too eh? Did he give you that cute little scar on your lip?'

Taking out a pack of cigarettes she stuck one in her mouth and pushed in the van lighter.

'No…please…my babies!'

'What…they want one too…bit young ain't they?' She laughed at her own joke but lit up anyway.

'I don't like them breathing smoke.' I mumbled.

'Nonsense! They have to get used to it sometime. They'll be at it behind the bike sheds as soon as they are 14 anyway.'

I wound down the window just an inch. I guessed it was the price I had to pay for the lift. I was wrong.

She flicked her finished stub out of the window. 'Good job it is raining. These moors get dry as tinder with all that bracken and heather in the summer. Pity it is dark too. Yorkshire Dales are stunning. You been before?'

'No.' I tried to see out of the windscreen but the windings of the road made me sick. My body ached trying to support Sarah slumping in her warm, jiggling sleep. Icy balls machine gunned on the roof and made the wipers swish faster.

'How long to Harrogate?' I asked as Ben stirred awake, his open mouth searching for milk. She wiped at the windows with an old torn tee-shirt. 'Oh 'bout an hour!'

I changed Ben to my left arm and discreetly eased out my swollen breast. He rooted around and latched on, sucking greedily. Maeve took an interest. I wanted her to keep her eyes on the road.

'Hurt do it?'

'A bit sore.' I tried not to look at her.

'Never had no kids me like.'

When I changed breasts she turned her head from the road again.

'Nice pair you got there.'

I kept my head down and tried to put my shoulder between her and the baby.

We both listened to greedy sucking noises. 'It fascinates me that like, you know, breast feeding. Erotic…like red lipstick.'

I felt the van slow a bit and wondered if we had reached somewhere, a village or petrol station. I wiped the moisture from the window but saw only darkness and faint outlines of hills.

Maeve cleared her throat, her voice sounded deeper. 'You know I usually get paid off hitch-hikers.'

I panicked then, knowing my purse had only a few coppers.

'I have no money…sorry…'

'Well then, let's see. What else have you got? A little feel of them might do it.' She nodded at my milky breast which had just been spit out by Ben.

Mortified, I lifted the baby to my shoulder to wind him and cover myself.

'Or maybe a little drink as you want to come all the way to Harrogate with me.'

My mind spun as it tried to make sense of the reason panic churned in my stomach. I did not know why she was saying these things.

'Oh go on, just a five minute suck, not much to ask for a lift now is it?'

I stared ahead, my mind raging with fear.

Her hand came over and caressed my breast. Appalled with what she was demanding, I pulled my hand from beneath the baby and slapped her hard across the face.

She was furious and shouted. 'Stupid bitch! You should catch up with the rest of the world, a hundred years' time when you meet some-one your first question will be 'Are you straight or queer? Maybe both?'

I wasn't listening. I wanted to hit her again and shout 'That is for all rabbits and pheasants you have deliberately

squashed!' But her meaty arm came between us as she put
her foot down hard.

Just then Ben filled his nappy and the air thickened with
pungent baby poo stench.

'Ergh…that's it! You don't want to pay and now you are
poisoning me. I can't bloody stand it!' She slammed on
the brakes and Sarah slid forward. I only just managed to
stop her sleeping head hit the dashboard.

'Get out!' She flung open her door then dashed around to
grab at the handle beside me. 'Now!'

Fresh air hit us like a fist.

A confused, protesting Sarah clung to me in her
floppiness. Trying to hold onto the baby and my almost
dry coat, I stumbled onto the wet moss. Maeve went
around to the back of the van, threw open the door and
grabbed my two bin bags, tossing them angrily towards
me. They slid down a hill into the darkness.

'That'll teach you to look down on some-one just cos they
are different!'

The tyres threw mud and gravel at me as she sped off into
the night. I watched the tail lights disappear then it was
total blackness. I could only feel my two children as they
whimpered and clung to me, their hopeless mother who

had taken them from hell to darker hell. Now I was here praying for sleep.

Blackbird and robin song woke me when it was light and dripping. Somehow I had slipped into uneasy slumber. I was glad to wake from the nightmares that would always remind me of what I had done. I looked up through the hole in the roof just along from us. The clouds had streaks of blue too thin to be warming but it meant the rain had stopped. The memories of my actions had not fled in this new day. Both baby eyes were watching me, charmed by the birdsong and stillness. After feeding Ben, while I kept Sarah and Humph still with the story of two fairies making their home in a dirty bird's nest after they had swept it with their wings, I took us all outside. I judged it to be about 6am. The grass was wet and sparkling with little peeps of sunlight. There were a few trees of greening beech but the oaks were still dormant. I could hear water running over rocks, a sound that had thrilled me all my life, this time it meant survival. We took the baby cup and drank greedily as we looked about. The ancient building was so tumbled down but there were two litter bins on posts, people must visit. The brooding moors where I had been thrown out into the rain were to the north, a little wood crowded the land to the west.

Sarah was asking for food but I told her to wait whilst I cleaned the baby near the stream.

'Stay away from the water chicken, mammy is the one to get the drinks. The stream can whoosh you away, then mammy would cry if she had no beautiful girl to kiss.' I hoped this would make her cautious. She toddled off looking at daisies and buttercups in the grass.

Ben was not pleased as cold water hit his bottom and he yowled into the crisp air. I had to keep him quiet, if any one knew we were hiding here I would have to suffer the terrible consequences of what I had done.

'Sarah!' My shout was a panic as I realised I had not seen her for a couple of minutes. I stood up just as she reappeared with chocolate around her mouth and a grit studded, half eaten Penguin biscuit in her fingers. I slapped the remains from her hand and she cried.

'Me want brekkie mummy, tummy sore.'

'Where did you get that?' I was snappy but she had to learn. She pointed to an overflowing litter bin with wrappers and Tizer bottles lying in the sodden grass.

I took the children back to the cellar and soaked a rusk in the cup full of water so she could eat it quickly. There was only one left. I had to ignore my own rumbling stomach, I would fill it with water.

I was still exhausted, so much that my mind was not functioning properly. I had to lie down as much as possible as my legs would not carry me to the road. Stiffly I sat us all down on the drying grass in the weak sunlight. Each cut and bruise stung, I must have looked a mess. My mind sunk into an awful reverie, I was pierced by the spike of shame of what my freedom would cost my children. And my dad. I may never see him again. I felt numb, shell-shocked by the truth of what my life had become. But I had to concentrate on survival, and what was in front of me. I showed Sarah how to make daisy chains. I looked down at her chubby hands not yet deft enough for the task, they were full of daisy heads. 'No chicken, you have to go right to the bottom, get a long stalk, like this.' I helped her stick her little nail in to make the slot in the stalk and she persevered succeeding in about half the flowers. Her tongue poked out of the side of her mouth in concentration and I saw real pleasure glow from her. I remembered how this simple task had thrilled me when my mother had shown me. I had decorated my hair, her hair, dad's neck and all our wrists. How I wished mum was here to take away some of my desperate fears.

I heard a car door slam, excited voices and nimble feet explored the fallen stones of the abbey. I heard a father shout. 'Race you up the hill!' Then a happy mother call. 'Be careful you two!' I picked up Ben and Sarah's hand, scattering her precious daisies from her lap to the ground and dashed them back into the cellar. I listened intently in case people ventured near the bend. I heard the excited feet and breathing enter the opening.

'Ooh, looks spooky in here!' A girls voice, then a boys.'
Oh great! Might be skeletons and chains!' Then the
mother's voice came close. 'Yuk it is smelly, come away.
You might get hit by a falling stone.'

I cuddled the children close, Ben was soon snoozing but
Sarah was restless.

'Me want necklace!' She cried and ran out to find her
treasure. I put the sleeping baby down and dashed after
her straight into the family sitting on a rug eating. They
looked more shocked than I did.

'Oh!' The mother stopped pouring Lucozade into plastic
beakers to stare at me.

'Sorry. I thought we were the only ones here!'

Sarah looked down at her half made daisy chain trampled
in the dirt. She yelled. The lady got up. 'Oh dear. Such a
lovely daisy chain. We are so sorry, we didn't see it until
now.'

Sarah burst into full crying.

'Here,' she handed her a packet of Tudor crisps.

Sarah stood snuffling with the bag in her hands. I had
never given her crisps before, she had no clue. The lady
turned her head to one side, opened the crisps and said.

'Look in here, see if you can find a tiny blue packet.'

Sarah sniffed and peered then handed the packet back.

'Ah, I will help you.' she said shaking the packet. 'Here it is look!'

After twisting the blue paper she sprinkled the salt over the crisps before handing them back to my dumbstruck child.

I looked at the woman's soft brown hair kept back by a red Alice band, her fingernails were clean and shaped. Her husband looked on supportively and I felt the old longings tear at my heart.

'We didn't see another car.' He smiled but his eyes raced around my scratched face. 'How did you get here?'

I hid my dirty torn fingernails behind my back searching for ways to sound normal.

'Oh my husband dropped us off this morning. He is coming back after his business…in Harrogate.' I saw the man's eyes move around my sleep matted hair and pushed my hand in to find bits of thistle and twig. How many scratches and bruises showed? 'Oops', I tried to smile. 'Been playing roly-poly.'

'That is where we live, eh Margaret? Where is his work, we will know it.'

I felt like a liar and hoped I did not look like one. 'Oh, a few places…selling…wool.' I stammered after noticing the clumps of fleece dotted about from the animals who freely grazed here.

The children were staring then lost interest in favour of chocolate Swiss roll.

'Well don't let us spoil your fun.' The man said lifting a tinned salmon sandwich to his mouth. The bread looked fresh and crusty and the smell hit my empty stomach like a jagged sword.

'Bye!' I said taking Sarah further down towards the stream with the promise of even bigger daisies. She loved the crisps and I ripped open the packet so she could lick the remaining salt and bits. When I heard their car go I am ashamed to say I went straight to the bin to see what they had left. There was a Littlewoods carrier bag crumpled around their scraps. I found empty crisp bags, two apple cores and grease proof paper covering the crusts the children must have left. There were edgings of salmon and I was thrilled as I shared them with my daughter. I imagined Margaret that morning cutting the sandwiches in her immaculate kitchen. Now they had sped off to their immaculate life. I felt even more alone.

I tried not to be seen after that. My straining ears became expert at listening for the cracking of stones beneath tyres and the banging of car doors. I could be in my hidden dark place for the short time it took people to look around at the view, climb the stones of the ruin and stuff what would become our poor supper into the bins.

The nights struggled by me, marked only by various degrees of shivering.

We formed a routine. Sarah grew attached to a brown paper carrier bag with one torn handle that was stuffed above other litter. She called it her 'uggage', after she heard some noisy people re-packing the boot of their Morris Minor with their luggage. That was the afternoon we had been seen going to the stream so that I had to pretend I was out for a walk.

Each night we explored the bins. We feasted on tiny bits of cheese triangles stuck into the corners of the foil, dusted down bits of Cream Crackers, crusts bitten from the tasty bits of pork pies and once a half a banana. This reminded Sarah of her favourite treat which she used to call, 'nana b'sandwiches'. She asked for these repeatedly over the next few days but we never found another banana or enough bread.

Into her 'uggage', she placed all the bits on the ground that had fallen from the bins or been left carelessly on rocks. She became expert at sifting and I told her how proud I was of her. When she was asleep, I cried that this had to be my measure of how clever she was.

She helped me stash a little pile of stones beside where we slept so that I could toss them into the dark places where scuttling and squeaking woke me from my stiff half-sleep. I began teaching her how to count these and get her to place them into piles of threes and fives.

The stone throwing never rid us of the feeling that we were not the first ones to hide here. I felt comfort and fear in equal measure from the energies oozing from the thick stones keeping the weather away from us. We were constantly cold.

One day Sarah found a Coconut Snowball, squashed underfoot in its wrapper so that the white marshmallow had to be licked from the cellophane. She shared this with Humph who luckily did not seem hungry. His ear was getting thinner and soggier.

I struggled with a flat, heavy stone which I managed to push onto two rocks embedded into the soil. I took the inspiration from the staddle stones at a farm I had played at where the grain barns had been built on lines of these so that rats could not climb the horizontal shelves. Now I had somewhere to keep the baby safe. My hands were bleeding with the effort. I had pulled a muscle under my shoulder blade so that it hurt to lift Ben.

I lulled Sarah to sleep in the coldness every night with stories made up on the spur of the moment. I kept an especially thrilling tale about a squirrel with shiny paws for when I had to keep her quiet when visitors peeked her curiosity. She could smell meat-paste sandwiches if the wind was in the right direction. If someone was biting into chicken legs her nose would lift to the breeze and I had to hold her back physically, nuzzling squirrel secrets into her ears so that she would wait.

After a few days of sun and breezy mildness the rain dropped again. For three days no visitors came. The only van was of noisy council workers emptying the litter bins. There was nothing to eat. Sarah became fractious and so did Ben, my milk was not filling him.

I tried to calm the hunger pangs in my daughter's little tummy with water, but still she cried. Desperation wound my mind into frantic whirling. I remembered when I was out with dad in my school holidays and he showed me how to chew wild sorrel leaves to freshen my mouth. We had dug ground nuts up after he told me how to recognise their ferny tops. I had to go down the moor to the woodland where the ground was more nourished and not cropped by sheep.

I fed Ben and waited until he fell into his morning sleep. I lifted him onto the safe shelf to keep him away from rats before I took the hand of my hungry little girl.

'We are hunters now, like squirrels. We have to find delicious things to eat under the ground.'

This peaked her interest but she was too cold and hungry to get up.

'Maybe we will see Cyril Squirrel in the wood, see if he really does have shiny paws!'

I tried to make my tired voice sound excited but the truth was, I was exhausted and weak with hunger myself.

She dragged herself from beneath my coat, she was already dressed against the cold. She put Humph beside her baby brother, picked up her beloved and crushed paper carrier bag and went silently to the cellar entrance.

Our coats were already drenched when we reached the wood. There was a double barbed wire fence to keep the sheep out but I grew up squeezing through these, I would not be stopped. We walked around until we found a section less taut than the others and I held the wires apart so Sarah could pass through. I bent and turned, snagging only once. I had lost none of my manoeuvres to release myself or my clothes. It took a while to find anything edible. If it had been autumn there would be blackberries and nuts. I looked up at the dripping lamb's tail hazel flowers and the bright green, just opening beech buds. How I loved the spring, but I had to rush to get back to my baby and out of the rain. Sarah was delighted to see some new bluebells and white stitchwort flowers, she began picking a few but we could not eat these so I had to hurry her away. I almost cried with relief to see a small clump of sour docks, fresh and clean. I picked a leaf and rolled it like dad had shown me before putting it into my mouth to chew. Sarah was not impressed and turned her head away when I put a leaf to her lips.

'Yum, mmmm,' I lied as I ate another. She studied me and opened her mouth, took a little and grimaced at the lemony sharpness. She struggled on more to please me than to eat but something was taking her emptiness away and she carried on. I tried several brittle bits of branch before I found the strong stick I broke across my knee to create a sharp point for digging. We passed new vigorous nettles which I knew were delicious in soup but we had no gloves or fire so I just told Sarah to stay away from them. On the edge we found plenty of dandelions with their yellow heads hiding from the rain. I picked some of the newest leaves which were less bitter and faked the yummy sounds again. Sarah, bless her tried but spit them out. I ate as many as I could bear, I needed to make my milk flow. I ate fresh chickweed which I did not enjoy and a few primrose leaves. Sarah would only pick the flowers which she carefully placed into her soggy bag.

I was overjoyed when I saw the tops of a few ground nuts and began digging with urgency. The roots were small and dirty but I knew Sarah would like these. I nibbled away the outer skin and soil spitting it out onto the grass. When I gave her the cream flesh to eat she took it, crunched and swallowed.

'Sarah like 'ound nuts mammy.' That was all the encouragement I needed and dug like a mad woman. We had quite a collection of roots and had eaten the larger ones in a rush. We had to get back to Ben.

Her wet paper carrier bag was disintegrating in the rain. She pushed our poor harvest into the crumpling sogginess, it fell through back to the ground.

'No! 'uggage mammy! Sarah's 'uggage!' her face and voice showed so much despair that I could not bear it.

I showed her how to carry the groundnuts by the tops and she tried so hard, gripping her wet paper to her chest with her crushed flowers. After negotiating the barbed wire where I tore my coat at the arm, we headed back, guided by the urgent wailing from Ben. He had woken alone. Panic sped us up the hill in case anyone was there. But the rain had some use, we were still alone. After washing the dirty tubers in the roaring stream we took them back to the cellar, to crunch and nibble our way to a peaceful night.

The dripping stopped, they were both asleep on the shelf safe from the rats. I only had one nappy left for the baby so I carried the five soiled ones to the stream to wash in the dark.

I let the gushing water rush through the terry towelling, it cleared away the baby poo but the stains remained. My fingers and wrists ached at the vigorous rubbing and wringing out. How I missed that twin tub washing machine I had hated so much. The towelling would take days to dry, it would be a case of putting a damp nappy onto my son again. I was chilled and forlorn, looking only at bleakness, torn by my ragged misery.

As I reached the top of the stream bank I thought I saw a light, I stopped and looked hard but the night was dark. Maybe it was a star appearing from the clearing clouds.

Just when I turned the cellar corner I saw the flash again. There was a man standing over my sleeping babies. Their innocent faces glowing in his full beam from a heavy torch. He had a shotgun slung across his broad back and some kind of thin hound snuffling at his feet.

Chapter Three

I screamed louder than I knew I could and he turned, grabbing the gun and aiming it at me all in a split second.

'Stop that! AAAAAAH! It is only audible to bats and my poor rescue dog here.' The hound shivered and leaned into his legs. The checked shirt emphasized the breadth of his shoulders, the faded denims the length of his legs in muddy walking boots. He looked powerful, this terrified me. He eased the rifle to his side. The dropped beam blinded me before he retrieved it then shone it upwards making him look ghoulish and angry. I used the only weapon I had; protective fear and wet nappies. I lashed out and stung him across his cheek with a flick of soaking terry towelling.

He almost laughed. But his manners allowed only a reassuring smile. He fixed his eyes to my own, they were sharp and sparkling with amusement. My fear began to subside, I knew then that he would not hurt us. I could only think then that he was vividly handsome in an outdoor sort of way. I was ashamed of myself. I judged him to be about thirty, maybe younger.

I suddenly became aware of my bedraggled appearance. Crumpled clothes, mud stained and torn, hair unwashed except by rain for five days. He saw a ragamuffin woman worn with grief. No wonder he was studying me in puzzlement.

Sarah sat up. 'Mammy!'

'It is all right darling.' Sleepily she sank down again but kept her eyes on the man.

'What on earth are you doing here?' he barked.

I detected surprise in his voice, maybe a little concern but no malice.

'I have as much right as you.'

'Yes, you do. But it is eleven at night and you have two children in haunted cellars of an ancient ruin on the moors.'

'Haunted?'

Just then a black and white collie dog ran out from the very back of the cellar. I gulped air as my eyes widened in new fright. This brought Sarah to her feet and she ran towards me clinging to my legs. He studied our fear and looked softened by it.

'Haunted with rats I'd say. Freddie was off like a shot which is what brought me in here.'

He picked up the dust covered, sodden nappy with two fingers and handed it to me.

'Not the most effective weapon I have been threatened with.' That smile again, broader now. 'Are you in trouble?'

Terrified he'd discover the truth I flung words at him.

'No! I am …on holiday.'

He almost laughed again. 'Why are you on your own? Where is your husband?'

'I… he is…I am a widow.' I spluttered. That word stung me, it was my new title.

'So this is all you can afford. Where is your suitcase?' He asked looking around at the mess of drying baby clothes and the piles of anti-rat stones. I saw it all through his eyes and wanted to die of embarrassment.

'Please go away! We just want to be in peace!' I shouted.

'Yes well, I just want to walk my dogs after the rain has had them cooped up all day. I didn't plan on meeting some mad woman who thinks freezing in soaked clothes in a rat infested ruin is giving her children a holiday.'

'It is none of your business actually. Please leave and never come back.'

'Well your holiday is not doing much for your manners, is it?'

He was staring at me. His voice softened.

'Do you need help? Do you want me to tell anyone you are here?'

'NO!'

He looked shocked at the voracity of my answer.

'Do not tell anyone! I do not need help, I am managing very well without it. Just get lost!'

'Please yourself.' He whistled up his dogs and they all pushed past me. Wet black noses sniffed the air, I knew I must smell awful. I turned to see his tall frame pass easily over the rocks into the night.

I felt even more alone when it was quiet again. As I calmed my thoughts they had a new direction. My coursing blood carried flashing pictures of the man who had frightened me. But fear was not my only thought.

Some things we do not know, we just feel them….I felt a strange loss at his leaving.

Adrenalin kept me awake for ages and my head hurt without dry nappies to use as a pillow. I woke rubbing at a stiff neck. I think it was Monday. Dear God, I was losing track of time. No one came all day. The nappies took ages to dry on the rocks so I took them down to hang on the barbed wire whilst we hunted for more roots. Sarah was not pleased with the same food she had to swallow yesterday and ate little. Ben looked about at his new surroundings. He gurgled something in baby language and laughed. He was happy. For all he knew every-one was breast fed and lived in a ruin. He was plump and sturdy for now but he'd need solid food soon, what did I have to give him? Nothing. We sat on a low swaying branch spreading from a beech tree, lolling up and down, it was soothing and rhythmic. I tried to teach Sarah the different greens of the new leaves and which trees they belonged to but she was too hungry. We swayed idly, my baby loved it. We listened to the burr of insects excited as us by a little sun. Sarah bobbed off and ran down the hill, her feet crunched a familiar smell into the air, it was wild garlic in bloom, a feast waiting for us. I had to call it something else for my child to eat so I encouraged her to pick the white flower buds then said. 'This magic bud is what the fairies eat to make sure they can fly high. Shall we taste some?'

She pulled a face at the smell and taste, but watched me eat with relish and copied my lip smacking and 'mmm'. She ate two new leaves and I ate a dozen hoping all these fresh spring greens would not have an adverse effect on our tummies or my breast milk.

The wind strengthened, so as we waited for the nappies to dry we went deeper into the woodland. It was woods like this that had taken away my childlike peace of mind when I was twelve. But I could not let those chest-contracting memories be in charge now. I had to give all that was left of my mental strength to saving us. Here Ben smiled and gurgled watching Sarah picked wildflowers. I loved the way his tongue came forward when he laughed, he would have crinkly eyes when he grew up as his expression always glowed from them. Sarah was delighted to find a patch of Forget-me-Nots in soft grass but I could see as she bent to pick some that her spirit was dwindling. She was hungry and although she trusted me implicitly, I knew I was failing her. I should never have done what I did. I should have waited, hatched an intelligent plan to rid me of that man who had been her father but in name only. Now we had to hide forever. My lacerating guilt combined with my hunger to drag at my stomach.

We drank water until we were bursting, Sarah filled her plastic cup for the blue flowers she had carefully carried back, then she balanced it on a fallen stone with scrolling chiselled into it centuries ago. We fell into the only awful half sleep that our rumbling tummies would allow. My mind spun with muddled possibilities of what I must do to save us. Some new noise tore into my nerves, it seemed other worldly, kindly yet threatening. Was it real or my trauma and hunger manifesting? I could not hear for listening.

Muffled footsteps and scuffles pulled me from painful half dreams to protect my children with urgency.

A bounding Freddie entered the cellar first then a skipping brown mongrel snuffled around a delighted Sarah. The man from last night laid candles and matches beside the Forget me Nots. I tried to look alert but I felt only embarrassment flow to my skin. I tried to smooth my rumpled hair.

'You have different dogs tonight.' I said sitting up, my face felt raked with strain.

'Yes, apart from Freddie, they are all rescues.' The collie gazed up at him with open mouthed undisguised adoration showing canine black lips and a pink lolling tongue. His coat was mostly black and white with tan under his sharp eyes.

'Here I brought you stuff.' The man shone his torch onto the roof so that it dimly lit everything. His longish dark hair was blown onto his forehead and curled slightly. He pushed it back. I noticed his strong forearms extended from his rolled up sleeves. I could not bear the look of pity mixed with a slight hint of his wondering if I was mad.

'Thank you but we can manage on our own.'

He looked at us, forlorn and shivering.

'So you have no use for eggs nor servant?'

Sarah's face lifted at the word eggs.

'No, of course not, certainly not a servant.'

'That is what you need most of all.'

He put the overflowing gondola basket down and went outside again returning a few seconds later with a different kind of basket. Sarah, hardly able to take her eyes off the eggs, looked over as he opened the front of the basket and out walked a very relieved, huge black and white cat.

'This servant you do need, got him from a farm down near Reeth, he was on his own for eight months after Old Jack the sheep farmer died. That eight months he spent honing his craft, rats ran from him and there were no mice to be seen by the time a new man took over. He wanted to shoot him as he was worm and flea ridden and driven mad with loneliness. I got him just in time, now he is clean and loving, slept on my pillow for two months after he was out hunting.' His voice softened with love for the ugly creature staring at us. 'Climbed the wisteria up to my bedroom to get to me. He'll sort out this place for you. You'll be doing him a favour. He has killed so many rats there are none left round mine, he is bored.'

The cat blinked in the darkness and Sarah took five steps towards him hunkering down to reach his shining fur. The cat reared up in welcome and rubbed his face against hers, he had a half moustache of black under his nose and a black triangle around one eye. She squealed in glee and he ran off, catching some alluring scent deeper into the cellar.

'I do not want your stuff! I can manage.' I mumbled through thick lips, trying to focus through embarrassment and heavy, sleep deprived lids. I was longing for the eggs myself.

'Yes I can see that.' Something flickered in his eyes but it was gone.

He laughed, pulled out the pillow from the basket, shook it and dropped it onto a waist high stone and turned to go, leaving with a smile that infected us all. I watched his broad back and long legs, strong with work and health. I could never say that I wanted him to stay.

'Wait! …what is the cat's name? How do I call him?'

'I told you his name, Servant!' He whistled up his dogs and left.

Sarah ran a little way after the cat, but was thrown back by the darkness. I was pulling things from his basket. I lit three candles and she saw the eggs. 'Chucky eggs mammy, for Sarah?' She picked one up. I had tried to eat a raw egg once as a dare, my stomach churned at the thought of it.

'We have no way of cooking them darling. Put it back, carefully.'

As she did it dropped from her hand onto a rock but did not break. I went over to retrieve it, it was soft boiled and still warm. After peeling the egg, Sarah ate with such lip licking joy that I hated myself for taking out of her little life even the simplest of pleasures.

'Sarah want nuvver egg mammy.' How could I resist her yolk smudged face or take the excitement from her eyes. I had to stop her at a third. I thought I should eat one myself. My stomach juices squealed and wailed. Taking the egg carton out of the basket, I moved a tea towel, a packet of cream crackers, butter and embarrassingly, two toilet rolls. I pulled out a tartan thermos flask. The lid was screwed on too tight and I had a mighty struggle before I could see what he had left us. I never thought that I would smell chicken vegetable soup again, especially not home-made. The aroma beat me into submission as I poured a lid-full, it was hot. There was a bent silver plated spoon, patchy with wear, in the bottom of the basket beside two bread rolls. Sarah ate some after I had blown it cool enough, but the eggs had filled her little tummy.

I cried with joy at another human's kindness. Then harder and longer at my misery.

But this was the first night I did not have to go out to search for food.

It was lovely sharing the cat's pillow with my little girl. How low had I sunk us that this was a measure of luxury? All cuddled up together on the harsh floor, we slept late and would have been even later if it were not for a weight on my chest and a loud motoring noise in my ears then a lick to my nose. My eyes opened to see the largest greenest cat eyes close to mine, the purring ratched up to mega, he was delighted to have company and stepped up to lick my hair. Sarah laughed. 'Me like 'vant mammy'.

I moved my feet but they felt extra warm and furry. Sitting up quickly I saw two big and very dead rats lying across my ankles. I shook them off screaming which woke the baby and scattered cat and rats.

'Puppies mammy, 'Vant bringed puppies!'

Sarah, grumpy that I would not let her cuddle the rats, sucked at Humph's ear whilst I fed the baby. When he had settled, I propped him up between two rocks then I fed Sarah the remains of the soup, only just warm but so welcome. Servant went out on a walk of his own as I used toilet paper to move the stiffening rats to one of the litter bins. I tried not to look at their bared yellow teeth and blood stained necks. A late frost had hardened the grass leaving a blue sky into which my breath clouded. No-one had visited the Abbey yesterday, the bins were empty. I shuddered to think how hollow our tummies would be if it wasn't for the man last night.

I didn't even know his name.

No visitors came. We spent the day washing clothes and ourselves in the freezing water, then walked down to the wood to dry everything. I placed us all in a sunny patch for stories as we watched the washing flapping and flopping in the new breeze. Ben was rolling over and trying to crawl, I should have been joyous at this natural development but instead it filled me with worry. There was nowhere safe for his little hands and knees but there would be no stopping him.

Our tummies were full of cream crackers and eggs that teatime as we gathered strength enough to plan how to improve our lives. I did not even know where the road was now. I had to find it then set off for our future. Tears threatened but I fought them back. I had to be braver than that. Braver than I really was.

That night, when I was slaking foul smelling nappies in the stream. I thought I saw car lights up the hill. I made a note of the direction. We would be walking that road soon.

I could relax enough to try to get the nappies cleaner as I knew Servant would not be allowing any rats near my children. I began to worry that the cat would be left there when I went. Hopefully the man would be back for him. I would be long gone.

The lights lit the sky as if the car was turning to come down to us. In panic I dashed to the nearest pile of stones, cowering behind. I held my breath in a trance of anxiety.

A car door slammed, it was as loud as the heartbeats in my ears. I heard steps and then quieter walking on the grass. A man's voice filled the still air.

'Here….put it here. It won't take long…maybe a fox will help us out.'

A whine from a female.

'Stop it! Here, give it to me! Do you want your father to kill us both?'

There was a bit of scuffling and a woman crying.

'Let go!' Hard words then sobbing.

'Shall we put it in the stream?'

More crying. 'No, no no! On these flowers, it's soft.' The female voice was wracked with sorrow and had an accent I had never heard before.

'Come on…for heaven's sake! Leave it.' Scuffling and dragging sounds reached me through my hard held breath.

The car door slammed again and I heard urgent reversing and saw the lights raise then disappear.

I thought my heart would explode. The relief that they had gone made me slump on the stones. I would see what they had left in the morning when it was light. As I made my way back with the wet nappies I heard a slight noise. It must be Servant mewing over some catch. I spread out the washing then went to lie on my rocky bed. I checked on the children and saw Servant fast asleep on Sarah's legs. I was just wondering what night-time creature sounded like that when I heard it again. I went to the mouth of the cellar. It grew louder, there was no mistaking what it was this time. I flew towards the noise with the winged feet of some maternal angel. There, on a patch of wild violets, wrapped only in a woman's yellow cardigan, was a new born baby. The little black fists tried to push into the hungry mouth and failed. I lifted the cold, tiny body. I pulled it into my chest and felt my milk begin to flow. It was the most natural thing in the world to warm and feed this tiny lost soul. I eased the cardigan away so that I could warm the little dark body next to my skin, I saw it was a girl. Her hair was dark and crinkled and she was snuffling and gulping with her first drink of her life. She was truly beautiful.

I held her close all night only leaving loose when Ben woke for his feed and Sarah scrambled beside me as I fed him. I absorbed the love of my two blond and blue eyed children, how they drew magic from me. There was a little mew from the bundle near my feet and Sarah's eyes widened.

'What that mammy?' She was so sweet. Up she got and went to the bundle, drawing in breath at the surprise.

'That baby for Sarah mammy?'

She put her little finger out and the tinier fingers grabbed it.

'We have to take care of the new baby sweetheart, can you help me.'

'Oh thank you mammy. Me have two babies now.' I was as thrilled with her new counting skills as I was with her loving acceptance.

I wrapped the baby in one of Ben's Babygros and it swamped her. I shook out the yellow cardigan she had been in. It smelled funny, not perfume or human smell, something oily and strange, I had never smelled it before.

Sarah kissed the little dark cheeks and asked to hold the baby. She seemed to see in that new face, a look of utter helplessness and Sarah felt needed. I wished I could have her thrilled look. I was struggling to look after two children. Now I had taken on another. How would I cope?

The babies were sleeping next to each other on the rock when it grew dark and in bustled an excited Freddie snuffling awake Sarah and touching noses with Servant. The man brought in a cloth shopping bag which he proceeded to empty. He pushed that falling hair back with big hands, I tried to work out if he was trying to be modern by growing it or it just needed cutting.

'I have a flask of Bovril, some chocolate tea-cakes and some Nimble bread.' He laughed embarrassed. 'Oh and some Primula cheese spread.' I examined his face with the eye of my heart, he did not have to do any of this. Two Golden Retrievers plodded in beside him, brothers I think.

'The village shop doesn't have many shelves or much imagination I'm afraid.'

He looked at the babies and his mouth opened.

'Good Lord! You kept that secret. Is this why you are running away? Do you need medical treatment? I could bring Dr Brookes out to you.'

'No! Do not bring any one.' I flung the words at him in fury so that he took a step back. I saw the renewed curiosity in his eyes.

'Look, I am no judge. If you needed love after your husband died then have to hide the evidence that is up to you. But this is no way to bring up your ever increasing family.'

'I have no choice.'

'You do, stop having babies for a start! There are…things.'

'What do you have against babies?' I bridled so that he took one step back and put up his hands. The retrievers looked scared and sat down at his feet.

'Hey, nothing! Children are the future of humanity. I feel…like animals and arsey women… they are a great part of life.'

'I am not arsey! I am fighting for survival.' I shuddered and only then realised that it was true. Tears brimmed and I prayed they would not give me away by spilling out.

He softened. 'Look it is your life. If you want baby after baby it is up to you.'

'Did I look pregnant to you? And Ben is only months old...how could it be?'

'Well, last year I took in a lovely skinny bitch, she followed me everywhere, she got a bigger shock than I did when she dropped five puppies on my coco-matting doormat.'

'Well I did not drop this baby, on a doormat or anywhere else. She was abandoned here last night, left to die.'

His eyes widened. 'So you are taking her on then, just like that?'

'Well she needed body warmth and breast milk and I have both. Do you suggest I should have left her out there to starve and freeze?'

The truth was dawning on his face and it grew more caring. 'No of course not. But if this is true then you have to give her to the authorities…the police or some-one.'

'IF it is true! IF!'

'Sorry, I just meant… what shall we do about it?'

'What chance do you think she will have if she goes into a home?'

I looked down at the baby who was now being hugged rather too tightly by Sarah.

'Anyway, I have fallen in love with Violetta.'

'Who? You have given her a name? Why?'

'She was lying in a patch of primroses and violets, and she is beautiful.'

'Good God! What are you taking on woman?'

'Nothing a man would understand! But you got it right there, I am a woman, any woman would do the same…especially one who has milk flowing from her and arms to fill.'

'I would think your arms are full enough as it is. But I get your point.'

He smiled then, through a lingering look I saw his admiration and something else.

'Violetta eh? Good job she wasn't left in a nettle patch.' He laughed and I saw how good he was, how his face changed to softer yet stronger. I felt a pull deep in me and knew I had to smother it. He seemed to look at all this with his understanding. It relaxed me a bit.

'Or dandelions! Thank goodness there aren't any deadly nightshades around here….or…..' I laughed. Ben giggled then, his little baby double chin shiny with dribble. I beamed love at him.

'That is the first time I have seen you laugh…or even smile. It suits you.' He was staring admiringly. I pushed back my grease straggled hair and grew conscious of my creased and grubby clothes. But he noticed none of these. I saw it in his eyes, or so I thought.

'I will bring shampoo tomorrow.' He said as he turned to go.

Who was I kidding?

The next night he brought half a bottle of Silvikrin shampoo and a pile of old tea-towels. 'Sorry that is all I have. I suppose you have to use Pears shampoo on babies. I thought you could use these as nappies, I have no clue where you buy these things and I can just imagine the gossip if I did.' He put them down along with another bag.

My relief at such a thoughtful gift brought fat tears welling up in me and a great hope that they would not reach my face. He turned his head to the side as he noticed my struggle. His eyes searched mine then moved to my mouth, I felt a butterfly of desire and hated myself for it. He would have been looking at my scar. What was I thinking for heaven's sake? I was struggling to remind myself how dishevelled I looked when he looked nervous and said.

'I was going to ask you...'

He took two steps forward. He smelled of soap, fresh air and the secret maleness he exuded from every pore.

I took two steps back which he noticed. His embarrassment clustered and clanged around him.

'What?'

'Well,' he hesitated, uncomfortable and unsure. 'Come back to my place, I have a little room you can have. Anything is better than this.' He threw his arms around at my makeshift home.

I saw strength in him then, it was nailed into him. He had understanding and empathy, kindness and gentleness. Everything I ever wanted.

There was an undefined promise of happiness in the air. But it could never be mine. I would never give over my life to another man. Never.

I could not drag this caring human being into the trouble I had created for myself. If he knew what I had done he would not even ask. What if he told some-one that I was here? I could not risk being found. I would lose my babies. I could never lose my babies.

'No I can't. I have to make a life for us all. I am leaving tomorrow.'

I saw disappointment as well as pity cross his face. He would be glad to see the back of me if I told him everything.

'Where will you go?'

'Err…Harrogate.' It was the only place I had heard of near here.

'Do you have someone you know there?'

'Yes of course.' I lied. He said no more but left a bag with another flask of soup and more bread on the ground.

The morning was dry but windy as I took us all to the stream for a shivering wash. My cuts and scratches seem to have healed very quickly in that cellar. Maybe it was all this fresh air. Sarah and I combed through our wet hair which dripped about our shoulders. It was so unpleasant, I wanted to sit on a rock and cry but I rushed us through it singing 'Fuzzywuzzy was a bear, Fuzzywuzzy had no hair, if Fuzzywuzzy had no hair he wasn't fuzzy wuz he?' She loved this song and I had to make sure we would be clean when we got to Harrogate. I seemed to have developed a cough overnight and felt sure that it was the dust in the cellar or maybe cat hair.

My nipples were unbearably sore, rubbing against my clothes as I gathered the still damp baby clothes and shoved them into one straining bin bag. It was too much for me feeding two infants, I would have to get Ben onto solid foods as soon as I was able. The other bag, a bit more worn, took the dry tea towels and the stack of cheese spread sandwiches I had made from the supper last night. On the safe rocks I left the bag, old knife and the thermos flask we had drained for breakfast. At least our tummies were full. Servant was out hunting, no doubt the man would take him and the rest of his belongings home tonight when he went for his customary walk.

I motivated Sarah with stories of shop windows full of pretty clothes, cakes and fancy bread. I had never been to this town but I knew I had to get her cold legs moving. I could not tell her that we had no money to buy these things but I would try with every breath in my body to make enough to keep her happy.

My arms were full of babies so that I could only hold one of the bin bags. I gave the lightest one to Sarah who struggled to hold the neck of the bag in her hand and clutch Humph with the other. I was coughing over the babies as we walked towards where I had seen the car lights. We stopped to fill the Tommy Tippee cup at the stream so I could sip to wet my sore throat. My nipples stung and burned against my torn coat, my arms ached as I clutched the two babies, Ben wriggled to sit up so I put him on my hip. It was almost impossible. Sarah could only manage to half drag her bin bag and she kept dropping Humph as she struggled up behind me. I could hardly bear to look at her. She was so strained and yet determined not to let me down. She started crying. We had only gone a short way up but she sat down in the blustery gusts hugging her bear to her heaving chest.

'Me want to bring Vant mammy.'

It broke my heart to see her. I thought about it for a moment, at least he could walk. But could I bear another burden? She was so like me, wanting to save anything small. She was only tiny and she was already a heroin.

'Servant can't live in a town pet, he would get squashed by a bus. He likes it here and he will go home with the nice man.' I put the babies down in soft grass wishing I could have gone home with the nice man myself. I tried to tell her of toys, dolls and picture books in shops but the wind stole the words from my mouth.

As I hugged her close, pressing her wet head onto my cheek I realised that I still did not know the name of the man who had fed us the last three nights. Now I never would.

I had a coughing fit then and sweated with the effort I had to make to get us all going again. We trudged and stumbled with aching legs to the brow of the hill where there was the narrow road full of pot holes and tufts of wind bent grass. It must have been made years ago and may have been the reason such few visitors came to the Abbey. The wind was fierce up here, it was hard to keep both feet on the ground and my hair whipped across my cheeks and eyes. Even the fleece of the sheep parted but not enough to stop them from eating as we passed them by. Ben was struggling to keep his eyes open when a strong gust came and he gasped, his little mouth dribbling and working. My arms ached so I put the babies down to stretch them out as I waited for my tiny daughter to catch us up. I felt that at any moment she would be lifted up off her feet and carried away. But she struggled on as she had seen me do. Violetta needed feeding again. Sitting with my back to the teeth of the wind I almost screamed in agony as she latched on to my sore nipple but I had to bear it. Sarah was trying not to cry as she plonked down beside me. She put Humph to her chest and told him he was a good boy.

There was a finger signpost, rotten, splintered and worn lying on the grass. I went over to it, it was hard to read but

I could make out. 'ogate'. The wind had beaten this too. It was impossible to tell which way it had been pointing but I could see by the weak sun which way was south. It would definitely be that way. Sheep lifted their curly-horned heads then looked at us for a moment before putting their heads down again, as if on a Godly mission to let no blade go uncropped.

I strapped on my enthusiastic face as I turned to Sarah. 'This way to the shops. Won't be long now.' I lied, looking at the snaking road with nothing in sight but hills, winding walls and scruffy wool covered sheep.

My legs wobbled with the strain of my loads, each one precious to me, yet they all rubbed against my cracked nipples. I looked down and saw a smudge of blood emerging around my chest.

Progress was torturously slow as our feet slapped the old tarmac. I had to stop for so many things. Numb arms, hungry babies, tea towel folding onto sticky bottoms, a worn out toddler or a dropped bear. My body wracked with coughing and I grew increasingly hot even though the wind whipped across my face. After what I reckoned must be an hour Sarah was hungry, I had no appetite but beckoned her off the road into a dip to shelter us from the wind and gave her a sandwich. I had no idea what would become of us or how I would get the strength. I only knew that I had to fight with all my might for my children's future.

The babies snoozed and Sarah cuddled up sleepily. Noisy gusts beat above us and lifted our hair but the high, grass covered mounds helped keep the strongest blasts from us. In minutes we were all lost in sleep to this lovely but terrifying world.

Tyres squealed breaking into my dream of trying to escape from a hot burning room. I had a fever, I could tell. I pushed prickling eyelids open to check on my children.

Sarah had gone.

Chapter Four

I stumbled up, sweat dripping into my eyes as I saw Sarah and Humph in the arms of our man. He looked like he had been shot at. Humph had a burst tummy, white kapok sprang from his torn seams and was taken by the wind. Sarah looked as though her world had ended.

'I ran over the bear! I almost ran over your child!' He was angry as he put Sarah to the ground with a filthy Humph. She ran to me.

'I thought you were going to Harrogate.'

'I am.' I muttered wearily.

'Then you'll have to walk backwards, it is the other way.'

He looked me all over, eyes lingering on the blood stained jumper. He went to the babies, picked up Violetta passed her to me then bent for Ben.

'Wow, he is a ton weight! How do you manage?' He took both babies then walked towards a dark green Landrover where Freddie was wagging his whole body. 'Come on.' he called looking behind as he easily climbed the embankment.

'Freddie! Rope!' The sheepdog leapt over the seats and snuggled into the centre of a coil of rope.

'He always lies there when his front seat is occupied. It made him feel secure as a puppy, stopped him rattling about.' He adjusted the babies then pulled open the passenger door.

'Get in!'

I pulled myself and the bags wearily into the passenger seat and he placed the babies in my arms then he lifted a tear stained Sarah making sure she was tucked up beside me. The road was bumpy, each wobble struck my sore head like a hammer. Through my misery I could see the beauty of the Dales but I felt locked inside myself. It took only minutes to cover the ground we had trudged.

'Are you taking us to Harrogate?' I murmured through my burning tonsils.

'Maybe later.' He said keeping his eyes straight ahead. I could not have cared less as long as we were out of that torturous wind. We shot off to the left to a steep downward road where everything grew gradually calmer.

Further into the valley the sheep had lambs following them. Sarah cried out in delight as we slowed to see a new-born wobbling to its feet, then an older more sturdy lamb nose under its mother pushing and lifting the fleece as if it were a rug being shaken out.

'That is where they get their milk Sarah, from their mum, just like Ben and Violetta.'

'Me want lamb mammy.' Her face was aglow at the wonder of this simple sight.

I was feeling sickly and even hotter as we came into a patch of gravel in front of an old stone built farmhouse and pub. It did not look open for business but the sun shone on the cream stone and newly painted white window frames. The wind was only a breeze here I thought as the door opened and warmth lay on my cheeks.

As he helped me out of the van my legs buckled, my head went woozy and I wanted to be sick. He lifted the babies from my arms. A lady wafting in delicious perfume took my arm and led me somewhere, I did not know where and I did not care.

'I'll take care of your children.' She whispered. She smelled of Aqua Manda a scent I loved but could never afford.

I woke to cheeping sparrows and early dusk. My eyes focussed on scrubbed pine drawers and side tables, I was under cream blankets and clean sheets wearing only my greyed underwear. Above me were heavy oak beams keeping up a high ceiling. It was agony when I sipped at water left in a glass beside me. How long had I been there? I heaved myself up onto stripped floorboards, trying to take control of my legs.

They stumbled me to the window. Blackbirds were tripping around a lawn and a red and black woodpecker was hammering away at a feeder filled with nuts. To the side there was a field filled with pecking hens and a wooden cree where they must sleep at night. Just over the wall stood a forlorn yet pretty old stone barn.

Panic rose in my chest. My babies! I heard Sarah giggling then saw her run across the grass with a tall dark woman chasing her. Sarah had on the cream cardigan that matched the lady's jumper, rolled up at the sleeves and almost tripping her up. I saw real happiness in my child's eyes as she was swept off her feet and swung high before being gently placed onto the ground. This must be the man's wife. How lucky she was.

This place was the start of a lightening of my soul. I could feel it. And yet I had to leave.

On a chair beside the bed some-one had laid out a soft blue shirt and cut off white trousers. Beside them was a bottle of Fenjal bath oil and a big white towel. Nervously I pushed open the door. I was on a big landing with a wooden stair rail rising up and continuing past me to other rooms. It had the look and smell of being newly polished, I gripped my toes into an expensive carpet and crept to the bathroom next door. Here was the pitiful toilet bag with child's tooth brush and comb. I looked down at my old stained underwear. Some-one had seen it. Embarrassment flooded my being. I turned on the taps and watched the water steam as it filled the bath. I pulled open a slatted blind, it looked onto a different garden. I saw a tartan rug spread on the grass and both babies lying there gurgling at purple catnip flowers just bursting. They wore a man's tee-shirt each and glowed with cleanliness. They both looked swamped in cotton and from here I saw how tiny Violetta looked compared to my robust son. Pear blossom petals floated onto them from branches above. The lady was showing a fascinated Sarah how to sew up her teddy's split tummy.

I was overpowered by heaven as I lay in the scented water. The warmth spread into me and I felt relaxation I had not felt since I was little. The steam helped my throat. When the water began to cool I washed my hair and face. The first soap and shampoo in warm water since that awful night. The little comb had a battle with my tatty hair as I watched the lovely scene from the window, how had I got here?

There was a pot of Pond's face cream on the chair and I slathered it across my cheeks and neck wincing at the healing scratches and cuts I had got rolling down the hill. My hands drank in the moisture as I smoothed them together. I felt tears well up. This had been my mother's only beauty aid and what I had used when I had been getting my weekly five pounds a week from working as the solicitor's receptionist.

The clothes swamped me but felt good and clean as I fumbled down the stairs to find the kitchen. The man looked up when the big oak door creaked. Our eyes met and everything in my veins said yes. But I had no right to want him. He would be angry and insulted if he knew. I could never infect him with the poisons of my life. I had to become a new character with a history I did not deserve.

'Ah ha!' You look refreshed. Quite glowing actually. Did you find all the stuff Carol left for you?' He turned back to the pan he was stirring on the old Aga. My breath caught in my raw throat.

'Carol? Oh yes. How kind, everything was so welcome.'

I was struck by his ease of being exactly who he was with no excuses. His eyes were bright and animated and looked at me over a straight, strong nose.

He sipped at a wooden spoon and jerked backwards. 'Yikes that is hot!'

'Did you like that chicken veg soup I brought in the flask?' I sniffed the air and my tummy commented on how empty it was.

'Yes, it was lovely.'

'Great.' he laughed. 'It is the only thing I know how to cook. It will ease your throat.'

He took a blue bowl from a dresser heaving with pretty but miss-matched crockery.

'Eggs.' I spluttered, feeling so out of place. 'You know how to boil eggs.'

He pulled a chair across the cream stone flagged floor.

'Sit here, ha-ha eggs, yes. I lived on eggs for almost a year when my mother died. I was 22 and had been spoiled rotten.'

He placed a steaming bowl in front of me. I peered down to see huge chunks of chicken breast and thigh with leeks, carrots and barley floating beneath parsley broth. He began sawing at a crispy cottage loaf. There was a knife stuck upright into a great chunk of creamy butter.

'Here.' he said passing buttered slices of bread, she glimpsed in his eyes such clarity and kindness. 'Your children are having a lovely time with Carol. You eat that then I'll take you out to them.'

'I saw them from the window, it was a beautiful sight.'

'Well, the wind dropped and the sun came out so we have to make the most of that in the Yorkshire Dales. I'll take them a drink.'

I watched his back as it disappeared and tried to analyse why everything just felt good when he was in front of me. I had to stem any thoughts of him as a man. My life would never have a man in it again.

Left alone when he disappeared with two glasses and a bottle of apple juice, I looked about at the rough yet comfy kitchen. The walls were whitewashed and the old units had been given a new lease of life with soft green paint. Carol had great taste in pans and the lovely cream jug which held fresh pink campions and forget-me nots.

The soup was delicious, I felt so full and just a bit sleepy but I needed to see my children. I felt my milk flow but dreaded the little mouths on my cracked nipples.

Carol looked up when she saw me approaching, her hair was swept back in a perfect French pleat. She bore a quiet elegance she did not seem to realize in her ease of being. I felt like a tramp.

'Oh you so suit my blouse and sorry the pants are so baggy. Most of your stuff is in the automatic washing machine. I hope you don't mind.'

Sarah ran to me to show me Humph who now had a line of big red stitches up his tummy. He felt different. I hugged her close and cuddled her bear, his wet, sucked ear brushing against my arm.

'Hello my lumpy friend. This is a lovely new look.'

Sarah laughed. 'Me picked red thread.'

Carol put her hand on my daughter's head, she held a joyous smile of greeting on her pretty face. 'We did have bear coloured thread but she insisted on this as she said it matched her coat. He seems to have lost some weight though.' Sunlight glittered off leaves everywhere, I had to shade my eyes.

I looked over at the babies who seemed far too contented after not being fed for five hours.

'I hope it is OK, I have given them a bottle and I have this for you.'

She handed me a tube.

'What is it?'

'Nipple cream. I got it from the surgery along with milk samples. You can use it three times a day as long as you wash it off before you give a feed.'

My face flooded with heat.

'Hey do not be embarrassed. I am the doctor here. I have seen it all before.'

'Well thank you.'

'I do need to talk to you about Violetta though. She is not yours is she?'

Terror rose in me. 'I did not give birth to her no, but she is mine.'

'I am afraid it doesn't work like that Rose but she needs you at the moment and you certainly saved her life.'

She took my hand. 'Don't worry, you are not in trouble, quite the opposite. If I had not brought a rescued spaniel down here I would not have been able to help.' A little gaggle of assorted dogs rolled each other on the grass and grabbed at sticks and balls.

'So many dogs here.'

'Yes, they come and go. I am the one known locally for looking after sick or unwanted animals but thank God there is a willing soul here to help.'

'Oh you mean your husband. I have noticed he has different dogs.'

'You have?' Her brows knitted. 'Well if it wasn't for Lancelot I would be swamped and lost.'

'Lancelot?'

'Yes, Lancelot Brookes, you just ate his soup.'

'Is that his name?'

'You didn't know?'

'No, it is not very modern, romantic though!' I should not have said that.

She smiled. 'Well there are lots of ladies around here who would agree with you there.'

I tried to look as if I was not jealous but her attention was taken by a yelping puppy whose ear was being chewed by an over enthusiastic collie. The dogs wagged their bodies in ecstasy as she bowled over to sort them out. They rushed past me after her thrown stick. Sarah ran after them into more fruit trees with pink apple blossom just ready to burst.

I sat beside the snoozing babies. One so fair the other so dark but each one pulled at my heartstrings. Violetta was scrunched in a way she must have been in her mother's womb. Her arms were up at the sides of her head and her knees up to her stomach with her tiny feet crossed at the ankles. It yanked my heart to think that this beautiful creature might be dead if I had not gone out to her that night. Or if I had not had milk or if I had not been there at all. I noticed an ancient wisteria vine clinging on the house wall, its purple fat buds just about to open and hang down luxuriously. I knew that must be his bedroom, where Servant climbed to sleep beside him. I looked around at this lovely place enclosed by an old dry stone wall. The cow parsley was still green but soon it would throw its creamy heads and scent everywhere. I had gathered armfuls of this for the old enamel jug on my mother's scrubbed wooden table. It seemed to be my childhood task to keep that chipped jug full of flowers all year round. In autumn it held sprigs of golden leaves and in winter larch twigs showing off their neat cones. But late April to May I was torn so that old jam jars were filled with cowslips, bluebells, periwinkles and anything else that lifted my heart. They crowded out our dinner plates. My parents hadn't minded, they loved what I loved.

The dogs had rushed back to Carol to drop various sticks at her feet. Sarah tried to throw some but they did not go far. I followed the dogs but my eyes were drawn to Lancelot talking to a visitor at the gate out onto the Dales. My heart stopped as the man replaced his policeman's helmet to his balding head as he turned to leave. Panic stricken I shouted abruptly to Sarah to come to me.

It was stupid. His eyes turned to me then he said something conspiratorial to Lancelot who looked at me too then shook his head. My heart crashed crazily inside my aching body.

He waved at Carol then went through the gate to the road. My mouth was dry, my lips sticking together as blood pounded into my brain.

'Hey, you need more rest. You look wobbly.' Carol's arm and that lovely scent encircled me.

'I have a sore throat.' I croaked.

She gently pressed practiced fingers to my neck and I winced. 'Have you ever caught your neck in something, some washing line or something to give it a hard squeeze?'

'No...I.'

'There seems to be some damage. We must keep an eye on it.' My mind flashed to the hundreds of times I'd had cruel fingers jerk and clamp around my neck.

'You are worn out, I will get Lancelot to make you some hot water and honey then off to bed again young lady. I will look after Sarah.'

I wanted nothing more than to sleep forever but even through my banging head and chest I knew I had to leave this place, leave fast.

The babies were brought to my bed by Carol. 'Are you sure, you can breast feed.' She asked as I took a mewing Violetta into my arms. 'I have checked her over. She is quite robust.'

'I need to, I am bursting with milk. Although I am worried that I have enough for two babies.'

'Well if you are sure. Do not worry about that, the more the milk is taken the more you will make. But put the nipple cream on after and wash it off before the next feed.'

'I will.' I said wondering what she would say if she knew I would be in the Dales again soon and would be washing them in streams and waterfalls.

I put Ben to my breast and cuddled up to Violetta with my spare hand. Carol pulled out an unwilling drawer completely from the pine chest. She laid a folded soft blanket to cover the bottom, then took a smaller cellular cream blanket and laid it over.

'Here is a drawer-cot for Violetta. Will the other two be OK with you in the bed? You can use the big pillow to stop Ben rolling off'.

She was deft and experienced. 'I suppose lots of babies started their lives in drawers in the olden days.' I smiled.

'Ha…and now. I had to do the same in January. A young girl with stomach ache. Her mum called me out and when she produced a full term baby refused to accept it. Thought I had brought it with me or something. Now she is the proudest Granny in the Dale.'

She turned to the door. 'Is there any one you would like me to contact?'

My dad flashed into my brain. He was safer knowing nothing. But I needed to know he was all right. I only managed a slow shake of the head.

'Well I have an evening surgery to attend to, see you soon. And rest.'

'Thank you for everything, you did not have to help me.'

Her laugh tinkled from her beautiful lips and teeth. 'Oh I do have to! Lancelot admires you and is so fond of you. I can tell. I would do anything for that man.'

So would I, I thought miserably. But soon I would have to sneak away from him. That was the kindest thing I could ever do for him.

I had just finished feeding Violetta when there was a hesitant knock on the door. 'Are you decent?'

I thought about that word and of course I knew what he meant but all I could think about was, that no, I wasn't decent. He was one person I did not want to find out just how awful I was.

I heard him start to move away. 'Yes, come in.' It felt strange telling him he could come in to what was his property. He held a steaming cup on a tray and a big spoon, beside them was a little bowl of black discs.

'Pontefract Cakes, you like liquorish I hope. I heard it has antiseptic qualities as well as the honey. They are a weakness of mine.' He looked around at the scene, my hair was dishevelled and Ben was asleep across my legs. 'Your washing is on the line and Sarah is fine. She is keen for you to come down though, when you're ready.'

He looked like he wanted to linger, like he had words on his lips but he turned and went, shutting the door behind him. The hot drink helped but I did not like the liquorice.

I went to the bathroom and washed then spent an agonising five minutes trying to sooth my cracked nipples with the cream. I read the label and saw the words 'Dr. Brookes'. Hardly able to bear my clothes against my chest, I made my way down to the kitchen. It was warm, the oven door was open, and on a rug on the floor was Sarah giving a bottle to a straggly lamb. She saw me and grinned, pulling the teat from the lamb's eager mouth to allow the air back into the pop bottle full of some milky drink.

Lancelot laughed. 'Ha, she has just learned that. This is lamb number two, she practiced on this one.' He pointed to a brown and white lamb in a cardboard box. It looked as if it was wearing a thin knitted dishcloth used to mop up spilt cocoa as a vest.

'You clever girl Sarah.' I went over and kissed her little head. She was beaming with the pleasure of it all. The lamb baa-d then and I jumped at the loudness of it.

Lancelot laughed. 'Well, he has to be loud to make his mother hear where he is on the hills. Only she will never hear him or his sister over there.'

We all looked sadly at the thin bodies and wiggling tails of the orphans.

'Mammy, I gived lambs names all by myself. This one Woolly and in box is Jumper.'

'Lovely names.' I laughed. I laughed! I had forgotten how it felt.

On the table was a pie and dish of potatoes. A pan on the range came to the boil and Lancelot rushed across to save it boiling over.

'Only frozen peas I am afraid.'

For some reason I felt acute embarrassment as I washed Sarah's hands, pushing up the oversized arms of Carol's cardigan. She had not wanted to be parted from Woolly and Jumper but Lancelot moved chairs around so she could stare at them. When she was balanced on two striped cushions he dished up the food on warm plates.

'Carol makes the best steak and kidney ever.'

She would, I thought enviously, she was pretty, clever and happy. Why would she not be a great cook? She had a lovely man to feed and a lovely home and a fulfilling job. I ate well, I had to make good milk, knowing it might be my last food for a while.

I was awake well before first light at 5am. I was becoming an expert at pushing everything into the disintegrating bin bags. It was all clean now except for the woolly I had found Violetta in, and it made me feel guilty. After gritting my teeth to feed the babies with my sore breasts Sarah and I crept out along the corridor and through the door at the front of the house. We were all dressed in our clean but un-ironed tatty clothes. Ben was awake and curious but Violetta was in a well fed sleep. We almost tripped over a long sign lying face down against the wall where sheep were feeding off the grass, their lambs keeping close on wobbling legs. Sarah ran to them and they scattered. She cried, wanting to take Woolly and Jumper with us, I had to promise her more lambs of her very own down the hill which I hoped was the way to Harrogate.

It was calm with a low cloud covering making the vast sky like watery milk. At least we aren't wet I thought as we struggled down into the view spread before us. There was a sort of road with big rough stones and sheep poo to avoid. Sarah gripped Humph hard against her and struggled to keep her bag off the ground. My arms ached, Ben was wanting to half sit up to see what was going on, I could have screamed at the rubbing against my chest. Violetta still slept in the crook of my elbow, her dark lashes across her cheeks.

I heard a vehicle behind us and stepped aside hoping some farmer might take pity on us. The green Land Rover pulled in front blocking our path. Freddie barked as he peered at us from the back window and Lancelot jumped to the ground.

'What are you doing out so early?' He looked at my tattered bin bags. Was that hurt across his face? Sarah looked alarmed at the loud barking.

'Take no notice, Freddie is a working dog and he is keen to get on. Like me.' He shook his head impatiently.

'You don't have to leave.'

I saw myself with his eyes then, wretched and struggling. I had the absurd thought that at least my hair was clean. But I was vividly aware of my torn, creased clothes. What must he see compared to his well-groomed clever wife?

'I am not your responsibility, I have to make a life for us all. I cannot freeload.'

He told Freddie to be quiet then put his hands up in submission. His look was indulgent, knowing and forgiving.

'OK. I understand that. I was going to interview you for a job?'

'What?' My shame smothered my self-esteem, what could I do that any-one would want?

'Can you cook simple but tasty meals?'

'Well yes…but…..'

'Ok you're hired!'

'That was the interview?' I said surprised.

'Yeah, I know your character already. No need for time wasting.'

I know I let my mouth hang open and I knew it was most unattractive.

'Mind there is no TV reception up here.' He laughed.

He picked a beaming Sarah up, her arms went naturally around his neck, and then he placed her delicately on the seat. 'I have a job for you too. Chief Woolly Jumper feeder.' He threw my bags into the back then took Ben. The relief in my arms almost made me sigh. Violetta woke as I clambered in. My nagging thought was of the policeman and when he would be back for me.

'You want me to cook for you?' I asked nervously, thinking of Carol's skills and beauty.

'Not just for me, for my pub.'

'Pub?'

'Yes, the front of the house you were in last night used to be an ancient pub, 'The Lark and Lamb,' two creatures we have many of around here. I have applied for a licence. That is why Tony came around at teatime, to tell me I have been successful.'

'Tony?'

'Yes, PC Trainor. Used to race about these hills on our bikes together when we escaped from school. I still see him peddling like mad over my land, trying to keep his beer gut in check.'

We jerked into action and the scenery rattled by as he turned the Defender around. Once again, the struggling journey I had so painfully trodden was travelled in minutes.

'Where is your land?'

He smiled. 'Here, all about. Ten thousand acres of beauty. Did you know that the Basilica in Rome has lead mined from beneath these dales near Richmond many years ago? I own everything on that land including the abbey hotel you stayed at for a few days. I could charge you rent.'

'I won't pay. The food was terrible.'

'Oh getting cheeky now you have a job are you?'

'Oh. No…I meant before you found us, other people's left overs and wild leaves. Cheese spread and eggs were Haute Cuisine after that.' I covered my embarrassment with new thoughts.

'I don't want any charity. I can make it on my own.' I regretted my tone.

'Good, I am not offering you any. It will be hard work and it is hard to get any one to work out here. It is a bit selfish of me to ask really.'

'I only cook basic stuff, like my mum made.'

'Great, that is what I want. A pub out here will only bring people in if they can get a good old fashioned feed. Pub food is the future.'

I did not dare say how much I hated pubs. How many nights I had strained thoughts of how our money could have bought the children much needed new clothes and decent food instead of being tipped into the tills of a smoky, beer smelling, rowdy drinking hole.

'Sounds lovely.'

'Well in the Dales we are way behind cities. They have a fad serving food in baskets. Chicken in a basket, scampi in a basket....you name it.'

'Soup in a basket?' I chimed in, shocking myself with the first glimpse of humour I had felt in years. I had been dwelling in deep unhappiness for so long I had forgotten that I used to be witty and fun. Ed had robbed me of that. He had paid for it now.

His laugh poured beauty and happiness through his lovely teeth. This man was a gift to any woman who could love him. I was so sad that it could never be me.

'Is Carol too busy to cook for you?' I asked reminding myself that he was already taken.

'Carol?' he turned to look at me in puzzlement. 'She is a GP. When would she cook for a pub?'

I felt embarrassed. 'I just meant...well that pie she made...she is such a good cook.'

'She can show you how to make that, then you can make it on a larger scale. Can you fit cooking in with your children?'

'I can try, but I do not want customers seeing me!' I knew I sounded anxious and he heard it too.

'I will employ a local barmaid who will serve the food from the kitchen. Why do you want to stay hidden? Your scratches are almost healed.'

I could not tell him the answer. He seemed to absorb what thickened the air between us.

'How long has your husband been dead?'

The sudden question pierced into my heart.

'Not long.' My voice was clotted by guilt.

'What did he die of?'

My heart caught on a fresh wave of pain. My mouth and thoughts were glued shut.

'Oh I'm sorry. Still raw I suppose. I just wondered why you had to leave your home and walk the moors.'

When I was silent he tried to change the subject.

'You know you have the same colour hair as Tony's wife, you will like her. They'll be coming round. Tony used to have the same way of talking as you when he first came here as a six year old, soon lost it in favour of a proper Yorkshire voice though.' He smiled.

'Did you tell him where I am from?'

'I don't know where you're from. I guessed Newcastle as you have a slight Geordie accent.'

'Did you tell him that?'

'No!' What is all this about? Is some-one looking for you?'

I felt my heart thud against my ribs and squeezed the babies tighter. What if he took Violetta from me? What if I lost all my children through my terrible actions?

'What do you mean?'

'Well family? Your parents.'

'I only have dad…he is lovely, and not looking for me.'

'Well any time you want to ring him, please use my phone. No charge.'

'Thanks, that is kind but he is not on the phone.'

It took only minutes of jiggling over rocks and ruts to find ourselves back at the door we had left almost an hour ago. He helped us out, holding Ben easily in his strong arms, then opened the gate so Sarah could run to see her lambs.

'I'll make the bottles as soon as I help your mother upstairs.' he called after her. He put our pitiful bags down beside the sign which he turned over with his foot.

'See, this will be above the door this afternoon. I designed it myself.'

'The Lark and Lamb', was painted gold on a dark green background. There was a fat lamb looking up at a tiny bird soaring above it. The clouds split a little then shining weak sun onto the lettering as if in approval.

'Ah skylarks are so elusive, I love their song but they are hard to spot so high up.' I said.

He gently put a wriggling Ben into my arms, taking Violetta and easing her onto his shoulder. 'Nice to see you have a natural affinity with nature Rose. It is important to me.'

That was the first time he had used my name, it shivered down me as if I had never heard it before either.

'Oh?' I tried to keep my voice normal. 'Why does a pub cook need to know about nature?'

'No, not that.' He said striding into the corridor to the kitchen to warm the lambs' milk.

I followed him in, he laid Violetta on the huge chintz sofa and I propped Ben against the arm with fat cushions. His wobbling head moved from us to Violetta.

I watched Lancelot's capable arms making light of the task he must have done many times. The smooth dark hairs disappearing into the turned back cuffs of his shirt. He eased the teats over the neck of the pop bottles and shook them vigorously before handing them to me.

'Here, you can help your daughter. I have to get going. I was up at four am to feed them. This saves me from dashing back to feed the lambs later.'

'Were you looking for us just now?'

'No, out to check on the sheep, the birthing is large scale this week, I had no idea you were even awake.'

'Will you be long?' I knew I sounded too hopeful.

'Don't know, I have two thousand sheep to check on and they go wherever they like. Yesterday a ewe had given birth in some-one's newly planted pansy bed. Ate the lot.'

He laughed. 'All cottage gates should be closed in the Dales'. He nodded towards the fridge. 'There are sausages in there...eggs on top. Help yourselves. Pans, under sink.'

He was almost through the kitchen door when I had a thought.

'Should I make breakfast for Carol?'

He stopped and looked back at me. 'No! Why?'

'I just want to be helpful.'

'Just look after you and yours.'

He was gone and the room shrank without him in it.

I did not see Carol for three days which surprised me. She probably wanted to stay away from the racket of a new pub kitchen being fitted and I went to bed early with the babies. I wanted to tell her how the cream she had given me cleared up my sore nipples, but I could never catch her. Ben was coaxed into eating a bit of scrambled egg with butter. Then thin oats with milk. He was able to push himself around the floor now, crawling would not be far behind. Sarah lived for the lambs and had taken over throwing the grain into the hen field. She had even been brave enough, with Lancelot's coaxing, to push her tiny hand beneath a chicken sitting on its eggs. Servant had reappeared having been met half way home and picked up in the Land Rover. Sarah was covered in his black and white hairs as she loved to pull him onto her knee and kiss him as he narrowed his eyes and purred so loud that we all laughed. I tried to do as much as I could to earn our keep, cleaning and cooking, but only just managed to stay out of the way of the many tradesmen who banged and clashed their way through the pub side of the house.

On Friday morning, when I was trying to get used to the new pub cooker, a little mini car pulled up. Panic hit my chest, I wanted to hide but the children were all around me. Violetta was asleep in a cardboard box with a pillow and Sarah was showing Ben how to bang on a pan with a wooden spoon. I had no time to act. A lady with a scarf around her brown hair and a busy demeanour burst in through the door.

'You Mrs Rose?'

I nodded so she handed me a brown envelope. That is your pay. I need more details from you and your papers. What is your first name?'

'Rose.'

'Oh, Mr. Brookes told me…..sorry, well what is your surname?'

Blood rushed to my brain and all I could think of was NOT telling her who I was.

'Linden…' I blurted, giving my mother's maiden name.

'Right, well we have to get it all sorted for next week. I do the wages on Thursdays and drive around with them on Friday mornings. Shepherds' wives have to get the shopping in.' She looked me up and down, then glanced at the children.

'See ya!'

As the door clanged shut all I could think was that I was no longer no-one. But I was about to have an identity. I did not want it.

Chapter Five.

News of me being here would be in the ear of every one
who worked for Lancelot and then spread to all ears in the
Dales. I looked at the envelope in my hands and opened it.
There were seven pound notes. More money than I had
ever held in my hands at one time. I looked at Sarah in her
too short dungarees and thought of all the old tea towels I
had to put on baby bottoms several times a day. I could
replace them all. Only I had not seen a shop around here.

My mind immediately turned to where I could hide my
money. I took us all into the house kitchen with one
urgent thought in my head. I glanced around looking for
hiding places and thought that under the mattress might
do. As I ran up the stairs I stopped. The thought hit me
like a slap. I did not have to hide my money. No one
wanted to steal it from me. I felt swamped in luxury.

I threw the notes into the air and let them rain down. They
were mine.

The house door cracked open and a rounded lady with her
grey hair poking out of a floral turban style scarf, bundled
in. She peeled off her old coat and slung it over the stair
newel post, went to the cupboard and clattered out a
cream and red Electrolux vacuum cleaner. She bent to
pick up two of the pound notes I had fluttered around me.
Only then did she look at up at me.

' 'ere, this must be yours. I suppose you are the new pub cook we have heard so much about?'

I balked at the thought of all that gossip. It had only been a few minutes since the wages lady left. They must have met on the step outside.

'Me name is Mrs Armitage and I cleans the 'ole house every Friday. Top t'bottom.'

She stared at me, taking in every feature of my being, no doubt to be able to regurgitate me to every person in the Dale.

'I 'ere you have lots of kiddies. Well I do not have kiddies get in my way, just as I don't have all the weird and wonky dogs get in me way when I am working. Ok? Clear?'

With what she thought was enough explanation to the newcomer she pushed her foot onto the switch and began pushing the long tubes and hard brushes across carpet and wood. The racket seared into my brain so I went back into the pub kitchen with the idea of getting out of the house until she had finished. I heard her rattle into the house kitchen and had a sudden thought, so pushed open the door.

'Mrs Armitage.'

'Aye?' she said keeping her eyes on her bucket as she tipped Flash cleaner into it.

'I am sleeping in the guest room, I will clean that myself if that's OK'

'Please yursel…the sooner I get 'ome to my Percy the better.' She said turning on hot water to steam loudly into her bucket.

I next saw Carol at the opening night of the Lark and Lamb. All the children were asleep, a hard task that night as Woolly and Jumper were taken to the next stage of their lives in a barn with the other four orphans which had been cared for by shepherd's wives and children. Sarah had cried when they had been lifted out of the kitchen but had to accept another hard lesson in her short life. Lancelot asked me to serve up the cottage pie and sausage and mash he had me make so much of. I was so busy I could not talk to the new barmaid, Babs, as she dashed in and out for loaded plates.

I had glanced out of the window when tucking Sarah up, Carol, wearing a flowing silk blouse in dusty pink and lipstick to match, was walking arm and arm with a tall man with black glasses and an obviously new suit. She was in the back garden showing him the long stems of purple cat nip where Servant had flattened his bed in the middle so he could nibble and squirm to his heart's contentment. They laughed, Carol's happiness tinkled up to me through the open window and struck into my heart.

I had never seen a woman so happy. I never would feel that same joy.

The new barmaid was fumbling around the beer pumps and giving everyone doubles instead of singles but Lancelot did not mind, everything was on the house tonight anyway. I could only see her back from the kitchen door and hear the high pitched giggle that I had heard on the day of the interviews. She had been the only one who turned up. Even though she was not the image Lancelot wanted to portray he had hired her, he had no choice.

I refused to go out into the bar or the front of the pub where Lancelot had put picnic benches with ashtrays. I looked out of the window when I checked on the children, looking nervously for Tony the policeman friend, but I never saw him. Carol was sitting with a gin and tonic and I saw her touch the cheek of the man who took her hand and kissed it.

I heard long strides taking the stairs two at a time and turned to see Lancelot behind me.

'There you are!' He was wearing a clean white shirt and smelled of something expensive and intoxicating. We need more food. Some late arrivals? What can you do?'

My thoughts ran wild as I ran through all the things in the pub kitchen. He looked over my shoulder and through the window.

'Ah that is where Carol got too.'

'She seems fond of that man she is with.' I said hoping I did not sound judgemental.

'I hope so! He is my brother…he is a geologist, usually away in Israel studying rock eating snails most of the time. She is thrilled to have him back.'

He turned back to me. 'Food?'

'Well we have lots of potatoes and eggs.'

'OK, then I can tell them that plates of egg and chips will be emerging in the blink of an eye, can I?'

He took my hand and helped me run down the stairs. It was a physical shock to realise the pleasure his touch gave me. When we reached the kitchen he let go. I felt this detachment from him sharply as if it was my right. I tried to be normal.

'Rock eating snails?'

'Ha. Don't ask…far too complicated.' He lifted the sack of potatoes over for me.

'Your food is a great hit already, I wish you'd come out later and let them see how clever I have been in employing you.' He saw my strained look and shook his head kindly. 'No?'

'I will leave you to the potato peeling then.' He dashed off to his guests.

I turned my hand over. He had only meant to hurry me
along but he could never know the electricity he had
zapped through me. I tried to rid myself of the guilty
feeling by opening the hessian sack to sort out the biggest,
chip worthy potatoes.

Babs barged in looking for the food. She was in the hot
flush of life and expert at getting all eyes on her. The oil
filled air parted to allow this confident, vivid girl to fill
the space she always took as her own. A tight white
blouse canoodled her breasts to present them high and she
smiled showing lipsticked teeth. Her labour intensive
curled hair was piled up just so it could escape
temptingly. She was what my mother had tutted and
called 'a peroxide blonde'.

'Where's the scran then? You must be Rose. I'm Babs.'
She said happily dismissing me as any competition in the
looks race.

She had alive roving eyes which seemed to stop roving
when they latched onto Lancelot. The kitchen door
slapped behind him. 'Plate them up! I will take these first
ones out!'

He disappeared with piled high plates of hot golden chips
with two fried eggs still slithering in shiny lard.

Babs elbowed me in the arm.

'I'nt he delicious?' She licked her lips. 'I mean to have
him!'

I looked at her as she hugged herself tight. 'He is as good as hooked.' She opened her eyes as wide as she could considering how much black mascara they carried.

'I took all the notices down that he put in the post office and shops 'bout this job. Made sure he had to have me if I was the only one who seemed interested.'

I stared at her, my emotions complicating by the second.

'Well, I've tried all the young lads out here on the Dales. Not one of them worth taking my knickers down for a second time. But him…ooooh! What I will do to him. That mouth! I want it all over me. And he has good money, can't wait to spend it for him.' She laughed and picked up the plates I had just loaded.

How could she manipulate herself into a job just to steal another woman's husband? I was shocked at her openness. She obviously thought me on the same level as her. I had to warn Carol.

It was exhausting looking after the children and making all the food the pub was selling. I developed a routine, putting the babies in a playpen made by Lancelot from high metal fire guards and a wooden clothes horse. Sarah grew in her responsibilities of lamb and hen care and wanted to learn how to cook mince and dumplings and bacon and egg flan that were the hits of the menus. I was making sticky toffee pudding with Sarah licking the bowls when Lancelot burst in.

He smiled at the children and then me, my heart expanded every time I saw him. He curled his finger around the runny toffee sauce bowl and tasted our efforts.

'Mmm! Sarah, you are a great cook, No wonder the fairies have left you surprises.'

There was one thing that peaked my daughter's interest more than animals and flowers, it was fairies.

'Where fairies, 'celot?' she beamed trying to get off the chair I had stood her on. I lifted her off and washed her hands.

'Oh in the garden. They visit when the rhubarb is ready for picking as they use the leaves as umbrellas. I think they have gone now but they have left you presents.'

She ran to the door. Violetta was asleep so I lifted Ben out onto my hip and we all went into the garden. Sun sparkled off beads of rain left by the early May shower all over the plants and grass. Hawthorne hedging threw its creamy blossom perfume into the warming air. The hens clucked over the wall excited to find worms encouraged out of the soil by the wet. Sarah took Lancelot's hand and skipped down the path to where he had planted neat rows of onions, cabbages and potatoes. Wooden stakes had been stuck through seed packets showing lettuces and radishes. There were two big displays of red stalked rhubarb holding enormous leaves up to the sky. On some of the stalks dangled thread with shiny paper wrapped sweets.

I saw a tube of Spangles on one and a packet of Refreshers dangling lopsidedly from a really thick stalk.

My daughter almost cried with joy as she pulled one then two sweets from the rhubarb. I watched and wondered at what kind of man could be so imaginative and kind to do this for a little girl. He turned to see my dreamy look and smiled with his eyes. When he winked at me I tumbled and crumbled, sinking deep into feelings I had no right to.

'Now Sarah,' he said turning to my girl who was sucking on one sweet and had the others crammed into her chubby hands. 'Put those into your pocket and help me pick the rhubarb. Mummy will make us all crumble for our supper and if it is as good as her other food we will put it on the pub menu tomorrow.'

He pushed down at the crown and broke off a juicy looking stalk then took a garden knife from his belt and swished the leaf off. He put this on Sarah's head.

'There now, best rain hat you ever had.' He picked three more stalks and cut their leaves onto the compost heap.' The fairies will take them to make new roofs for their castles.'

I could hardly speak for bubbling joy. Sarah glowed under this attention she had never had from a man. They say signs creep out of your eyes when you are falling in love so I was about to turn away from him when I said.

'You should have children of your own Lancelot.'

He looked at me, clean into my eyes and I could see a sadness. 'I would love them.' He murmured.

I wondered if Carol was too into her career to get pregnant. Who could blame her? She obviously wanted to do things the right way around instead of being like me.

When we got back to the pub kitchen Babs was just arriving for her evening shift. Her breasts were pushed up higher than usual and her eyes were rimmed in black and edged in thick false eyelashes which she batted at Lancelot.

'Evening Babs.' He said without seeming to take in her encouragements. 'Friday night will be our busiest so get ready to take all that lovely money from the farm lads' pockets.'

She was gazing at him as if he was the eighth wonder of the world.

'I'll meet you in the bar to go over the selling points of the two new real ales we got in today.'

She beamed as she left, already scrabbling in her handbag to squirt more of her pungent perfume from the quickly emptying bottle.

'Babs is going a bit far in the make-up department.' I said trying not to sound bitchy then realising how plain I must look beside her. He laughed.

'Oh she is a law unto herself that one. The customers love it. But I must speak to her about that cheap scent, don't want my ale overpowered.' He swung through the door and into her lair.

Carol ate in the pub with Lancelot's brother that night and came into the kitchen after I had put the children to bed.

'Lance told me you had a secret Rhubarb crumble in here. Where is it?'

She looked so keen I had to laugh.

'You are in a good mood.' I said spooning out tangy pie and topping.

'Yes! I have two days off. My first in six months.' She half sat on the edge of a chair.

'And how are the nipples?' She said through mouthfuls of pudding and the custard I had copied from my mum's.

'Almost healed, I am giving Ben soft food now so he is not latched on so long.'

'I know you do not want to hear this Rose, but we have to sort out Violetta. I would be failing in my duty if I did not make a report. I shouldn't really be pretending that I think the baby is yours. I could get into trouble.'

She saw how upset I was, put down the bowl and came over to put an arm around me.

'Rose you have too much on, along with your grief at your husband's death which I presume is what caused you to run away?' She looked me right in the eye. 'Why could you not stay in your home?' I shut them tight and hoped she would think it was tears not guilt I was trying to hide.

She pulled me to her chest. 'Ah, it is hard feeding two babies, and delightful though your children are, they will become more and more of a drain on you. Then you have to go home when you are well enough. I am not sure Lancelot is doing you a favour keeping you here.'

The thought of leaving was like a dagger in my sore heart. The peace, the beauty, my little job. I pulled them all into my mind but they did not push out what it was really full of. Lancelot. This woman's husband.

'Rose, I admire you. I really do but Lancelot is always taking in lame ducks, literally. He has had ten rescue dogs staying with him already this year. But you. You are the biggest animal he has taken in; ever.' Her laugh was thin.

She pushed me gently away at arm's length. 'All our animals are loved back to strength then re-homed Rose.'

Real tears came to me then. Carol stepped back and passed me a tea towel.

'You make a great rhubarb crumble Rose.' She said trying to lighten the mood. 'Lancelot will miss you when you go.'

She did not know that I could never go home because of what I had done. That I could not even let my dad know where I was even though he would be driven mad with worry. Or that she would be waving me off to homelessness.

She took the tea-towel I had used to dry my face and tossed it into the basket.

'That reminds me. You cannot go on without proper nappies. I am going into Darlington tomorrow shopping. Would you like to come? Pub is closed Mondays anyway.'

'Oh,' I had a thought then. 'How far away is it?'

'An hour, but lovely scenery. Have you never been?'

'No…I…'

Babs flung herself merrily into the kitchen then and the room filled with only her concerns.

'Any scran left?' She said opening the oven door and lifting pan lids noisily. She helped herself to a healthy portion of Shepherd's Pie taking it to the bar which must have been empty of customers by now.

We both pulled a face that woman did when they disapproved of another.

'Carol, I do not want to alarm you but Babs is rather too keen on Lancelot. I think you should be aware.'

'Is she? Well he needs a bit of female company, men sometimes like a brazen hussy.....can't seem to see through it like us woman can. Let him enjoy himself.'

I was dumfounded and puzzled. I would never be happy about such a thing.

'Aren't you jealous?'

'Why should I be?'

She put the bowl down.

'He is your husband!'

'Ha ha! Whatever made you think that?'

'Well you are Dr. Brookes and you live here.'

'I don't live here. I live in the village in the house where my surgery is.'

'Apart from your husband?'

'Who? Lancelot? No, Arthur is my husband…oh. That is funny, wait until I tell them.'

A thousand emotions crashed into my brain and heart making my face red and my eyes wide.

Carol stopped laughing. 'Oh I am sorry, it is easy to see just how you could have thought that. Did you not think when I was never at breakfast?'

'Well, no. Lancelot is out so soon and I just thought you had to be at work early too.'

'Oh dear, well I can see why you would warn me, I would never let a woman like Babs anywhere near my husband. No way would she work here if Lancelot were mine. But Arthur isn't as well off as his brother, nor does he have the sex appeal, thank God. But I adore him anyway.'

It was hard for her words to claw through my skewed emotions,

'That reminds me', she said putting her bowl into the sink. 'Arthur gave me only five minutes to eat that. He and his brother were playing darts. See you tomorrow, at 10am, is that OK?'

Alone then, I tidied up automatically as my feelings raged, zig-zagging in trying to find just what my situation was. Exhausted, I fell into bed to feed and change Violetta. Ben and Sarah were enjoying the sleep of the innocent. How I wish I was capable of that. Never again would I be entitled to dream of good things.

I wondered what people thought, me living with a single man in his house with no-one else around. Babs clearly dismissed me as out of the equation she so hoped to get into. All she saw was a struggling mother who cooked the food she served.

In the morning I was up early with one purpose in mind. I had to catch Lancelot before he went out. He was just going out of the door with Freddie at his heels. He looked up at me surprised.

'Hey it is only 5.30am! Hard to sleep now the mornings are lighter isn't it?' His smile curled my insides.
Somehow he looked different now I knew he was single. But he was as much out of bounds to me as if he had been married for fifty years.

'Yes, I just wanted to ask you something?'

He turned fully to me then, expecting something. His hair was still damp and that one bit fell over his forehead as if to tempt my fingers.

'Can I borrow some writing paper and an envelope, please?'

There was a keen wondering came over his face but he decided not to ask. Freddie bounced and whirled impatiently around his legs.

'My room…desk…third drawer down.' He made for the door then turned. 'I understand you are going into town today with Carol, do you have enough money for the things you need?'

'I…what…? I thought about the two weeks wages I had lying casually about my bedside table. 'I don't know….I hope so.'

He registered my embarrassment and added. 'I just meant…if you need more, whilst you are already there, ask Carol and I will repay her out of your next wage. Hate you to miss the chance to get all you need.'

As I listened to the racket of the Land Rover fade away I felt like an intruder who lurked in some-one else's space. I had never been in Lancelot's room and he had just given me permission to enter his hallowed space. I crept up the stairs, turning the other way to the one I took every night. It felt wrong to turn the handle and enter but I had to, I had to write a letter before the children woke.

His room was flooded in just rising sun, it lit the giant oak headboard carved with leaves and acorns above white sheets turned back to air the bed. His bed. It felt wrong but I imagined him sleeping there, his kind eyes shut, his dark haired chest rising softly. At the foot of the bed was Freddie's cushion, chewed and hairy. There was a door open to a steamy bathroom which smelled of the same herby smell Lancelot always wafted with him. The window was flung open with all the confidence of a warm spring day and no-one about. Books were everywhere. A pile beside the bed and a whole wall shelved out and lined with books interspersed with family photos. I wanted to look, search each one for clues of who this man was but it made me feel like an intruder. There was a pair of denims folded neatly over a chair back in front of his desk. He had worn these last night and I wanted to touch them. I shook my head and quickly opened the third drawer down on the right, it was full of money. I slammed it shut. If any went missing...he would suspect me! I went around

the chair and pulled open the third drawer on the left.
Here was a pile of Basildon Bond note pads and a packet
of envelopes. There were also two Air-Mail letters in thin
blue paper, untouched as yet. They all lay on top of a pile
of opened letters, read and stacked.

I pulled a sheet off one pad and took the top envelope. I
pushed the drawer shut and looked at the expensive
fountain pen laying on his desk, then dashed out onto the
landing with a thumping heart. Why did I feel so guilty?

After quietly checking the children I crept downstairs into
the kitchen, picked up the pen I used to write the menus
and thought. This had to be perfect. It had to be right. I
could not let one tiny hint of where I could be found
escape onto the page.

Darlington was bustling and I had all three children with
me. Carol kindly drove me to a Mothercare shop. She
could not believe I had never heard of them never mind
entered one. I hated to tell her that everything my babies
had worn or used was second hand from hard up mothers
or kind families. I said nothing. She sat in her pale green
Hillman Minx with Ben and Violetta whilst I took Sarah
into the colourful shop. My daughter's eyes glistened with
wonder. At last she had reached the shops I had promised
her during our trudge across the Dales. She showed
Humph all the shelves and asked me how much
everything was. I had no idea if this was an expensive
shop or low budget. I had never had money to spend

before, now I had because I had worked for it. It gave me a confident glow.

Feeling the new robust cotton and velour between my fingers was such a delight. I could hardly believe that I had money in my purse to make them mine. I piled up nappies and Babygros in two sizes, asked how much that would be before I told Sarah to choose something for herself. She picked a bright blue cotton dress which made her eyes pop. I added new cloth shoes and a cardigan. The sales assistant was quite taken by Humph and his thin soggy ear. She rummaged beneath the counter and came up with the tiniest baby jumper I had ever seen. 'This was in the window display and got dusty, would your ted like to wear it?'

Sarah was even more enchanted and helped the lady pull the wool down over Humph's big head. It covered his huge red stitches. 'There now, your ted looks handsome, did he have an accident?'

'He got runned over by Land Rover when we were lost on the moor.'

The assistant giggled, 'Oh kids have such imaginations don't they?' She pushed everything into bags and I paid.

Carol had Ben on her knee letting him play with her pearls and the gearstick as he bounced energetically with his feet on her thighs. She passed him to me and he gurgled, picking up our happy mood. I could have cried at the shabbiness of his clothes compared to the things I had seen in the shop. I would burn everything tatty first chance I got.

Carol left us in the car whilst she shopped and I fed both babies. A bag with sausage rolls and fruit drinks for us girls came back with her. We ate greedily sprinkling the clean car with flakes and empty bottles. Humph sat on the dashboard as if to show off his new jumper to every passer-by.

'Would you like to go to Binn's department store for stuff for yourself, I'll watch the babies for half an hour?'

'No I don't need anything.'

'Excuse me! You do. You need new tops, some trousers and a bright lipstick. I won't let you back in the car unless you have them all when you come back.'

She shoo-ed me out with Sarah who was thrilled. My little girl tried two perfumes on her wrist and asked an assistant for 'sticklip'. She came out carrying my new Miner's Coral lipstick and wearing a pale pink slick to her tiny pursed mouth.

Carol wound down the window. 'Did mammy get clothes?'

I held up the bag and she opened the door to let us in.

'Oh Sarah, you do smell delicious. Did mammy buy scent?'

'No I did not. I have better things to spend my money on.'
I saw Carol's eyes meet mine in the rear view mirror.

Embarrassed at her compassion I spoke too loudly. 'Oh, I have a letter to post.'

On the way home, the car stopped after a mile at a little village Post Office. Carol offered to pop out but I could not chance her reading the address. I fumbled my way from underneath the babies and a sleepy girl who'd had too much excitement. After buying the stamp then slotting the letter into the old red post box, I felt a relief from one thing at least.

I did not see Lancelot until the next afternoon when I was cooking hot-pot for the pub. Sarah was pretending to give Humph tea at the table and the babies were in their makeshift play pen.

'Wow!' His eyes widened. 'You all have new clothes...even Humph.' His eyes crinkled as he picked the bear up. 'You look very smart Mr Humphrey, just like the rest of your family.'

His eyes went to me. 'You look lovely, I...' His words were taken by the door bashing open to allow Babs her usual entrance.

'Who looks lovely?' She quizzed looking around and deciding that it could not be any one here.

'Rose, they all went shopping in Darlington yesterday, do you like the new clothes?'

Her eyes raked me in a way that told me she did not. They softened as they returned to Lancelot, determined to keep his eyes off any one but her.

'They're all right I suppose. You wanted me in early to talk about rearranging the dining tables.'

'Ah yes, we have more people wanting to eat now they know we have good food. Let's get to it.'

He turned to smile at me as he left, noticing that both Sarah and I were wearing lipstick. 'Pretty lipstick.' he said to Sarah who beamed and put a ginger biscuit to Humph's mouth.

The smell of the lamb and potatoes was just starting to rise from the oven when Babs dashed back in. It could not compete with the pungency she had sprayed onto herself from some unknown bottle.

She peered at me, closer than I wanted her to be. 'You wearing lipstick?' Her sneer hurt.

'Any one would think you were trying to catch a man.'

'Pardon?'

She fixed me with her black rimmed eyes heavy with sooty lashes.

'I told you, he is mine! Don't you forget it.'

That night Babs deliberately left plates of food to cool before serving them and did not take some orders in at all. She was determined to spoil the Lark and Lamb's good name for food. Or perhaps mine.

Twice I had to put plates of dinner into the oven, then as jam roly-poly cooled in dishes I decided to take it out myself. She smirked when she saw me enter the pub. There were five tables waiting for pudding they would never get if it was up to her.

'Who are these for Babs?' I asked but she just continued to rub lazily at a glass with a cloth.

I walked to the dining area. 'Two Roly-Poly?' I called.

A hand went up and I caught my breath. It was Tony, the policeman, with his wife.

I tried not to look at him and turned as soon as I could but a female voice piped up.

'You must be Rose the wonderful cook!' I had to turn back and push a smile onto my stiff lips.

'Thank you.'

'I wondered who was lucky enough to get to live with the lovely Lancelot, didn't I Tony?' She laughed in a friendly way but I felt blood colour my face. Tony's eyes never left my face, I felt scrutinised. I could see his policeman's mind ticking.

'Oh…it is not like that…'

'Aaahh, I am just teasing. Nice to put a face to the name. Where you from then?'

Thoughts whirled through lies I should tell but the words froze in my mouth.

She put up a hand. 'No! Just talk a bit more and I will guess by your accent, I'm good at that eh Tony?' he nodded faithfully. 'What did you put in that lovely supper we just devoured?'

I wanted to get away, to tidy up, to hide, check on my children in bed and then fall into my own.

'Well, neck of lamb, carrots and taties…'

'Stop there, taties tells me all I want to know. You are from somewhere between Durham and Newcastle! Am I right?'

She was bang on, my father had worked in Chopwell Woods and that is where I had grown up.

'Yes, Durham-ish,' I said. Hoping to throw Tony off the scent of Newcastle should he hear anything about what I had done.

Lancelot came over then and casually draped his arm around my shoulder. I almost jumped at the intense pleasure. I hoped it did not show in my posture or eyes.

'What are you horrible pair doing making my treasured cook blush then?'

I felt like an intruder into a long ago bonding of people who grew up together. Babs came over to the table and picked up empty glasses. She glared at me in fury whilst the others were laughing about something Tony said.

I felt an energy burn through my shoulder from Lancelot's arm. At the same time I wanted to escape and stay there for ever.

Just as casually he lifted his arm and began pushing in chairs at surrounding tables.

'Enjoy your pudding.' I smiled at them then left for the sanctuary of the kitchen.

I was hardly through the door when Babs flew at me.

'What the bloody hell do you think you are doing?' She put her arm to my chest and pushed me against the wall. Her jangling bracelets caught on my neck.

'I told you he is mine!' Her face came closer as she bared her teeth, whisky breath shot out at me. She had been helping herself again. 'Stay away from him!'

I brought up my fore-arm and hit hers away. She looked shocked.

'Don't you ever do that to me again!' I said quietly with a confidence I did not feel.

'I won't as long as you stop flirting with Lancelot.' She followed me to the sink where I turned my back on her deliberately. I did not have to see her to feel the sneer.

'Do you think for one minute that he'd be interested in a worn out mother of three squawking kids who has no sense of style and straggly hair?'

She grabbed my elbow to spin me round. 'Have you seen yourself? You are nothing…that is why you have to lie on your back to get those assorted kids of yours.'

She knew when my eyes flew open that she had hit a sore spot. She laughed.

'Plannin' to get a little Lancelot to add to your breeding pack are you...plannin' to trap him into keeping you here? You are the talk of the Dales. Living here alone with such an eligible man.'

'Go away Babs' I felt shaken but forced my words to be steady.

She obviously thought her words had not thrust deeply enough so she said. 'I have already had him, you didn't know that did you? A few more times of me giving him the thrills of his life and he will be curled around that.' She held up her little finger, wiggled it then changed to two fingers which she almost poked my eyes out with.

'He is going to be driving me home after work from tomorrow. My dad's car has to go into the garage for repairs. Good time to get extra cosy. As long as he doesn't have any of those annoying rescue dogs in with us. So you can get stuffed!'

My heart caught on a new wave of pain.

She flounced out then leaving me with fresh agonies, wounds I had no right to hurt with. I went to bed in a fuzz of soreness and hopelessness.

Over the weeks I cooled towards Lancelot. I could see he was hurt and puzzled.

'Aren't you happy here anymore Rose?' he asked as we met too closely at the garden door, me coming in to get the children drinks and him coming out with a tray with glasses for himself, Sarah and me with the baby cup for Ben.'

I backed out allowing him to bring the tray into the June sunshine. He put it on the old weathered table and turned to me handing me popping ginger beer with ice.

'Rose, I know you have your sorrows but you were starting to smile and make funny quips. Where has it all gone?'

I took a sip nervously.

'Is it Babs?'

I looked at him quickly. Pillow talk, no doubt.

'Babs?'

'I noticed you don't get on these days. She is OK you know, do not be fooled by her brash appearance. She has a heart of gold. The customers love her.'

My mind struggled to find something that did not sound jealous, there was a heavy space between us. I occupied it by lifting the glass to my mouth.

'I know by your silence that I have hit on the truth. But I do not want to lose either of you. Your food is bringing in the people who have money to spend. They love your dumplings'

'Ha…is that what they love about Babs too?'

He laughed. 'See, you are funny and I love it. Keep it up. That is the Rose I have grown to love.'

As he walked the few steps to the rug on the grass to give Sarah and Ben their drinks, his last word sunk into me. Of course he did not love me in the way it sounded. But reality hit me like a train. That is what I felt for him.

Love. I was in love. I had never experienced this before. It was different to what I had felt for my parents or the ground into my bones love for my children. This was what 'In Love' felt like. But I was in it alone.

It hurt.

It hurt if I saw him and was agony if I didn't so I just let things work out in their natural way. But I still lay in anguish listening for his Land Rover to return after taking Babs home. Had he been walking the dogs on the Dales or had he been wrapped in this awful woman's arms? I needed my sleep to look after the children and do my work but it was hard to find.

His eyes changed as we sat down at the kitchen table one early morning at his request to update the menu to something more summery. He'd left the door open to let the early sun wake us up.

'Don't you have to get out to your lambs today?' Freddie was out in the garden sniffing at the new smells the night had kindly left for him. Servant pounced on him playfully from the laurel hedge and the two ran off for more fun.

He poured tea for us both into blue and white striped mugs. 'No they are all steady and strong. I just need to drive about once a day now to check they are safe and take their supplements.'

As he handed me the tea my eyes focused on the long fingers then the soft dark hairs just showing from his turned back sleeves. He was getting browner.

He turned his eyes to me and all I could think of was that I had not combed my hair yet. He was usually already out when I padded down for 6am tea.

I put a finger to the corner of my left eye to remove some hardened sleep always there. I had to hold back a yawn and he smiled. I straightened my back pulling my cheesecloth shirt across my swollen breasts. Neither baby had taken breakfast yet.

'You are funny.'

'Oh how?'

'In a good way I mean, you look all soft and cosy but you try to act like you have been up for hours. Just relax.'

I felt him absorbing my presence and wondered if this was how he looked at Babs.

'Do we have time to chat or will the babies need you?' He asked nodding his head towards the ceiling.

'You'll hear when they wake. Have no fear about that.' I laughed. This brought about such an appealing look to his face that I could not drag my eyes from it.

'I really admire the way you cope with everything Rose. It can't be easy for you. I just want you to know I will help in whatever way I can.'

'You already have.' I said trying not to show my feelings for him. 'I was lost and had a very uncertain future before you found us in the abbey.'

'I often walk the dogs up there at night after Babs has finished with me you know.'

Images crashed unwanted into my mind, my smiled dropped and he noticed.

'Oh sorry, you must hate that place. I was going to ask if you fancied a run up there one morning, take a picnic for us all. Slay your demons.'

'I will never go back there! Ever!' I flung the words at him as if he had offered me a trip to hell.

He was concerned that he had upset me. 'I am sorry, I should have known. Well the seaside then, Sarah would love to make sand castles and paddle.'

When it was obvious this suggestion caused me even more pain he asked.

'What is it Rose, why does this upset you so much?'

Tears brimmed but I could not speak. How could I tell him what had happened at Scarborough. He would never understand. My life before here was one he did not even know existed.

'Talk to me Rose, let it out. It will make you feel better you know.'

But I couldn't. If I let one little thread escape from the hurt of the past it would catch on something, some sharp or careless word, and all unravel until my truth was laid bare for all to see. How Babs would love that; my horrible truth.

I wiped away my tears and said with false cheer.

'Summer suppers.' I sniffed. 'I have some ideas.'

Two days later, the morning the ingredients for my new meals had arrived, I went into the bar. Lancelot had his broad back to me writing on a blackboard with white chalk. The writing was beautiful and perfect. What else?

He headed it 'Summer Suppers', underneath he had written the three ideas we had agreed on.

Babs came into the not yet open pub and crept behind him jogging his arm so that the chalk streaked across the board crossing out three carefully written words.

'Hey' He turned to look at her and joined in her amusement as she tried to wrestle the chalk from his hand.

'No you don't young lady.' He easily overpowered her, grabbing her handbag in revenge and placing it on the top shelf where he knew she could not reach. Her mouth, jammy with lipstick, split into a grin as she turned to me to make sure I was watching this bit of fun between lovers. She was wearing a new dress in a headache pattern of red and orange.

I left them to it, increasing giggles digging into my hurt heart.

I returned to the kitchen where Sarah had left Humph in the playpen for Ben, he dangled the bear by its worn legs. She climbed up onto a chair to see the new ingredients. Lancelot had made her Chief Cooking Assistant to cheer her up from her desolation when the lambs no longer needed bottle feeding. She took this new job seriously.

'What these mammy?' she asked holding up a bag of fat pink prawns.

'Prawns, for a prawn cocktail salad.' I said.

'Can Sarah make 'awnocktail' for pub?' I said she could and got her mixing the mayonnaise, tomato puree and Worcestershire sauce in a big bowl. Carol had suggested this as she had eaten it at a friend's house. We were to make sample dishes for Lancelot's lunch but as he had written out the board it was a bit late if he didn't like it. We made one sample of poached salmon with watercress sauce, buttered new potatoes with peas and rump steak with fried onions and round chips. These chips were named by Sarah who liked potatoes boiled whole then cut into round slices and deep fried.

The smell brought Lancelot into the kitchen to satisfy his hunger along with his curiosity. 'Why is Babs here at lunchtime Lancelot?' I asked trying to keep annoyance from my voice.

'Oh, I thought I would try opening for a few days, see if walkers come in. If they do I was going to ask if you would do sandwiches.'

'Oh, OK.'

'What smells so delicious Sarah? What have you made?' He lifted her to stand on the chair. I had put plates of each meal into a warm oven, except the prawn salad which was waiting on the table for him. Sarah studied his every move. Her eyes moved from the two fat prawns she had placed on top of the rest to the fork in his hand to his mouth, she stared at his face as he chewed.

'Delicious,' he laughed seeing her tension was about to burst. 'Here try it.'

Sarah copied his actions, his fondness for her showed when he tilted his head and asked.

'How many prawns shall we give our diners Sarah?'

I had already made her count them out to ten.

'Nine.' she said, taking one off. She saw my surprise.

'Sarah eat one to try first.' It was great fun trying the salmon and steak from one plate, both of which pleased us all.

Babs bundled in, seemingly unable to be away from the man she considered hers for more than ten minutes.

'Here Babs try this.' He said handing her the plate with salmon and a clean fork. 'You have to be enthusiastic to sell these when you take the orders.'

All our eyes were on her. 'It is a bit tasteless. What tin is this out of then, not the one my mum gets at the Co-op. That is delicious.'

Lancelot shook his head in amusement. 'This is fresh salmon, from a fishmonger. Rose has poached it.'

'Well I wouldn't pay for that, or that steak there. Looks raw to me.'

'It is cooked medium rare as I like it Babs.'

'People will be sick with this stuff. Where's the Shepherd's Pie gone?'

He stood up then and turned to me. 'You have worked wonders,' he smiled.

Babs' face turned to thunder. 'I will not be putting that in front of people!'

He turned abruptly to her then. 'You, young lady, will do as I pay you to do.'

Fury sped her to the door and the big slam after her rattled my teeth.

The Summer Suppers were a big hit bringing in lots more customers, some of them from Richmond, Leyburn and Darlington on a drive into the country. I made sure I never entered the pub when all these people could see me, I could never be sure who was in. I was glad my food was well received and Sarah loved washing the slugs and caterpillars from the lettuce and scrubbing the new potatoes with a stiff brush. She kept anything alive in a jar with the tough outside lettuce leaves.

It was a sunny June morning when I settled the children on the rug beside the lupins and fading lilac blossoms. Lancelot came out with a mug of tea and a toasted teacake, Freddie curling about his legs. Carol followed him out with her own tea.

'Hello there Rose. What a lovely sight you all make in the sunshine.'

I walked over, glad to see her in her flowing white dress and crimson cardigan.

'Arthur went back to Israel again on Saturday. Came to cheer myself up.'

'Oh dear,' I sympathised.

'I will miss him too, he promised to help me with the garden.' said Lancelot standing and brushing crumbs from his shirt. 'Well the weeds won't pull themselves up. Any little girls about that might help me.'

Sarah ran to his side and the two went over to the flowerbed against the stone wall. We watched as he pushed grubby gloves onto her tiny hands and showed her how to pull from the bottom of the weed so that the roots came out. She adored him. The sight did something to my insides, a sort of tugging and then the mental slap of my own face. I had to pull my thoughts back to the reality of my life. I bore a heavier burden than most, my hopes could not include anyone but myself and the babies. Never.

Carol touched my arm.

'We have arranged to take the dogs to Scarborough for a run on the beach tomorrow Rose. I suggested that Lancelot invite you and the children but he said you would never come.'

'No I can't Carol. Sorry.'

She watched my face. Did she see my pain at the very mention of the seaside town that meant joy to many? The boating lake at Peaseholm Park, a climb to Oliver's Mount to see the town spread out and the sea…endless, as if you could see forever if you stood with your back to the tall cenotaph. Then the miles of sandy beaches promising sand castles, family picnics and paddling with squeals of icy delight. Oh those beaches, those dark, agonising beaches.

My lips sealed themselves but it was really my heart that clamped shut.

Her soft hand stroked my arm.

'Tell me why Rose. It will go no further.'

She waited, with her keenness to help glowing as she turned to look me warmly in the face.

I could only choke back my thoughts as I silently walked away from her and sat down beside the babies.

No-one found the pub at lunchtime so I was spared the discomfort of having Babs around during the day. That night, after making fish pies as a Sunday night special, I asked Lancelot for some more writing paper. His face was glowing as he came into the kitchen having just won a very raucous darts match against three of his employees.

He filled a pint glass with water and drank it down almost to the bottom.

'Yes, of course. I will get you some. I'll just see this rowdy lot off the premises first. Don't tell them I am on water, not a good example for a pub owner. Shepherds are hard drinkers.'

The door swished behind him and my spirits returned to somewhere near normal, which was low and suffocating. Babs thundered in with empty plates clattering them on top of the big dishwasher. Unable to leave without taunting me she said. 'My darling is in a great mood tonight, gonna ask him for a lift home later, me dad's car isn't working.' Her eyes glittered through false lashes and her new orange lipstick clashed with her latest new bosom squeezing blouse. 'A gentleman like Lancelot wouldn't let a lady walk home on her own now would he. I'll have to think of a way to use up some of that energy he seems to have so much of tonight.'

She looked at me, decided that this was enough to sink my heart and keep me awake, then flounced out letting 'Goodnights' and 'Go on! Just one more Scotch', waft into the kitchen.

Just as I was finally fading into sleep, listening to the three little breaths and snuffles, I heard footsteps outside the door. I was up like a shot, grabbed the candle stick and flung the door open.

'Hey whoa!'

It was Lancelot, he had left a pad of writing paper and six envelopes on the floor. Freddie flung himself out of his bedroom and was at his master's side in a flash. He wagged his tail when he saw it was me.

'Sorry, I meant to give you these sooner but I got caught up.' He was grinning.

I tried to drag my imagination from painful images but failed. His eyes softened as he looked over my tousled hair and just scrubbed face. My eyes lifted to look at him through unpainted lashes. I must have looked so boring compared to the rouged cheeks and sooty eyes he so obviously preferred.

'Rose, who are you writing to?'

I smiled and shook my head. His voice was soft. I picked up the pad and envelopes and closed the door on him. But I could not close the door on the images of what he and Babs had been up to in the hour since they had left the pub.

I could not sleep so I went down to the kitchen to write the letter I hoped would keep us safe, if only for a few months longer.

Chapter Six.

Carol drove up to the front of the pub and waved at me over the garden wall. It was 9am and a perfect day for the seaside. A clear blue sky promised heat and calm, exactly as it had been on that awful day.

She struggled to get out of the car. I could see two bouncy terriers put their paws up to the windows wanting to see what was going on. She wore stylish white cut off trousers and a blue cotton top synched at the waist with a brown leather belt. She saw my eyes widen.

'Oh, those two came into my care last night. They are not starved or beaten, just homeless. I bet I am in for a big pull on the leads today.'

'They look cute.' I said hoping Sarah did not catch sight of them. 'Can you post a letter for me please?'

'Of course, we pass the village box on the way, I can pop it in for you.'

'No! In Scarborough, post it in Scarborough please, you must!'

She looked shocked at the voracity of my plea but decided not to pursue it.

'I'll come into the kitchen for it, shall I?'

As I handed her the sealed envelope Lancelot came in with an Irish wolfhound on a lead. The dog was nervous and at first did not drink from the bowl he had just filled with clean water. Freddie decided to show him how.

'I wish you'd change your mind Rose, it will be a lovely day for the children. Plenty of room in the Landy, the dogs will be in the back.' He smiled as we walked back outside.

'I have plenty to do here, the children are already in the garden.'

Just as I said that Babs pulled up in her dad's car. It seemed to have been fixed miraculously soon. She bounded out wearing a big straw hat with a leopard print scarf wrapped around. Her strappy sun dress was revealing her bouncing bosom, her shoulders and her legs. She posed meaningfully before closing the door. No man on Earth stood a chance against this woman. A strong smell of suntan lotion hit me as she wafted over to Lancelot, the wolfhound shivered and cowed behind his saviour's denim clad legs.

'Ooh, not too early am I. Never been to Scarborough me...so pleased with the invitation.'

The car sped off without a thanks or a wave, it had served its purpose and was then forgotten.

My tummy sank to my boots. I turned to Carol who was still taking in the sight and smells of the whirlwind now putting her red and white striped bag into the Landrover.

'Oh, I didn't know she was invited.' I said meekly, feeling annoyed that my refusal to go left it wide open for her.

'More likely asked herself.' Carol muttered behind my envelope.

Babs didn't even speak to me but her sly look from under the brim of her wobbling hat told me that she was thrilled I was not dressed for anything other than a day looking after children.

Lancelot strode over to his vehicle, put his hand in through the open window and pulled out Babs's bag. He took it over to Carol's car and opened the door allowing two delighted, body waggling terriers out to bounce and sniff everyone and everything.

'Sorry Babs. You cannot travel with the dogs smelling like that. They will be sick. You go with Carol and I will take all the dogs.'

Carol flashed him a look that said 'Thanks a lot.' He saw it and smiled secretly.

The terriers flung themselves against my knees and I bent to ruffle their ears. They were soft and rough at the same time.

'This is Biff and Boff.' Carol laughed. 'We don't know their real names, they only came in from a deceased lady's house last night.'

'Probably bashed her to death!' I giggled as they tried to climb up my legs.

'Ha ha, that might be so. Sudden death. They don't seem to have noticed as long as they can bounce about.'

'I love them!' I said as they ran off to pester Babs. She shouted at them and they cowed before returning to me at super speed. She teetered over on high heels then flung herself into Carol's car and shut the door against them. Her face was like thunder.

'Looks like I am in for a cheery ride. I don't know why she is dressed like that for dog walking and lead training on the cliffs. I can't see her crashing into the waves to help remove the fear of water from the dogs either.' Carol muttered to me.

Lancelot whistled up Biff and Boff who jumped into the back of his Landy where the wolfhound was already lying majestically in Freddie's rope circle. They scrabbled over him and chewed his ears immediately but he seemed to like it. Freddie bound into the front seat which he knew was his from birth.

'Have a peaceful day Rose.' He smiled to me and his eyes clouded. 'I wish you were coming.'

I wished I was too. I felt sick and left out as the pair disappeared into the distance. I returned to the garden where Sarah was drawing on an old envelope, the babies were lying in the shade. We could have an hour or two out here but we would have to go indoors away from the mid-day sun.

'ook mammy, me drawed flowers.' Sarah held up a scribbled red and green picture that may or may not resemble any flower I had ever seen. Ben rolled onto his tummy and began to crawl into the soil where he took a great handful and put it to his mouth. I dashed over as his puzzled look turned to a crumpled face. As I was cleaning his mouth and hands Violetta began to yell and Sarah fell off her chair. All this childcare was getting hectic.

So many flying insects felt the same urge to enjoy the day as us and buzzed about so that I felt I had to go in for the sake of the babies. In the quiet and cool of our bedroom I held Violetta to my breasts. She was growing ever more beautiful, her curled dark lashes fascinated me as she gazed up with sparkling and adoring eyes. I loved her as much as I loved Ben and Sarah. I stroked her cheek with my finger and promised her that I would do everything in my power to make her life good. I just had no idea what that would be.

Ben fell asleep on the rug where he had been peering into an old bag I had filled with wooden spoons, small candlesticks, a potato masher and anything else chewable and harmless. He took them out one at a time, felt them with his mouth then dropped them to the floor before repeating this until the bag was empty. Sarah refilled the bag and he started his important mission again. It had worn him out. Sarah climbed up beside me for a story.

It was hard to make up, on the spur of the moment, a story about how we could get another baby but that's what she wanted. My thoughts kept straying to a striding Lancelot followed by dogs and a tottering Babs. The story mustn't have been any good as Sarah declared she was hungry and slid down to the floorboards. I laid Violetta into her drawer and covered Ben with a blanket.

In the house kitchen Sarah helped me make her 'nana b'sandwich'. The fruit bowl always had bananas, delivered once a week with all the shopping on Lancelot's list. In the quiet of the hot day I heard a car approach the pub entrance which I knew was locked. I peered out of the side window where I could see a bit of the police van and Tony in uniform putting his fist up to hammer on the pub door. I froze. The sound echoed through to me.

I heard gravel crunch and the squeal of the garden gate then a knocking on the kitchen door. I put my finger to my lips to silence Sarah and prayed the babies would not wake. I lifted Sarah, clinging to her sandwich, into the pantry and pulled the door almost shut. She giggled thinking it was a game and I drew the only smile I could muster from my fear raddled mind. Then the sound that almost stopped my heart.

'Rose! You in there Rose! I need a word with you.'

Tony's voice hung in the hot air. My chest almost burst with holding my breath then just as Sarah dropped her crust and scrabbled down I heard the footsteps crunch, the gate creak and the car door bang. At last the engine rattled into life and the sound faded away.

I drew my first proper breath in minutes.

'Who dat mammy?' Sarah asked as she examined her crust for dirt. I took it off her and cut another slice from the loaf.

'Oh just Lancelot's friend sweetheart. He didn't want us.'

'He said 'Rose', mammy, that name is my mammy.'

She was getting too bright and grown up, I distracted her with a new banana.

Chapter seven.

It was almost 10 pm, the cat was blissfully enjoying my ear rub as we both listened to ewes baa-ing deeply for their lambs to come close for the night, then the higher pitched excited, milk anticipating baa of their off-spring. I heard the familiar Landy and a few seconds later Carol's car. I was having a cup of tea in the garden trying to get the stunning June sunset to calm my troubled mind.

Servant dug his claws in my knee as he went from snoozy
to excited. The gate flew open and dogs bounded in,
obviously refreshed by sleeping the long journey home
and in need of a sniff and wee-wee dance. The cat
jumped on the wall and disappeared to a space where
young terriers could not find him. I ruffled one high head
then two small ones as they dashed in excitement to my
knees. They had become the best of friends. Lancelot
came in carrying a cool box. He looked rosy and warm.

'Phew!' He said almost standing on Freddie who was
tempting the terriers to dash about. He lifted the box to
the table in front of me. It was the first time I had noticed
how green his eyes were. It must have been the extra
colour on his cheeks and the way he smiled at me.

'Did you have a nice day?' he asked.

'Yes thanks. You?'

'Great, just a minute.' He strode into the kitchen with all
four dogs keenly at his heels. Carol came into the garden
looking exhausted but pink.

'Hey you, did you get sunburned?'

'I am not used to being out so long. Just dropped Babs off
at her house.' She gave a little laugh. 'Poor girl broke a
heel on her shoes and had to buy rope sandals. She is
lobster- like despite slapping on more foul smelling
lotion.'

'Was it a good day?' I asked enjoying the picture she had just described.

Lancelot came out with two pint glasses brimming with cold water, gave one to Carol and drank his in one go.

'Wow. That is better. The dogs have learned so much. Wulfy is gaining trust and will make some-one a lovely pet. We wished you had come.'

I saw Carol look at my discomfort. 'Here.' She offered me a bulging carrier bag. Inside was a red, blue and yellow bucket with happy crabs and lobsters painted on the sides and a little spade. A pink stick of rock wrapped in crackly cellophane poked out of the bucket. 'We got this from South Beach, the shops and cafes are so near the beach, it is beautiful sand on both bays. We walked all the way up to Oliver's Mount, the view is spectacular. Have you seen the twelfth century castle from there?'

'No...I...thank you for thinking of us. Sarah will adore this.'

'Oh don't thank me. Lancelot bought it.'

He waved his hand at my thanks. 'Well if the lady won't go to the seaside. The seaside must come to her.'

I was touched by his thoughtfulness.

We all took our glasses and mugs into the kitchen where the basket of eggs Sarah had gathered at tea time stood awaiting his approval. 'Ten!' he grinned.

He went to the pantry and took out the bowl of pennies he stored there. He put six eggs in a box, gave them to Carol and then the rest in a new dish. He laid ten pennies in their place. This was Sarah's pay. She was saving up for a black baby doll for Violetta.

'Omelette any-one?' He asked taking out a frying pan and breaking the fresh eggs into a bowl.

Carol called Biff and Boff and fastened leads to their collars, they immediately put on a sad face. 'No thanks I must be off, get these two settled. Are you hanging onto Wulfie?'

'No, he needs company, you take him. He might teach those two hooligans some manners.'

There seemed to be a spell in watching Lancelot gently melt butter in the pan and whisk up the eggs with salt and pepper. He put two plates into the oven to warm. As the eggs sizzled and began to rise I said.

'Well goodnight, and thank you.'

He came over and took my arm, it felt scorched by his masculine energy.

'Now just you sit down, you did not say no when I asked so you have to eat half of my omelette.' He took the plates out and placed them on the table before me.

'Secret number two, warm plates so that the egg does not lose air.'

He slid a golden fluffy omelette onto my plate, cut it in half and put that onto his plate.

'Eat.' He commanded.

I did and it was delicious but something was stopping up my throat.

'What is secret number one then?' I asked taking my second forkful.

'A pretty lady to share it with.'

'Oh, well that one failed.'

He looked at me. 'Why do you say that Rose? You are a lovely human being, your strength and gentleness shine through mixed in equal quantities to show on your sweet face.'

I felt blood rush to my cheeks.

'Don't you ever look in the mirror Rose?'

'Not if I can help it.'

'Then you should. It is a very comforting sight.'

He slid off his chair and took my plate, ate a forkful and tossed the rest to Freddie who had never taken his eyes off the food. He put the plate down and looked at me.

If I could have reached over and taken his hand to place against my beating chest I would have. If I was not a breast feeding mother who worked for him, a runaway fugitive and a liar. But I was all those things so I simply stood up and left the room. I could not even say goodnight.

It was a week before Carol came to see us again. Biff and Boff had a new home with some-one who could take all the bashing and bouncing and walk for miles. Carol laughed as she saw my disappointment.

'You won't look so sad when I show you why I have come today. Bring Sarah out to my car.'

I checked on the babies and told Sarah to come with me. She clutched Humph to her chest and held my hand. When we squinted our way out into the late June sunshine Carol put a basket in my arms. She peeled back the pink blanket to show us three creamy puppies with soft mouths and no teeth. Humph hit the dirt.

'I was wondering if you knew anyone who could feed these little orphans with bottles.'

'Yes me! Sarah squealed in delight. 'Me feed lambies and chickens.'

Carol smiled. 'Oh I thought you would be too busy Sarah, with your egg collecting and babies.'

'Sarah want these babies now, please.'

She was allowed to help carry the basket into the kitchen where she sat next to it on the floor. Servant came over, sniffed then left in disgust. Sarah examined each puppy with tender consideration.

'What puppies called?' She asked Carol.

They have no names. Maybe you can think of something pretty.

She came up with Daisy, Buttercup and Bluebell. Two were boys but they wouldn't care.

Carol brought out milk and little bottles the vet had left for her yesterday, then showed Sarah how to hold the puppies to make sure the milk did not go into their nostrils.

She joined me at the table for a mug of Yorkshire tea. Lowering her voice, she leaned towards me. 'The mother was knocked by a car into the side of the road. She was found dead with her puppies suckling her. No one knew where she came from.'

My heart burst with sadness. What if they had not been found, not brought to Carol?

We watched Sarah kissing the soft noses and wiping dribbling mouths with a towel from the basket.

'Did you post my letter Carol?'

'Oh, yes I think so...at least...'

She saw my alarm.

'Don't worry...mmm, oh yes. Babs posted it.'

'What? How?'

'Well she got me to stop at a village shop for Dandelion and Burdock pop. When we got to Scarborough I was looking in the car for your letter, thought it must have slipped off the dashboard onto the floor. She asked me what I was looking for and when I said it was your letter she told me she had posted it when we stopped.'

'Oh. What village? Where?' My mind was racing. What post mark would the envelope have? How near to here? Could it be traced?

Carol looked thoughtful. 'Oh, so many pretty places on the way…it had a chestnut tree on a green and one of those Post Offices that sold a few groceries… do you know I took no notice. I was too busy watching Lancelot and his Landy disappear over a hill. That is why I did not notice her take your letter. We had to motor a bit to catch him up.'

She scrunched her eyebrows together. 'Why? Is it a problem?'

Not wanting to seem ungrateful or raise any further suspicions in Carol, I shook my head.

'Of course not and thank you.'

When Carol left and I was cuddling up to the babies watching Sarah fall asleep beside her new loves, my mind raced through every encounter with Babs that week.

Had she been even more triumphant than usual when she talked about how in love she was with Lancelot? Had her sidelong glances been even more conniving? Had she posted my letter or hidden it to read later?

I tried to recall every exchange with her. But I realised the cold truth and it was even more frightening. She had been avoiding me.

All the confidence I had been gathering about me, in my stupid idea that at last I might be able to have a safe life, deserted me.

Panic flooded my brain, she could not be trusted. How much did she know about me now?

A chill of fear ran through me as I heard Babs high voice announce her arrival at work at 6.30 that evening. I had to confront her. I had no choice.

She looked shocked as I flung through the kitchen doors into the bar. She knew I never wanted to be seen in here but it was too early for any customers. I smelled the sickly sweet perfume of Coty L'Aimant that floated around her in waves. She turned her back on me and started to stack mixer bottles.

I stood right behind her and pulled at her arm to turn her. Was that a flash of fear before she managed to pull her sneer over her face?

'Babs, did you post my letter in Scarborough?'

She shrugged me off. 'Never seen no letter.'

'Yes you have. It was in Carol's car when you went to the coast. Carol said you posted it.'

Her eyes widened. 'Well she is a bloody liar then.'

Lancelot came in from sorting out the picnic benches outside.

'Who's a bloody liar?' His eyes scanned us both. Babs was furious that he had heard her be so nasty and about some-one he cared so much for.

He stood still taking in the fact that we had both clammed up.

'Babs. Who were you talking about?'

She looked about and then at me.

'Ask her.'

He looked at me and then said. 'I am asking the person who said it. You Babs.'

She tried to smile at him but it did not work. 'Just some girl in the village, nobody you know.'

He let it go then, obviously not believing her but feeling that it was beneath him to investigate further. I just wanted to get back to the kitchen. He followed me and as I turned to hold the door open for him I saw the threatening look Babs fired at me.

The smell of lamb hot pot wafted over us when I opened the oven to check on it.

'Mmm,' he said appreciatively. Then he took a banana from the bowl on the table and peeled it, he took a bite and swallowed.

'Rose, you have never been in the village have you?'

'No. Only to the post office.' I said before realising what he was leading up too.

'Then how do you mutually know some-one?'

'I don't.' I said turning into the pantry to hide my embarrassment. My mind searched for ways to deflect him from discussing this, I was flustered. I came out with the first thing my hand touched, a black rubber torch. 'She is just gossiping.'

He looked at my hands. 'Why do you want that? It is for when the electricity fails. It hasn't and it will be light for another four hours yet. It is almost mid-summer.'

I was making myself look even more foolish.

'I have to put the babies to bed and then I will come back down.' I said walking out with the torch. I was digging a big foolish hole for myself.

Sarah wanted to play with the torch but soon lost interest when the beam could not compete with the sun. She left it on the lawn where the puppies' basket had been. I saw it later from the window, a symbol of my lies and stupidity. I was sick with worrying what Lancelot must think of me.

Where was my letter?

Three days later almost at closing time Carol pulled the kitchen door and stood with it open.

'Any good food left Rose? I have been on a call out and have not had anything to eat for hours?'

We both turned as loud laughter sprouted from the bar. Babs had pulled Lancelot close to deliver the punch line on one of the jokes she learnt from her dad's day at the building site.

Carol let the door swing shut.

'I have plenty. Ham salad or salmon fish cakes?'

'Oh... em, salad please. Getting a bit late.'

She sat at the table and I put a thick slice of the ham I had roasted that morning on a plate with tomatoes and cucumber on top of two lettuce leaves.

I watched as she put salad cream on the side of the plate and began to eat.

'I think Babs is reeling in her catch.' I said trying to keep the jealousy from my voice.

'Who, Lancelot? No!' she looked at me. 'She is not his type, he only humours her to keep her happy and therefore his customers.'

She filled her mouth and smiled, lifting her perfectly formed eyebrows appreciatively.

'Are you sure?' I asked trying to clear my eyes of any relief or vain hope that might show there.

'Yes!' she laughed. 'I am sure. His heart was well and truly hooked years ago. Still gasping on the pier even now.'

I was puzzled. 'What do you mean?'

'I mean Cleona, a beautiful Irish girl he met when he was at York University. She went to Florence to study portrait painting. He writes every week.'

Carol put her hand to her mouth. 'Oops, I think it's a secret. Don't let on I told you will you? He can be quite cross about gossip. Hates it.'

The crashing of all my hopes, secret dreams and stupid, stupid feminine emotions clattered at my feet like rusty armour. I'd had no clue. And why should I? I was just a homeless bitch and her pups who Lancelot had found a use for. Maybe he just humoured me to keep his customers happy too.

I knew then why I had seen so much writing paper in his drawer.

I could not sleep for imagining him in younger days swanning around York with some dark haired, blue eyed beauty with a stunning figure and captivating wit. I had never been to York but it must be romantic. I wondered why he had not followed her to Florence, which must be romantic too. I had been stupid to ever imagine in my most private and hidden thoughts that he would ever have the slightest inclination to look on me as a woman.

Sarah and I were on the lawn a few days later watching the puppies having a life or death tussle with each other. Tiny mouths grabbed at tiny tails with tiny new teeth as they rolled and pounced, making little growls and yelps.

She picked one up needing two hands to get around the barrel-like tummy and wriggling legs. I would have a terrible time when it was time to find them new homes. Ben was taking an interest too as he rolled closer from the rug where Violetta wriggled limbs and cooed at floating rose petals above her. My heart swelled as I noticed his hair. It was growing into the style Sarah had at eight months, one thin curl on top of his head and one above each ear, sticking out like question marks. It was so cute I could cry. I wanted to smack kisses onto those round red cheeks of his.

The gate clacked and I looked up to see Tony stride in wearing the uniform I dreaded. All my happiness drained away.

A knot tightened in my chest but I forced a smile.

'Ah Rose. I tried to catch you the other day, but you must have been out for a walk.'

I looked at him, frozen in agonies of what he was about to say.

'You know this dale is a large yet small place. Well, I was surprised when some-one told me that you had a toddler and two babies. I would never have guessed it. I just thought you were the cook here. Where did you come from Rose?'

I did not answer.

I tried a smile but none came. It could not get past the banging in my chest. I wished he would get on with it.

'Well for ages I have been looking for some-one like you and now I can relax. I have found you. This makes my job a lot easier.'

My legs began to shake.

'Please come out with me to my van.' I thought about my children and what would happen to them. I thought about Ed lying splayed out on that chair. I thought about my father and his crippling shame. I wish I had never done what I did. I was about to pay for it.

'I am willing to pay my dues Tony.' My voice was thick with dread.

He put his hand up. 'Say no more! Not yet.'

I saw Lancelot look out of an upstairs window, I hoped he would come down to look after the children.

I supposed I would have to answer questions at the station. When we reached the van I went to the passenger door.

'No not there. The back.' I was to be treated as a prisoner.

He opened the back door and I bent to get in but it was full.

Tony had brought an old second hand Silver Cross pram, it had two large wheels and two smaller. There was a curved handle and a sun canopy with fringe. The body was silver and navy blue. I know that my mouth hung open in confusion.

'Please say you will take it off my hands.'

'What? I thought you were on duty...'

He pulled a face. 'Well I am, do not say anything to Sarge Bates if you see him will you?'

I almost fell to my knees as my shaking legs felt the relief. He was too busy to notice.

He eased the pram out of the van and set it before me. I adored it.

'But I can't...'

'Yes you can. We don't want any money for it. Just big up my portions of steak and kidney when I next order it, will you? And double that delicious gravy too.'

My mind was whirling around trying to re-think the last five minutes.

'Lancelot said that you never got into the village what with the bairns and all, so I said to Doreen. 'Can we give that lass our white elephant?' She was thrilled, she really liked you. You should call for tea and whatever it is that you women with children talk about.'

I stared at the thing I thought I would never have. 'But I can't.' I repeated, feeling like some-one said I had won the football pools when I hadn't even filled in the coupon.

'Glad to see the back of it. I can get into my entrance hall now, the first time in five years. You are doing us a favour.' He turned to leave then. 'Oh, I almost forgot, here is a child seat so you can add your bigger baby…and a sun canopy.'

I had always wanted a Silver Cross. I had seen the proud looks of mothers as they had lifted their babies out of their luxury prams to allow the nurse to weigh them at the clinic. I had felt slightly beneath them with my worn Marmet pram with the scuffed hood and scratched body. A neighbour had sold it to me. It was sticky, with some awful things, and I had to scrub and disinfect it for hours. It was a dream come true to have my babies ride in one of these.

'Our two made good use of it mind you, there are a few scrapes and dents. Please say yes. If you don't I will pay you to take it.'

I saw then that he was kind man and must have thought I was so buttoned up so I kissed him smack on the forehead.

'Hey! Careful now!' he blushed, putting his helmet back on 'I am a Constable on duty you know.' He plonked into the driver's seat and turned the key then wound down the window.

'Just love it.' he called as he drove off.

I would. I should also try to relax and not think the worst.

That pram changed my life. The babies loved their walks. Sarah claimed the seat when her little legs grew tired, sitting Humph on her knee to show him the world. Even the puppies had a ride in it although they slept all the way nestled at the bottom where tiny feet could not kick.

We strolled and bumped along rutted lanes to smell the wild roses and blackberry flowers. I lifted Sarah up to the pale petals so she could sniff and see the bees working. I wanted to give her a great childhood. It was a joy to be out and this is when I felt a tiny glimmer of happiness. It reminded me of when I was living with dad. Before I had ever met Ed. When I had not known how one human being could spoil the life of another.

I hoped my dad was happy with his new love. I longed for him to be part of my children's lives but I knew that could never be. My letters to him told him I was well and happy but he could never know where I was. The Darlington post mark of the first would put any one searching for me off the scent and I hoped that the second was not posted too near here, if it was posted at all. I had a strong urge to write to Jane who had been so kind to me. She deserved to know I was still alive but she might tell anyone, even without interrogation. I could not wrap that lovely soul in my lies.

But how long could I hide here?

Chapter Eight

It was a shock to me when Carol told me that Violetta should come into her surgery for immunisation. I had been so wrapped up in caring for my babies that I had forgotten about this most important thing to keep them safe from disease.

'Ben has not been done either.' I said feeling ashamed and panicked.

Carol had held both babies and put them down into our makeshift play pen in the kitchen. 'They seem healthy to me Rose, you are a wonderful mother but we do have to make a big effort to have Violetta settled into a secure life.'

'She is secure with me!'

'In your love, yes. But you are a widow with an insecure future, the authorities will not see what I see. How are you going to cope when both babies are crawling or toddling? It will be chaos.'

She saw my distress. 'No one can take your biological children from you Rose.'

But she did not know what threats followed me. My children had a very high chance of being left motherless. I plunged deeper into that awful broth of fear, hopelessness and sorrow.

Babs made a huge effort to stay out of my way. She lowered her eyes to the food when she came into the kitchen to whisk away the orders. As she brought the plates back she stacked them noisily near the dishwasher. This continued all week until Thursday when the rain fell in sheets and thunder rumbled across a bruised sky keeping people in their homes.

Lancelot wandered into the kitchen as I was sorting out the unsold food and asked what he could eat.

'I can do you your favourite steak and chips if you like, we have some big juicy onions, arrived today.'

He looked pleased with that so I started cooking. He took the potatoes and knife out of my hand and took over. 'Eat with me Rose? Please.'

He made that smile, the curly one which made him look boyish. I turned to the bench as much to deny to myself how he made me feel as to stop him from seeing it.

I sliced the onions and tossed them into melted butter as he handed me three perfectly peeled potatoes. They were free from eyes and clean, I tried not to touch his fingers as I took the largest from him. He watched as I held the potato in my left hand and cut the chips with a sharp knife in my right.

'How on earth do you do that Rose?' he asked admiringly as if I had just discovered penicillin.

'I don't know…just how my mam did it. I don't know any other way. Is there another way?'

'Well I put them on a wooden board and slice them.'

The onions began to waft their mouth-watering smell into the air as I tossed chips into the hot beef dripping, easing the pan basket out to stop the dripping from foaming over with the initial hit of wetness.

I saw him slice two steaks from the sirloin he had taken from the fridge.

'Not too large for me. I have to get to sleep after I have fed Violetta.'

I slid the onions into a dish and put them into the oven then buttered the hot pan. When it was almost burning I dropped in the seasoned sirloin.

'Wow, the smell has me ravenous. He said setting the table with steak knives and forks.'

'Would you like a glass of red wine with this Rose?

'No, I do not drink anything with alcohol thank you.'

He disappeared into the pub and came back with a large glass a quarter full of wine.

'Moderation in all things.' He raised the glass.

He sat where I had just placed the plates piled with fragrant steak, onions and chips. Holding the glass up to the light he said. 'This is an Italian Valpolicello. I discovered a taste for it when I visited Florence last year.'

He began to eat voraciously and did not know that his words had sunk my appetite. I could not let Carol down by saying that I had heard he had a girlfriend in Florence. I ate some of my supper watching him enjoy his with the hunger men have after working in fresh air all day.

The door swung open and Babs swanned in bringing with her the usual pungency and what she thought was a tempting smile. Her face dropped as she took in the scene. Jealousy, of the kind only women recognize, oozed from every pore.

'I am bored'. She said seductively to Lancelot. 'There's only one old dodderer and a couple having a whispering row in the corner. It is an hour until dad picks me up, can you take me home…please?' She purred in what tone she thought she might get her own way.

'Oh, I have just drunk a glass of wine, I wouldn't have if I had known.'

'Please.'

'Rose and I were just enjoying supper together.' You would have thought he had just said that we had got married and gone to live in the South of France by the look on her face. He did not notice, keeping his eyes on the slicing of his steak.

She was now deadly determined to get him out of my company.

'I have an awful headache, must be the thunder, 'she wined.

Must be the stolen whisky, I thought.

'Ok, I will bring the Landy to the front so you don't get wet.' He pushed his knife and fork together. 'That was delicious Rose, Thank you.'

Her demeanour changed when he left. Her mouth tightened and she came right up to the table and shoved her twisted face into mine.

'Why don't you want your dad to know where you are Rose? What are you hiding?'

The shock of her words caused my mind to spin, what was she talking about? Then I said quietly.

'You have been reading my letter.' She looked flustered, caught out.

'Well it was all torn and open after scooting onto the floor of the car.'

'You had no right to read some-one else's letter. It is illegal.'

She looked a bit scared then pulled on her insolent expression.

'I had to read it, see if it was all there. Your poor dad. I love mine. You obviously do not give one jot to keep yours from seeing your kids…whatever colour they are!'

She felt safe in her indignation that I would not harm her. If she knew what I was capable of she would have walked out of that room and never come back.

'Did you post it Babs?'

'Yes I bloody posted it.'

'Where?' I hated the way my voice grew louder.

'In the damned village of course. It got caught up with the rest of my stuff in my bag. The woman in the Post Office stuck some Sellotape on.'

'What postmark do they get from that post office?'

'What? I don't bloody know do I? Never sent myself a letter, what would be the point?'

Lancelot bounded in with a wet Freddie who shook himself near us both.

'Hey filthy mutt! This is a new dress…you're all stinky. I'm not going in the Landy with you!' She brushed at her clothes as she stepped back.

'Please yourself, the last customers have just left. Go clean up and set the tables for tomorrow until your dad comes.' Lancelot pushed back his dripping hair then sat in his seat at the table.

'Pudding for me I think, now I do not have to go out into that summer storm.'

Babs looked like she might explode all her make up off with all the pressure rising to her face. I imagined eyebrows, dollops of blusher and crusts of foundation hitting the fridge and walls, to slide down in big greasy dollops.

I did allow myself a smile as I turned my back on her to open the fridge door. She clattered out and began loudly pushing chairs around the stone floor of the bar.

'Oh that was not very gallant was it Rose?' He pulled a grimace which melted into laughter.

'You are supposed to be gallant as you are named after a knight?'

'Who me?'

'Yes, you and your brother Arthur. Your mother obviously liked tales of the Round Table.'

'Ha…no Arthur is named after the surgeon who pulled him out of my mother's womb and I am named after her favourite gardener.'

That puzzled me. 'Gardener?'

He smiled. 'Yes, Capability Brown the 18th century garden designer.'

'What? Your name is Capability?' I was confused.

'No, Lancelot was his real name. He became known as Capability as he always told clients that their estates had great capability for improvements.'

'Oh, sorry…never heard of him.' I felt uneducated. What had I been able to learn in my, as yet, short life of struggle?

'Oh my mother had big books about him and pinched some ideas but a Dales farmhouse was not quite posh enough to have the spectacular gardens of Mr. Brown. Anyway, he once moved a whole village out of sight of one of his expensive projects. That would not go at all well with Yorkshire folk.'

'Oh.' I must have sounded disappointed as he replied.

'He was a master gardener to King George the third. He has improved landscapes throughout the country. That is who I am named after. Sorry I cannot be your knight in shining armour.'

He could never know the secret I was trying to hide even from myself. He did not think of himself as better than most men, a knight of chivalry and protection.

But he was.

Later, lulled by the sweet breath of my brood as I listened to the rumbling of thunder pass right over the Dales, my mind raced at the new dangers that foolish girl had put us in. Tomorrow I would send myself a letter.

Chapter Nine.

The next night was Friday, it was a lovely evening with the Dales freshened by the rain. Some of the roses had lost their petals onto the wet grass so Lancelot was showing Sarah how to snip the dead heads off after giving her a stern lesson in scissor safety. I walked over to see her little tongue poking out of the side of her mouth as she snipped and tossed the dead heads into a waiting bucket. Her hands were hardly big enough for scissors. She smiled when she saw me, her tiny, perfect teeth adding to her prettiness. My little girl deserved this happiness and I wished she could keep it forever, but I doubted it.

'I hope you have plenty food Rose, this is the kind of evening the world and his wife fancy a drive into the Dales for a drink.'

'I have it all in hand. A whole new piece of sirloin arrived today and plenty of new potatoes. We have enough prawns to feed an army.'

I was reluctant to leave the sun and the heart lifting sight of Sarah's blooming love for the man who taught her so much. The babies were awake in their makeshift playpen in the shade of the stone wall, placed there so I could watch them from the kitchen window. It was a lovely scene but I had to earn my pay. I was off to Darlington on Monday for more baby clothes. Carol had kindly agreed to take me again although I was sure she must get a raw deal when she could be enjoying a grown up trip with peace and no squeaky children.

Lancelot was right. The customers flooded in and Babs could not cope with all the orders for summer suppers and the steak and chips. I think the rush was because I had learned how to make onion rings in beer batter. I was forced to dash into the bar and lounge with plates of hot food which I plopped in front of people as quickly as I could without being rude. Exhausted, I gave the babies their ten o'clock check and suckled Violetta as quietly as I could, glad to get off my feet for a few minutes. My heart swelled in love for this tiny being who gazed up at me in adoration. I stroked the wide nose and glowing cheeks I loved to kiss. It was calm and warm outside as I listened to gentle snuffles and tiny snores. I was nodding off when the baby slipped my nipple out of her mouth in deep satisfied slumber when suddenly there was a voice almost beneath my window.

'No, no. No!'

It was a voice I had heard before, a sad sound I had played over and over in my mind every night for weeks. As gently as I could I lowered Violetta into her drawer then tiptoed to the window. I could see a couple. He was shaking her and shouting under his breath.

'I am sick of you like this! You had better get over it or I am off. I am warning you.'

There were little female cries which I also had burned into my memory and I knew exactly who it was out there.

'God woman! You have been a pain in the arse ever since that night. I have had enough!'

I flew down the stairs and out into the garden where I yanked open the gate that led to the front of the pub. It made a loud squeal and the woman who was alone in front of me turned in fright. The face, lit by the window, was almost the same as Violetta's and the eyes, widened in fear bore the same curled lashes. They were wet with crying.

In her relief to see it was a woman who was moving towards her she almost slumped.

'I am sorry. I did not mean to trespass.' She turned in embarrassment and took a few steps before I stopped her with my words.

'I understand a mother's pain.' I made my voice quiet and reassuring even though my pulse was banging in my throat.

She froze, then turned gently.

'What?'

'I am a mother too.' I spoke softly so that she would not run away.

'I am not a mother...I am a disgrace, a bullied spineless shame on women.'

'No, I have a daughter too. I could never be parted from her. But I know how men can intimidate us.' She turned to me and came really close. There it was. That smell, the same one that was on the cardigan the night I found Violetta.

'Who are you?' her brows came down in suspicion.

'Never mind. I have a surprise for you.' I took her arm as reassuringly as I could and led her into the house.

When we reached the bottom of the stairs she pulled back, wrenching her wrist from me.

'What is going on?'

Of course she was scared. Some woman just appears and lures you upstairs.

'Wait there!' I dashed up the stairs and dragged the unwilling drawer open as gently as I could. The smell was still faintly clinging to the yellow wool. I flew down and to my relief she was still there. Her eyes fell to her cardigan, puzzlement knitted her brows then she lifted her eyes to question me. The energy between us buzzed with unanswered worries.

'I want to give you back your happiness.' I tried to put myself in her position, she must be shaking inside with horror and hope in equal measures. She took the cardigan, pushing her face into the soft wool I had made sure never to wash. I saw dread loosen her face. She thought this was all I had for her, that I had found only this on the moors where she had left her baby to die.

'Please, follow me.'

I began to walk up the stairs and for a moment I thought she wouldn't come but as I gently cracked open the bedroom door I heard her feet on the wood. I held open the door and her eyes tried to adjust as she scanned my two blond children asleep on my bed.

I went over to the cot drawer. 'Come over here...see what I have for you.'

Cautiously she took the four steps to where I was and peered into the drawer. If I live to be a million I will never see such an expression again. Delight, confusion, relief and terror crowded her face. She stood stock still.

I bent and placed my hands gently under Violetta's limp body and head, her tiny arms wove about in sleepy surprise. I offered her to her real mother. It broke my heart.

For a moment she did not take her baby. It was as if she was trying to work out landing in another universe.

'Here.' I passed Violetta to her so she could not avoid the woman's natural lifting of her arms to take the body she must have craved for so long.

She spluttered and choked as if emotion would kill her but she lifted her baby to her face and breathed in her delicious scent. It was Johnson's baby lotion, milk and her own scent that she probably shared with this woman holding her. It would bond them even though neither of them knew it. 'Thank God! Thank God! My baby. My beautiful baby!'

Tears sped down cheeks and air was gulped into an emotion wracked body.

'I do not understand. I thought she was dead. We did a terrible thing that night.' Sobs wracked her chest. 'How did you find her?'

'Oh, it is a long story. I was sheltering in the Abbey that night and heard you, that's why I came downstairs just now. I recognised your voice. After I heard your car leave I caught a slight drift of a baby cry. I was already breast feeding my son so her need made my milk flow as I snuggled her into my warmth.'

A stricken look came across her face like a blackout curtain. 'All these weeks, I thought I was a murderer. I thought I had killed my baby.' She looked down into the face so like her own. 'I never wanted to abandon her out there on the moor but Alex forced me. He said my dad would kill us both. He said he would leave me if I kept the baby.'

'Where did you give birth?'

'On my bathroom floor. In Leeds, we are both art students there, only I had not been to any lectures for the last two months I was pregnant. I was showing too much. I kept painting though. It was my only solace.' Her face changed swiftly around elation and guilt.

That is when I knew what the yellow cardigan smelled of. Oil paint.

'But why did you go to the Abbey to leave your baby?'

'Alex borrowed his mate Chris's Ford Capri for the day, we just kept driving and driving until he could stand my snivelling no more. It is Chris who brought us up here tonight, said he heard the food was good and we would enjoy the run out. The truth is, I haven't enjoyed anything since the day I gave birth.'

'What will you do now?'

She looked at her baby and I could see that she was caught in the same spell of every woman who had ever felt a baby grow inside her and delivered them through pain into this hurtful world.

'I want her…she is part of me. She has coiled herself into every dream I have had, broken my heart every day. Alex can take a running jump!'

We beamed at each other. We both felt the strength of womanhood seared to unbelievable heights by the magic of being mothers.

'Of course my dad is another problem. But I will just have to be brave and tell him that the father is white and my baby will never be parted from me.'

We both gazed at the wonder in her arms. The beam of love was identical, only one was losing and one was gaining. I tried not to let the depth of my pain show.

'I love Violetta so much. It will be hard for me to lose her.'

'Violetta? Is that what you have named her?'

'Yes, you left her on a patch of violets. It seemed appropriate.'

'I was going to call her Jennifer, after my mum but I love Violetta. What is your name?'

'Rose.'

'Violetta Rose that will be her name. I will tell her why when she is old enough.' She gazed at her baby and gasped with pleasure as the tiny fingers curled around hers.

'My name is Melonie by the way. This is such a shock. I have so much to work out. Can you keep her until I make arrangements to take her home? It will not be easy persuading my father.'

'Of course I will, she will have to be breast fed anyway. You can start her on the bottle when you take her.'

A shout came up through the open window. 'Mels! Mels! Where are you? Do not do this to me. Chris wants to go back now. It is a long drive! Come on!'

'I had better go. I won't be telling him yet but I can never stay with a man who left my baby to die. I should have been braver. I will be back as soon as I am able. I will ring you at the pub number. I'll get it from Yellow Pages.'

She put Violetta back into my arms then kissed me hard on the cheek. 'You are a true angel Rose.' I listened to her light footsteps fade then some talking and a car door slam.

I gazed down at the child I adored. She made squeaking noises as she woke then waved her chubby hands around, they were paler in the palms and I kissed one as it came near my face. Her dark skin glowed and made the whites of her round eyes even whiter, she did a little gurgle and a half smile. My heart ripped open. Sarah loved her too, she would take her departure as hard as I would. I went to bed before Lancelot could catch up with me. He was used to me falling asleep as I fed Violetta. I had many things to sort inside my whirling head.

I walked down to the village the next morning. I watched Ben and Violetta pressed up against each other as they lay side by side beneath the fringed sun canopy I struggled to fit onto the pram, they were both getting bigger. Ben had four teeth now and he used them daily on me. It broke my heart that I would never see Violetta's teeth or watch her take her first steps or say her first word.

Beneath the buttery sun Sarah was travelling in style on the seat holding in one hand Humph, wearing his just washed jumper, and in the other the letter I had written addressed to myself. She made a big thing out of allowing Humph to post the letter pushing his fat paws into the red slit of the pillar box then letting him peer into the deep darkness to make sure it was safe. I pushed the pram uphill past thirsty weeds and dusty paths. The verges were thick with summer, I stopped to let Sarah pick fists of purple periwinkle and white bird's eye flowers.

I passed two women chatting about a new washing machine over their dividing fence. One had a florid well fed face and the other the pinched mouth of a heavy smoker.

'Good morning.' I said cheerily as I strode by. Their conversation stopped and I knew that I would be the topic when it started up again. I heard them mention Lancelot and hated that I had brought his name down to the lips of village gossips. I knew then that what they thought was my story would be threaded through every gossiper in the dales.

I was glad when the Lark and Lamb came into view as the uphill struggle was more than I had bargained for. I was just going to push into the garden gate when I decided to go around, still on the stony ground. The old stone barn I saw from the window had long fascinated me but I had never been able to explore with the three babies. It was a hard, bumpy push that almost woke Ben and Violetta but Sarah was as excited as I was to push open the rotting door and look inside. It had no glass in the two windows at opposite ends and the floor was a mix of rotting manure and soil. The cream stone was not so weathered inside. I adored it.

'Mammy, can Sarah have play in here?' she beamed feeling the cosiness.

'I will ask Lancelot pet.' I said as I picked her up to look out of one of the windows. We could see in a different direction than from the house windows. It was a charming view sweeping down towards where the river had carved deep cliffs out of the dale. Somehow this barn wove a spell on us both. Yes it had a wounded look about it and seemed forgotten, like long burst party balloons. But I had bandages of love and a purpose to inflated it back to bright and bouncing. We giggled and talked for the five minutes it took to manipulate the pram home. It was then that I knew what I wanted to create in that old building. I would have to get some money to buy it first.

Carol brought more puppy milk for Daisy, Buttercup and Bluebell that teatime. I was busy with vegetables and watching Sarah try to snuggle the puppies up to a now naked Humph who was supposed to be their mum. They wanted to roll each other over and bite at tiny tails but she was determined. They sniffed at his big red stitches. As soon as she got one into place another scrabbled away to new adventures beneath the table.

We laughed together as Sarah's legs disappeared in search of her naughty charges.

As I poured us both tea beside the wilted flowers in a jam-jar I said. 'I have news about Violetta.'

Carol looked into the playpen where Ben was watching the baby trying to get her fist into her mouth.

'I have found her mother.'

Carol's pearls almost strangled her, so fast was the turn of her head towards me.

'What? Are you sure? How?'

I recounted the story as her eyes opened wider and wider.

'Well, this is great news. I think.'

I was puzzled then. 'What do you mean?'

'Well I have not said too much Rose but the mother has committed a criminal offence. Serious charges could be dropped on her.'

She studied my face.

'And us Rose…we should have contacted the authorities. You to report that you had found a baby. And I…I should never have pretended not to know she was not really yours. It was just that breast feeding a baby is the best start you can give any child. I am trying to persuade every new mother I treat to do this but the fashion is for bottle feeding. I tell them to not be so vain, they think their breasts are for ornaments. Some say that their husbands want to keep them for themselves and forbid them to breast feed. Can you imagine?'

I couldn't. To me it was the most natural thing in the world. I would miss it so much.

'We have to handle this carefully Rose. When is she coming for Violetta?'

'I have no clue…she has lots to sort out. It will be so hard for me.'

'I know, you love Violetta like your own. We all do.'

That acid flush of terror flooded my stomach, how could my doing a good turn get me into even more trouble than I was already in? What if it went public? Got into the papers? There would be no hiding then and my children would be taken away. I felt that whatever I did in life would find me out.

'I haven't told Lancelot yet Carol. He has been so busy with shearing.'

'Yes, I noticed the bald sheep looking clean and relieved as I drove over here.'

She sat at the table as I poured us both more tea. 'I wonder if we could make this seamless. What is best for Violetta?' She bit her lip gently. Hope rose through my dread, but only a little.

'That is what I care about. Surely we can check out that Melonie will be a good mother and hand her baby over without alerting any authorities.'

Carol blew on her tea thoughtfully. 'When she rings, get her address and phone number. I will look into it.' She turned her wrist to see her watch. 'Eek! Is that the time? I'll pick you up at ten on Monday, OK?'

On Sunday tea time, I watched from the window as Lancelot was training Freddie and showing him off to Sarah who was bare-footed on the grass.

The sheepdog was leaping over a stick held at hip height. His overflowing vigour had him dashing this way then that before winding through his master's long legs. On one command he jumped over the wooden seat and back again. Sarah's adoring gaze could have warmed up a snowman. I hoped she did not get that openness from her mother. He would see straight through me.

At two years and three months old she was allowed to let her love show for this man, I was not.

I brought both babies down to the lawn and found Humph was now the subject of strict training although he was not doing as well as Freddie.

'Hello my lumpen friend.' I laughed. 'Too fat for jumping are you.' I stroked his little teddy head.

Lancelot smiled when he saw me. He would never know what that smile did to me. The puppies were now instructed to copy Freddie but were only capable of rolling about and waving short, fat legs into the air.

Lancelot helped Sarah put the puppies back into their box to sleep in the shade then picked up my beaming daughter and swung her around. He trailed an air of capability whatever he was doing. Just like his namesake it seemed.

From his pocket, Lancelot took out the whistle he used to instruct Freddie to do exactly as he wished to herd his sheep.

'Sarah, do you know why Freddie is such a good sheep dog?'

She shook her little head and I noticed how much her hair needed cutting.

'Well, the sheep like him. He has a kind air and never nips at their legs or fleece. That way he gets cooperation.' Sarah looked at Freddie whose long red tongue was flopping out of the side of his mouth. 'He has great turn out and speed and a powerful but lovely pace.'

It was lost on her but I loved watching what passion did to this face, it pleased me so much. Foolishly, I let it feed the fire of wanting him that warmed my heart.

'Freddie has a good gearbox and doesn't waste time. Would you like to hear?'

He peeped at his whistle and Freddie went left, a different peep and he went right, hugging the ground as he turned. 'I trained him myself from a puppy. He is so special. But we need sheep to demonstrate and I will not allow them into my garden.' He laughed at her concentration and swung her up into his arms. 'I will take you all out to the moors to show Freddie off to you one day.'

She beamed at him, showing the tiny teeth I loved to see.

'Now,' he laughed looking about to find new pleasures to entertain her, 'shall I show you how to scent your feet?' He put her onto the moss covered low stone wall behind the lavender hedge and jumped up beside her, flicking off his shoes as he did. I had never seen his bare feet and somehow it seemed way too intimate, erotic even. I tried to drag my eyes away from them but failed.

'Careful with the bees.' He laughed as he showed her how to swing her legs into the lavender spikes and catch the perfumed oil onto her skin. She lifted a foot as near to his face as possible.

'Mmm, divine!' he smiled.

Ben started his belly laugh in my arms, he was developing such a sense of humour. I held him tighter and he clung to me. His pink gums and four little teeth made me laugh even more.

'Mammy come here and smell 'slot's feet.'

'No! I am sure they are lovely but...' I turned to put Ben down on his rug.

Lancelot lifted her off the wall and shouted. 'Well if the mammy won't come to the feet; the feet will have to come to the mammy.' They bounded towards me and wrestled me down until I had to sniff two pairs of feet through my giggles. I felt my stomach swoop.

As he touched my arms my heart clattered in alarm. It was only fun but I had wanted his strong fingers to stay on me forever. Having him this close was excruciating.

Was the dormant spark of my life, held back with cold winds and frost, about to bloom?

The squealing and tumbling made Servant wake from his flattened catnip plant and jump up to the wall where Freddie leapt playfully to push him off. The cat batted at his nose and we all laughed. It was a lovely family scene for anyone who might have walked through the gate right now. But it could never truly belong to me. No matter how much I pretended.

Unfortunately, the person who did walk through the gate was Babs, her face like black thunder. Her glare lowered the temperature by several degrees. She brought with her a traumatically potent scent. I half expected the flowers to shrivel.

'You asked me to come in early to practice making cocktails.' She said to Lancelot whilst completely ignoring me and the children.

'He lifted Sarah to her feet, then brushed bits of cut grass from his jeans. 'Ah yes, is it that time already? I'll see you in the bar.'

Babs managed to get in one filthy look before she turned and left but as usual Lancelot missed it.

Later, when I took the amended menus into the pub, Babs was standing behind the bar. It was early and only Tony, out of his uniform. was in enjoying a pint. She pursed her mouth and sniffed but her eyes never left me as I placed the new menus in front of her.

'Aye Aye!' Tony said when he saw me.' You've caught me enjoying a sneaky one, don't tell the wife will you?'

I laughed as I knew he was a kind man but I also knew he had the power to break my heart if he ever got a whiff of who I really was. I opened the pub door and went out to replace the menu in the glass case on the wall.

When I had finished I looked about at the lovely evening in the Dales. The stone walls stretched up and down the vast, sheep strewn hills. It all seemed timeless and I wondered at the men who had developed such skill in building dry stone walls that had lasted centuries. How long had it taken them? Where did they get all that stone from? Did they freeze and shiver in winter then sweat and droop in summer? Did they take their chilblained hands home to wives waiting for them with warming soup and a blazing fire or did they have to snatch broken sleep in the tiny, forlorn shepherd's cottages dotted about? Whoever they were, I admired them and loved them for the practical beauty they created. They could never know how long their dedicated, clever work would last. It felt great to look at this vast working history. I felt small and inadequate by comparison.

Babs did not look up as I stepped back in, but I saw her murmuring to Tony, they both looked over at me then Babs said something behind her hand.

Acid pooled in my stomach, that woman was determined to make trouble. She saw me as a threat to her dreams of landing Lancelot but she had no idea that it was some other woman who held his heart. Neither of us would ever come close to having him.

I went quietly into the kitchen, checked on the children and gave into Sarah's request to let her stand at the sink to wash the soil off the new potatoes. She'd be soaked and dirty by the time she had had enough but I had to let her learn, she had a strong need to feel useful. I had been the same, my poor mother had to change me every Sunday as I begged to wash caterpillars off the dark green cabbage leaves dad brought in from the garden. I learned to recognise the different caterpillars and what butterflies they would become as I studied them in a washed out jam jar before setting them free to their futures. How innocent I had been of life. If I had known what was to come maybe I would never have gone on.

The door sneck clacked and Tony walked in.

'Ah, so this is where the magic happens.' He laughed looking about at Sarah, the babies sleeping in his old pram and the puppies trying to get out of their chewed cardboard crisp box. This was my world and he had the power to take it from me.

'Rose, you always look so shocked to see me. Am I so alarming or have you a terrible crime you are covering up?' He laughed and I could see how much fun he must be. Luckily he missed my guilt stiffened face as something caught his eye.

He wandered over to the salmon lying on the table.

'Ah ha! This is the crime; poached salmon and not in the cooking way. Who caught that for you? Did you ask to see their licence?' He saw my scared face. 'Just kidding. Wish I was eating here tonight.'

I was trying to recover my composure and was losing. He took my silence to be annoyance.

'Oh sorry…I will get out of your hair. I was hoping to see Lancelot to tell him I won't be having the station anniversary dinner here after all.'

I knew nothing about this but knew Lancelot wanted to encourage business.

'Oh, why is that?'

'Babs said you would not be able to cope with it. Said you were too tired?'

'Really?'

'Not to worry. I can find somewhere else. Lancelot will understand.' He turned to leave.

I pulled at his arm. 'Don't you dare! I can cope, I have no clue why Babs told you that.'

He looked thrilled. 'Really! Great. Can we have that juicy gammon and pineapple ring with your fabulous chips?'

'You can.' I laughed he was so excited.

'And Black Forest Gateau too?'

'Of course. That is easy, we can buy that in. I only have to cut it up.'

I made a note of the date and another to order the gammon from our wonderful Dales farmer. When he left I wanted to make a third note not to look so guilty when I saw him. He was nice. But I spoiled the thought with the plain fact that he was a policeman and would have to act as such when the time came. Then it sunk in. I had just arranged to have a pub full of policemen for one night. Why had I agreed to that? If one of them had seen my photo or had contacts in Newcastle, I would be sunk. I would not be leaving the kitchen for one minute.

The drive across the Dales that Monday, through Richmond with the cobbled streets and crumbling castle fed my soul. I was treating every day of my freedom as my last. One day it would be.

When we came near to the town, traffic churned and turned with mysterious efficiency. Darlington was busy because of the sales. Carol did me the favour again of baby sitting in her car with Violetta and Ben whilst I treated Sarah to the delights of shops and a bustle of people and cars she found exciting. I was thrilled to get a white Babygro with pink rosebuds for Violetta at half price and something new for the rest of us. I felt rich as I purchased stuff I would never have been able to afford this time last year. There was nothing to spend my money on in the Dales so I splashed out carelessly. I was proud to take juice and a sandwich back to the car. After we had eaten Sarah fell asleep on Carol's knee as I fed the babies.

'Ah bless her. She is not used to the high life is she?' We both smiled as we gazed at her limp mouth.

'She has been looking forward to this trip for days. It is such a treat for her.'

Carol adjusted her seat so she could see me, 'Talking of treats. I have two rescue greyhounds I want to socialise and train. I am going to suggest Whitby next Monday. Sarah will adore a day on the beach, she has never used that bucket and spade we brought back from Scarborough has she?'

She was studying my face. She took my frozen expression to be exactly what it was. Fear.

'Is it all sea-sides you have an aversion too Rose?'

I dropped my eyes to Ben who was playing with my hair.

'You know talking these things out always helps. Tell me why the mention of Scarborough strikes terror into your heart.'

She was so kind and her voice so soft that I wanted to tell her. But still it froze in my mind.

'Is it because of lovely memories you have with your husband Rose?'

I expelled air so quick it sounded like a donkey braying. I had not one lovely memory of Ed. Only desolation.

She read me right. 'A bad memory then. It always helps to get it out Rose. What happened in Scarborough?'

'It is time for your appointment, surely.' I shifted uncomfortably.

She looked at her watch and eased Sarah onto the seat still snoozing.

'Ok. I will be an hour at the most. Will you be OK?'

I smiled and nodded. I must have had a little snooze myself because when she came back straining with heavy bags and parcels, I was startled awake and had dribble down my face.

The babies and Sarah woke up too, we must have looked a right dopey lot. Carol plonked down into the driver's seat and eased her arms up and around.

'Ooh. Those bags were heavy.' She said taking a Ladybird story book out of her handbag. Sarah's eyes lit up as it was placed into her hands.

'I have such a sore shoulder Rose. Can you drive home?' She held one arm then rolled her shoulder about.

I must have looked shocked as she smiled and said. 'Don't worry, I will tell you where to turn.'

'Oh Carol, I am afraid I cannot drive and never will.'

'Oh, sorry, I thought…what do you mean never will?'

I tried to look at the pages in the new book as I said. 'Well I am too stupid to drive.'

Carol lifted my face and must have seen the pain there. 'Rose I have not known you long but stupid is not what you are. Quite the opposite in fact.'

I swallowed hard and turned my eyes to the pictures of Red Riding Hood looking at a wolf in bed.

'You know Rose I have had quite a lot of training in psychology and you are showing classic signs of mental abuse. Tell me now and honestly, was your marriage happy?'

I felt flattened by a steam roller but I had to say something.

'No…' I whispered.

'Tell me why you think you are too stupid to drive Rose.'

I was shaking. The memory stood out before me wrapped in all the hopelessness it had soaked into me. Carol was so reassuring that I felt I had to speak.

'My husband had a work's van sometimes and once on our way home through quiet lanes I asked him if I could learn to drive, he laughed and said it took brains to manage a car and traffic so I would never become a driver. I said I thought I could do it but he grew angry and stomped out of the car. I only had Sarah then, she was on the back seat in a carry cot.'

I looked at Sarah who was engrossed in her book but I lowered my voice.

'He dragged me out by my hair and made me sit in the driver's seat and told me to drive.' My voice and body began to shake.

Carol took one of my hands. 'Go on.'

'I asked him what to do and he said that if I thought myself so bloody clever I would know. I fumbled about and managed to turn on the ignition but I grew scared as I didn't know what to do next.'

'He yelled at me, 'Press the bloody pedals you idiot!' His face was twisted. So I did, he yanked my hand on the gearstick and the car jumped about as I tried to get into first gear then I pressed the accelerator.'

I tried to get the words passed my throat but they stuck.

'Go on Rose, get it all out.'

I looked her right in the eye. 'I managed a bit of motion but the steering wheel was turned into the hedge where he had left it so that is where the car went. Into the hedge. There was no damage and we all just stopped. He slapped me across the face and said 'I told you were too stupid to drive.' I was stunned. All the pain of that day visited me again and flowed through my veins into my heart.

Carol did not speak.

'He got out, yanked me out onto the grass, kicked me in the thighs then got the car back onto the road. It was simple, I had only gone a few feet. That was the end of my driving.'

Carol squeezed my hand harder. 'You do realise that he was abusive and wanted to make you feel small so that he could feel superior don't you?'

I had not realised that I had stopped breathing until I spluttered and gulped in air.

'Genuine controllers are an anti-life, killers of energy, living fire blankets that smother all endeavour.' She said taking my hand.

'I suppose you had mixed feelings when your bad marriage ended in his death. But you mustn't feel guilt Rose that your release came from him dying.'

At the word 'guilt', my mind became sharp with the need to say nothing further. Was this the stitch that caught on a thorn and would unravel the whole of my garment of shame? I had to stop this now and so I settled Sarah into the front seat and got into the back to look after the babies.

I was pleased to leave the town and get back to the peace of the Dales. Sarah was thrilled with her new clothes and wanted to try the rosebud sprigged Babygro on Violetta immediately but I had to discourage her. I had something in mind for that.

After we had tidied away the shopping I took Sarah into the house kitchen. On the table were letters, some opened by Lancelot and piled neatly. One letter was mine. It was set apart on the other side of the fruit bowl. I recognised my own writing and knew that there was a blank sheet of paper inside but that was not what interested me. I peered at the postmark I so needed to take a worry away from me. It was smudged, thick with ink from the pad of the post mistress as she bashed her wooden and rubber stamp into it before bringing it down onto my letter. I took the envelope to the window for a better look. I could make out the last few letters. My worst fears hit me. My heart thudded, then stopped. If Babs had slid my letter to dad into that same post-box it could be traced by anyone investigating where to find me. Nausea crept into my belly.

I no longer felt safe here.

Every time the pub phone rang my heart leapt in the hope that it was Melonie telling me she had arranged everything and give me a date to pick up her baby. I was shot through with feelings of dread and hope mixed in equal measures. I wanted to keep Violetta but I also wanted her natural mother to feel the joy of her beautiful baby. I wished I had told Melonie to ring when the pub was closed as I hated to think Babs would take the call. It had been two weeks. I was getting worried.

I was also worried about my dad. I wished he had a phone. I wondered if he was still getting along with that lady I met so briefly. Margaret…no…Maureen. She might have a phone. I could not remember her second name. I would ask directory enquiries if I did. But I only met her for half an hour and then my world spun out of control.

One day when the wind was too strong to take the children into the garden, I packed them into the pram with the hood up. Sarah begged that she and Humph could sit on the top seat and bravely pushed her hair out of her eyes all the way into the village. Not many people were about because of the gusts but she enjoyed seeing the houses and gardens. We made a counting game of how many plant pots had crashed to the ground and then how many gates were swinging back and forth. She could count up to 20 now, although she often missed 18 out. She was thrilled with her new life, thriving as I thought she never would. I prayed she would never be taken from me. But I knew I would have to answer to my crimes one day. I could hardly get thoughts of what would happen when everything caught up with me out of my head, so I turned for home where I mashed up different foods for Ben to try. Sarah spooned in mashed beef with cabbage and I laughed as he pursed his lips and spat out the lot. His left eye closed before he winced at orange and rhubarb and we

all giggled at the funny faces. But he put out his chubby
hand and pulled mine towards him after his first spoonful
of fish, potato and cream sauce. I cleaned him up and
lifted him out of his high chair. He jiggled his feet in
pleasure and Sarah tickled the fat toes.

'He is a nice baby mammy, all squishy and smiley isn't
he?' The love that beamed between them would last
forever, even if I was not there.

The next morning was breezy with fat clouds scudding in
fluffy groups. Lancelot came into the garden with his
breakfast at 10am, he had been out in the Dales since six.
Freddie sniffed at the puppies in their box then lay in the
shade to recover from his morning's work.

Lancelot put his cereal bowl down on the wooden table
and called Sarah from her puppies.

'Let us look at my sheep in the sky Sarah.' He lay down
on the lawn and she copied. They gazed up into the blue
and as I looked up I saw that indeed the fast moving
clouds looked like flocks of fat sheep.

'Is Freddie in sky too 'slot?'

'Let us see now...ah! Can you see the long grey cloud?'

She pushed windblown hair from her eyes then cast about
and although she looked like she couldn't, said she could
to please him.

'That is Freddie running flat out like he does when he is herding the sheep across the rocks. He is so fast he looks like he is flying.'

She saw the cloud then and asked if she could see Freddie doing this for real as promised.

'As long as mammy agrees. I can take you one morning, but you must get out of bed at five thirty. Can you?'

She nodded with great excitement. She was too young to know that she was flat out until seven or eight every morning.

I lay beside them. Here was something I was great at. Dad and I had spent many hours spotting elephants, angel wings and sunlit pigs when I was a girl. We laughed at the changing vapours trying desperately to get each other to see what we saw before the cloud morphed into something else. Sarah mostly saw puppies and babies, such was her experience of life so far.

Lancelot took her hand when she was pointing at a large shape she insisted was Servant running away. He tried to get with her eye line but failed.

'You know Sarah, you are doing a great job with Bluebell, Buttercup and Daisy but soon they will want to go to live with a family of their own. A nice mammy and daddy who want a little dog and will love him.' He tried to sound as matter of fact as he could to soften what he knew would be a big blow to a small child. There was no response but I knew from her silence that her heart had sunk.

He continued. 'I was talking to a lady yesterday, she lives in a lovely cottage two miles away and she said she was lonely and would love to have two puppies to love and play with.'

Still silence.

'I told her that we had three who were growing too big for their box if she would like to come to see them. If we like the lady we may let her have two of ours. What do you think?'

She let loose of the hand she had been thrilled to hold, scrambled up and went to the puppies who were slouched into a sleeping heap.

Lancelot and I got up and went to her.

'What lady's name 'slot?'

'Mrs. Handley, She has a nice smile and soft hands.' We both watched the little blond girl who loved these puppies as much as her babies and knew she was hurting.

'Anyway, shall I ask Mrs. Handley to come along so we can see if we like her and if she likes the puppies?'

Sarah ran into the house and we heard her feet on the stairs.

I checked the babies then ran after her. She was lying on our bed with her face in the pillow. I stroked her hair.

'Listen pet. It is what happens to all baby puppies and kittens. They have to have new homes to be loved in.'

She turned over and gazed at my face as if having to see truth for herself.

'My babies mammy? Will my babies have to have new homes?'

My heart almost stopped. I knew that she would have to lose Violetta soon too. There would be hard lessons but she had to learn them.

'Do you remember when we found Violetta?'

She nodded and pulled Humph from the top of the pillow and stuck his ear into her mouth.

'Well Violetta did not come out of my tummy like Ben did. She will go back to the mummy whose tummy she came out of.'

I saw my daughter shrink further into sadness. At her age everything was forever. She did not know that life was about change. I cuddled her close and told her that as we are so good at looking after babies, the puppies and Violetta had needed us and then they needed other people and we had to give them a chance to be loved. She sniffed along the back of her hand.

'Will Ben have a new home mammy?'

'No darling, nothing will ever take Ben from us. He is ours forever.'

She was a little comforted by this so I carried her downstairs to the garden and her puppies. She ran to the pram where Violetta was sleeping then to the box.

Lancelot was holding Ben who was dribbling down onto his bib as usual. I did not usually see my son in the arms of anyone else and it struck me how sturdy he was. His back was straightening, his arms and legs looked like sausages in a pan waiting to be pricked. His hairdo made of question marks brought a smile to my lips. My heart felt ready to explode with love for this little boy. He would never allow alcohol to pass his lips. I would make sure of that. He would respect women and never lay a finger on them with anything but love. This is how I would bring him up. He saw me as I stepped nearer and held out his arms. I put him on my hip and he snuggled close. Lancelot gazed at us and I saw in his eyes that he loved him too. If only I could have that love. But I was not a helpless child. I was a woman on the run.

'Rose, when I was young my dad made a wooden cart and fitted it with the wheels off our old pram. I used to pull Arthur around the garden and then the Dales in it. He was only just sitting up but dad padded it with cushions and although he wobbled and bounced he also squealed with glee. I am thinking of making one for Ben, is that all right with you?'

I was thrilled. 'As long as you don't use the wheels off our pram, we still need it and autumn is not far off.' I did not say that I might need it to carry all my stuff when the time came to leave.

Every time the phone rang in the pub my nerves jangled. It was answered by Lancelot or Babs but no one ever came to say that it was a call from Melonie to tell me she was coming for her baby. Each time I held Violetta to my breast I wondered how long I would have her like this.

I was not prepared for the arrow through my heart when Lancelot told me he was going to Italy for a few days. I mumbled something through my flooding thoughts of him in the arms of the lovely Irish girl he wrote to.

'Can you manage without me?' He asked studying my face.

I wanted to beg him not to go but instead I said 'Of course, you deserve a holiday. Enjoy yourself.'

'Well it is not a holiday exactly, I have something I must do, something I have been putting off far too long for my own happiness.'

I smiled a smile I had to dredge up from the bottom of my soul as I looked at his beautiful eyes. 'You are so understanding Rose.'

I waited for him to say something about Cleona as I had promised Carol I would not say she had discussed it. He never mentioned her.

The morning Mrs Handley came to see the puppies was a quiet one. I had kept the news from Sarah so that she would not have a troubled sleep and I waited until her cereal bowl was empty before I told her.

'When the little hand on the clock reaches ten,' I said walking over to the old freckle-faced grandfather clock, 'here.' I pointed. 'The lovely lady who really needs a puppy will be coming to see ours. If she loves them as much as we do she will be taking them to a new house to have a lovely life with her.'

She was silent until the knock on the door.

Mrs Handley had soft white hair and a lovely smile. She came into the kitchen and deliberately kept her eyes away from the puppy box although I could tell she was excited.

'Now then. I have heard that there is a special girl lives here who does a wonderful job looking after puppies until they are big enough to go out to people who want them so much.'

'Me have puppies.' Sarah was not smiling.

'Oh then it is you who does such a good job. I was wondering if I could see the puppies.'

She held out her hand and Sarah took it, leading her the ten steps to the box. Mrs. Handley's face lit up. 'Now what are their names?'

Sarah pointed and told her.

'My name is Wendy. I live near Reeth and I had a lovely dog for fifteen years, her name was Bundle. She died of old age last month and I was hoping to find two puppies who would play in my garden.'

Sarah lifted out Bluebell and Buttercup. They did not like being woken and spread out their little legs in protest. Wendy took one of the puppies and held it up in the careful way animal lovers do.

'Oh how pretty she is. Her ears are all soft and warm.'

Sarah placed the other puppy upside down in her arms and kissed it on the nose.

'Have you got a nice garden Wendy?'

'I do, yes.'

'My puppies love to play in the garden.'

'They seem perfect to me. Can I take these two home with me?'

Sarah looked at me and I nodded encouragingly.

'Can you take three puppies Wendy? I do not want them to be lonely.' There was a catch in her voice.

'Well my sister was looking for a dog to take for walks. She lives a mile away from me. She would love Daisy, I am sure.'

'You can take their box if you like.'

'Can I? That would make the puppies feel at home. I could put the new bed I have for them just beside the box, see if they like it.'

Sarah put a soft kiss to the heads of each of her beloved puppies then clattered up the stairs to bed.

There was a silence between us two women.

'Best if I go now. You need to see to your daughter. I will look after these little dogs and you must visit anytime you want.'

I held the door open so Wendy could carry the box through, then I opened her car door for her. It hurt me too to lose these lovely little souls but it had to be done. The house did not seem the same.

I did not go up to Sarah, she had to work this through in her own head. When she came down after ten minutes I tried to make my voice as upbeat as I could.

'Well aren't we lucky to have such a special lady for our doggies.'

She merely asked if she could make pancakes for lunch with golden syrup and icing sugar. As I took the flour from the cupboard I ached that I could never protect my daughter from the agonies that lay in store for her life. Some of them may be caused by me.

It was a busy night for food. I had seen some recipes in the pile of magazines Carol had brought up from her surgery. Being keen to try something new I made a chicken and mushroom cream pie, toad in the hole and quiche. Sarah had helped silently.

The week before Lancelot went away dragged at my feet and my heart. I did not realise how much seeing him each day meant to me. I had only been here a few months and I was his employee, not another thing, but I could not bear the thought of his smiling face turning to some-one else. This thought continuously yanked at my whole being so that I could not sleep or pay proper attention to anything. I heard banging one morning, it came from the garden. I looked out to see Lancelot making the little cart for Ben. I took him a mug of tea. He stood up then took it from me, placing it on the wall. 'I got the wood from an old barn of mine on the hills. There are no wheels though but I have put the word around and one or two say they know some-one with an old pram or pushchair. One day soon a set of wheels will arrive on our doorstep, just you wait and see. That is how things are done hereabouts.'

I pushed my hands through my sleep flattened hair. 'Ah, we call that a bogey where I come from. The children will love it.'

I dashed back up just in time to see Sarah sitting up and the babies stirring. I opened the curtains and soft light fell on their faces. How lucky they were to be here in this wonderful place with a wonderful man. If only their mother was just as wonderful. If only she had got here some other way than the way she did.

The day he was flying out was grey with heavy black clouds scudding low on the Dales, we were eating Sugar Puffs in the kitchen with Freddie curled around Lancelot's feet. Sarah drank her last spoonful of sugary milk and asked to be down from the table at the same time Freddie went to the door asking to be out. I opened the door and the sheepdog ran out to do what he had to do but before I could shut it Babs bowled in dressed in a new pink and blue shirt with pink pants. She must have got up really early to plaster that much make-up over her face.

'Dad brought me over to catch you with this before you left for your plane.' She took it all in as usual, the empty bowls, the teapot with the knitted tea cosy in the shape of a fat lamb and me with no makeup, wet from the bath hair and my cheesecloth shirt buttoned up wrong from when I was feeding Violetta. Her eyes darted to Lancelot who also had wet hair which, plastered to his head, only emphasised his green eyes and wide surprised mouth.

'I brought you this Saint Christopher.' She smiled then bustled over to stand in front of him offering him a little box, which she opened, took out a silver chain holding a medallion and went behind him to put it around his neck.

'There, he is the patron saint of travellers, to keep you safe in Florence.'

I am sure he tried to smile but it was so mixed with confusion that it did not reach his eyes.

The shiny disc looked strange on his neck. Jewellery was not for him. All I had ever seen on him was his big watch. She kissed him on the cheek and his eyes popped open but hers slid over to me in a triumphant, sly glance.

I could see that he did not know what to say about this unwanted gift or what the offering said about how Babs felt about him. We all looked at each other. Lancelot stood up and said. 'How kind of you Babs, I am sure it will keep me safe.'

'And this.' She beamed, handing him an envelope. He opened it and I saw a card and a photo which he pushed back quickly. 'That will keep you keen to come home.'

Babs was not good at reading him. But I was.

It went suddenly dark, there was the distinctive sound of rain pattering on the windows and then thundering on the roof, it grew louder. Freddie dashed in the still open door and brushed past the new pink pants leaving streaks of muddy undergrowth and wet dead leaves from the hedge which was the dog's favourite rolling about place.

'AH! AH! These are new on! You horrible filthy dog!'

She put her hand out to me as if asking for a cloth. I passed her a tea towel.

'He is a working dog. He should be locked outside in a barn not in here where people have good clothes on.' She growled rubbing vigorously at her knees making the stain worse.

Sarah took it all in then we turned to Lancelot as he cleared his throat.

'You know there is an old Indian legend that says when people die we all cross a bridge on the way to heaven. At the other side sit all the animals ever encountered in one's lifetime and it is they who decide, based on what they know of this person, who they let in and who they turn away.'

I smiled. 'That is so lovely Lancelot. I hope it is true.'

Babs's brows knitted furiously. 'It is the stupidest thing I have ever heard. What have animals got to do with God? They are only bloody animals after all!'

He looked at us both but said nothing. The rain eased as it grew a little lighter on the roof.

There was a toot of a car horn outside and Babs tossed the cloth to me, hitting me in the face. 'Dad has to get off to work so I have to go. Sorry. Have a safe journey.' She gave him a hug which he did not return and left, leaving the box and a cloud of stomach heaving scent. Lancelot pulled at his shirt and sniffed. 'I will have to change now, I cannot be knocking fellow passengers out now can I?'

He came down wearing a crisp white shirt that showed off his Dale's tan.

He sat down and pulled Sarah onto his lap. 'Now that the puppies have gone you have the most important job of your life.'

She gazed up at him and waited.

'Please look after Freddie for me. Feed him twice a day and plenty of stroking. Ricky, one of my shepherds, will be taking him out to work in my Landy after he has taken me to the airport and every day after that until I come back. I know I can trust you.'

She hugged him close, a hug he welcomed and returned and I must admit I felt a pang of jealousy.

He lifted her to the floor. 'And,' he said towering above her. 'I want to know exactly how many eggs you collect. Mammy will show you how to write the numbers down, won't you?'

He turned his smile to me and looked me in the eye. 'I will only be five days. It is all it should take. And I may bring back a nice surprise.'

My heart thudded to the floor. What would take that long? To get engaged? To marry his Irish girl? To break my heart?'

'Time to go, I have to pick up Ricky, so he can use the Landy.' He said heading for the door.

I glanced at the babies who were happily dozing away their breakfasts in the pen then I followed him. Sarah stayed with Freddie trying to distract him with bits of beef saved from supper for this very reason. The rain had stopped, leaving the garden washed and birds singing their gratitude. My favourite sound was drowned out by blood beating in my brain.

As he reached the vehicle he casually tossed in his bag in the way he did everything, with confidence and ease. How could he know he was leaving me in wound up and knotted dread? He came towards me as if to kiss me goodbye and I swallowed loudly. Then he seemed to think better of it, remembering that I am his employee and lifted my chin. 'Keep that up. I know this place will be safe in your hands. You have all the instructions about putting the pub takings into the safe, all the food is ordered and pub well stocked, OK? I will see you soon.'

He bounded into the driving seat and bashed the door shut making rivulets of rain tumble down. There was a smile but only from him as I was frozen with dread of losing something that had never been mine. My hopes and dreams about this lovely man were all I had, now they had been taken away forever.

The wipers squeaked then he wound down his window. We waved, eyes meeting in a melody of confusion and sadness which snatched at my heart as he drove away. I was finding it hard to understand my own intense looks never mind his. I was snapped out of my reverie by the sound of Freddie barking. I came in and saw the medallion box lying on the oak table at the bottom of the stairs. I opened it and was pleased to see the silver glinting. The card and photo peeped out of the envelope so I touched it telling myself I was only going to tuck it back in. But I could not resist. There on shiny paper fresh from the chemist's developing service was Babs. She was beaming and thrusting out her chest from a satin blouse two sizes too small for her. Lancelot had tossed these things carelessly onto the table, not bothering to take them with him which had been their reason for the early delivery. This delighted me immeasurably and I allowed myself a little smile as I popped them into the drawer where keys were kept along with any bits and pieces no-one knew where to put.

When I opened the kitchen door it was to see Sarah hugging a sad sheep dog and whispering. 'Will you let me into heaven Freddie? Will you?' I knew with certainty that he and many others would welcome her with waggily tails.

The house was different without Lancelot. It grew bigger and seemed to develop echoes and sighs I had never heard before. I was here alone now, just me, with my three precious babies feeling lost. My fear grew to monstrous proportions.

I hung two dozen nappies on the line to dry. As I pegged each white square to flap in the breeze I realised that Lancelot had never complained once that his much loved garden was daily taken over by washing. His bachelor life changed the moment I accepted the job. He had all the disadvantages of having a big family and none of the benefits. The woman he loved was in another country, he would be bringing her back. How would she feel to see us all here; a stray family taking advantage? Yes, that is what she would see. And she would not like it one bit.

My mind churned over what I must do. I could not leave here until Violetta was settled. The pub was Melonie's only way of contacting me. The moment Melonie had her baby safely in her arms was the same moment I should leave. I thought of the smudged postmark that made it unsafe for me to hide here and wondered where I would move to next to ensure Ben and Sarah stayed with me at least until they were grown up.

I was plagued with recurring images of a beautiful smiling woman sharing the bed just along the hall with the man I loved so much. I could never bear it.

The memory of his face and playing of his voice came over me at every quiet moment with such clarity that I could almost touch him. Even though I had never had this pleasure. His presence lingered in my mind, sapping my power to do anything else.

Two days passed by more slowly than I ever knew time could. The pub was quiet. As I closed the door after settling the children into bed I turned towards a noise.

Babs was coming along the landing with her handbag slung over her shoulder. She had honoured the day with a new tight blouse with a flared skirt and a cardigan slung over her shoulders. She had a skittish air in the surprise of being caught.

'What are you doing here?' For a moment, she stared at me, pouting. She looked at the floor.

'Oh...I was looking for you.' Her eggshell charm was cracking.

'You have no right to be in the house Babs, your job is in the pub.'

'You can't tell me what to do. You are not in charge here. You are nothing, just a runaway with kids to three different dads.' She spat the words with her nose in the air.

'What are you talking about?'

'None of your screaming kids look like your so called husband, do they?'

Silence, heavy with shock and dread hung between us. She looked scared like she knew she had gone too far.

'What do you mean?' I bore my eyes into hers in a way that had always worked against school bullies.

'Well', she stammered, struggling to keep her face mean, 'they all look like you...even the black one.' She tried to look calm but something caught in her throat.

Her eyes glittered with narrow minded sourness. Her face stained red with fury. I stared at all this. What did she know about how awful men could be, how hard it was to have so many babies? How I would lay down my life for any one of them.

'My life has been more difficult than you could ever imagine. What have you been interfering in Babs?'

Her eyes darted like an animal looking for escape. She ran down the stairs leaving only the smell of a new perfume smelling of expensive ingredients and good taste she did not have. I dashed to the window, opened it with a crack to see her below. There were clouds and the wind had slackened but still snatched at tree tops and whirled leaves across the lawn. I saw her standing near the gate, the wind twitching at her hair and rippling the folds of her skirt. She looked up, half scared and half triumphant. The sun reduced her eyes to slits as she scowled. She had escaped from my multitude of questions and it was more than my aching head could bear.

But she made me dislike myself because I felt something horribly close to hatred. And I felt fear.

I was busy in the kitchen but had my ears strained to listen for the phone ringing in the pub. Every time the bell pierced into my thoughts I went to the door and eased it open. Babs was muttering on taking table bookings or discussing cask deliveries. One time I heard her say 'Who?' I marched quickly into the bar just in time to see her plonk the handset into its cradle.

'Was that for me Babs?' She looked embarrassed

'Yeah, I thought you were upstairs.'

'Who was it?'

'Well it weren't Lancelot so don't get yer bloody hopes up. It were a woman…said she were a friend of yours.'

'So?'

'I told her you 'ad no friends and put the phone down.'

'It was hard to keep my anger back. 'You did what? You idiot! Did it not occur to you to give me a shout?'

'Hey! Don't you call me an idiot! I'm not the one smelling of sick and dirty nappies…and I am right; you don't have any friends.'

I had to exert great control not to grab her by her stiff, overdone hair and yank her to the floor. I walked away, back to the cauliflowers I was cooking for soup.

I was overwhelmed by a surfeit of mysteries and worries. I felt filled with general despair of the world and its people. I only had to hope that Melonie was intelligent enough to ring back. I wish I had given her the house phone number when she was here and not just agreed to her ringing the pub. It was a great strain.

Ben's tiny teeth were getting too sharp for my over-used nipples. He would giggle when I cried 'ouch' and pulled away from him. He thought it was a game and glowed in pleasure showing the dimple he inherited from my mother, he was developing the same wicked laugh too. It was like having a bit of mam back with me. I hugged him close. I would always have her near as long as Ben was with me.

The sudden peak of late summer ripeness got me out into the garden to give the children oatmeal for breakfast. There was still some pretence of summer and Sarah was thrilled to see windfall apples on the grass. Helped by Freddie and Servant, who were just as keen as she was to see what the strange new things lying on their lawn were, she dashed over. She brought them to the table one at a time in her little hands. Big, shiny and hard green apples with a blush of red overflowed her fingers and she glowed in the same way any successful hunter gatherer had done for thousands of years. She counted each one until she had seven. I turned them all over, two were immature and would be too tarte, one had definite beak marks allowing juice to ooze out and it looked like wasps had been busy too. The other four seemed not bad.

'Would you like to make apple crumble or pie Sarah? Just for us?'

This thrilled her. It would be a few weeks yet before apples hit the pub menu. I would make it her job to collect the apples from the lawn every morning. I was shovelling the last food into Ben who was busily trying to knock the apples off the table when I thought I heard the pub phone. It was so far away through two doors but I plopped him down on the grass beside Violetta.

'Watch the babies Sarah.' I called from my turned head as I dashed through the kitchen door, then the pub kitchen and finally the darkened bar just in time to hear the ringing stop. I almost cried with frustration. I half hoped it was Melonie and half hoped it wasn't.

What if she had changed her mind? I should have taken her number that night instead of just letting her go. I was annoyed at my stupidity brought on by my shock.

I propped open every door between the phone and the garden on my way back to the children. The apples seemed to be attracting the wasps so I gathered them to take into the house. Ricky suddenly whistled over the wall and Freddie leapt it easily, keen to go to work. I only got a polite wave from the shepherd and it made me wonder what he thought of me and how he must see me, as an intruder into the world he had grown up in or a hard worker who was struggling on her own with her family?

Happy the wasps had gone away from us and the babies snoozing, I wandered around the garden. Lancelot's mother had done a great job laying out the herbaceous border and planting fruit trees. How could she know how useful the vegetable plot would be or how her son would grow far too many of everything just to work there, to feel close to her?

I felt I had to strain for the bell of the pub phone every minute of the day. It was wearing. Every door between where I was and the bar was propped open with a chair, a pile of cushions or an empty drinks crate. I was down the garden trying to pick late gooseberries as quietly as possible with strained ears and constant stops for hard listening. All was quiet, even Sarah who was testing the riper fruits as she carefully avoided the prickles. When we got back to the kitchen to put our heavy bowls on the table I was annoyed to find every door closed and all the stuff I had used as door stops put back in their original places. I sniffed the air. There was no heavy waft of sickliness that told me Babs had been in but I did smell wood polish. I had forgotten it was the day Mrs Armitage cleaned the house. I checked the babies, only Ben was awake so I put him on the rug with Humph and some wooden clothes pegs in a tin. I could hear the vacuum cleaner droning in the bar and went in. I tried to speak to her above the racket but she just pushed on singing about catching a falling star as she cleaned the carpet to within an inch of its life. I went to the wall and pulled the plug out. She turned and saw me. Her scowling face had three downward curves registering her disapproval.

'Oi! What you do that for?'

'I'm sorry but you couldn't hear me. Has the telephone rung whilst you were here?'

'Aye.' She said picking up a small mat and taking it outside. I followed her out and she looked surprised but shook the mat good and hard. I spluttered and turned away.

'So?'

'So what?'

'Who was it on the phone?'

'I dunno, do I, I'm not a bloody secretary. I don't get paid for messages.'

'Well you could have answered it or called for me.'

She looked at me then. 'It were a woman.' She walked over to the plug and pushed it back into the socket before shouting over the noise.

'I wrote the bloody number down and put it on the table beside your mixin' bowl'.

'Well why didn't you say?'

She started to sing her Perry Como song again.

'…an' just in case yu feel you wanna 'old 'er.' She wailed on.

I dashed back to the kitchen just in time to see Sarah feeling sick after too many gooseberries. There was no note. I searched the whole kitchen. Frustration built up to make my head ache.

'Sarah's tummy is sore mammy.' She leaned against my leg and I bent to pick her up. That is when I saw Ben crumpling something into his mouth. It was a small torn off piece of newspaper. I had to wrestle it from him, it was soggy and he yelled at losing his latest plaything. Sarah started to cry too and this made Violetta wake then join in the wailing competition. I tossed the paper into the bin and tried to calm each of the children. I laid Sarah down on the sofa, gave Ben a wooden spoon to chew on and breast fed Violetta then placed her in the pram. They were all quiet. I heard the vacuum cleaner go off. The door swung open and Mrs. Armitage flung herself in to put her tools away and retrieve her coat.

'I cannot find your note, where did you put it Mrs Armitage?'

'I already telt yu', next to that big bowl.' I looked again.

'Must o' blown off then.' She said loosening the strings on her apron.

'Well what did you write it on?'

'There was no note pad around 'ere so I tore a white bit off that newspaper there, it is a week old. Can I take it for my Burt?'

'Yes of course.' I replied just wanting her to go. She looked around at my brood, did a sort of 'umph' noise, picked up the newspaper then left. I rootled about in the bin and found the number I had waited so tensely for. It was tiny writing and the pencil marks were faint, wet and creased. I flattened it out as best I could then picked up Ben whose eyes brightened when he saw what I had in my hand. I jiggled him onto my hip and leaving the sleeping girls I went to the pub phone. It was hard having to peer at the tiny writing and keep Ben from grabbing at the promotional figurines of white horses, black and white dogs and a tiny Babycham deer the drinks company had us display to advertise their various products. I had to lay the receiver down and dial with one hand while the black phone wobbled and edged dangerously towards the end of the shelf. It started to ring, the noise competing with the crackling of a packet of nuts Ben had managed to pull off the display card on the wall and the beat of my anxious heart as it geared up to discuss something that would change my life.

It rang and rang then just as I was about to end the call a man answered. 'Yes?'

'Can I speak to Melonie please?'

'No, she has just gone out with her mother, and I was washing the car before having to dash into the house to answer phones for heaven's sake.' he barked.

Cowed by his aggression I just asked that he would tell Melonie that Rose rang, thanked him and put down the receiver. If that was Melonie's dad he would be the granddad to Violetta. Maybe his sharpness and aggression were why he had not been told of his daughter's baby, maybe he was angry because he now knew what his daughter had done. What if the phone calls I had missed were to tell me that Melonie was never coming for Violetta? If she was so keen to be reunited with the baby she left on the moors that night she would have persisted. Wouldn't she?

My mind flooded with possibilities.

I was in a strange flux of wanting to prepare my affections for losing Violetta to another woman and loving her wildly. She loved it when I kissed her tiny feet as she wiggled them upwards when she was laying on her back. Ben always started his deep belly-laugh when I kissed his and pulled them away then thrust them back for more lip-smacking and toe nibbling. She started to try to copy him when they lay on the bed together as I dressed them. They tugged my very heart and soul into a whirl of maternal love. I never wanted to be parted from either of them.

Days passed with me pushing the pram around the dale and village where I swanned through the mumble of gossip and lingering looks. I cared less and less. These woman did not know me but I smiled at them all and cared not too much when not one of them smiled back. I always wondered if I had missed the call I was waiting for when I got back home, then as I cooked, my ears strained for the ring of the phone and the end to my worry.

Early one evening as I brushed egg across the top of my corned beef pies, I heard the phone ring in the pub and then Babs mumbling. My eyes flicked to the children and then I dashed full pelt to the bar where Babs' eyes met mine and guilt changed her stance from spiteful to embarrassed. I ripped the receiver from her hand and put it to my own ear.

'Hello, this is Rose speaking.'

Silence. Then 'Oh Rose, at last! I have rung seven times and got a peculiar woman each time. I was beginning to think I had the wrong pub. It is Melonie here.'

Relief did its best to calm my banging chest and I listened as I was told that everything was in place for Violetta's new home and family. Babs started clashing glasses and singing at the top of her voice in an ear-stabbing distraction. I took the address and phone number down on an order pad near the phone then stuffed it into my shirt. As I stepped away back to my babies I just knew Babs would be holding that pad to the light in order to read the impression of what I had written. Good luck to her on that, I had turned it upside down and wrote lightly.

Three days after Lancelot had flown out of my life leaving me in a turmoil of worry about our future, Carol swung through the kitchen door from the pub with a gin and tonic in her hand.

Freddie bounced up to her and looked pleased. He was demonstratively grateful for her enthusiastic loving. 'I have no rescues at the moment, feeling a bit empty handed in the dog rubbing stakes, aren't I boy? Yes I am!' She turned to me then.

'I hope you don't mind if I eat in here with you Rose, I am worn out and Babs is in a foul mood, she took no notice of me trying to order.' She lifted the glass. 'I had to go behind the bar and make this myself. She must be making a fortune in tips smelling of Chanel Number Five.

Arthur bought me some a few years ago, I eke it out, it is too expensive for every day.'

She lifted a pan lid. 'Is this the courgette soup I saw written on the menu outside?'

'Yes, I just made it up after Sarah discovered several over large courgettes under big leaves in the garden. We had to make three journeys there were so many.'

'Ah yes, it is the first time Lancelot has grown them. I told him two plants would be enough but he planted the whole packet of seeds.' She laughed.

'Well there are many more growing. The locals were suspicious of anything with a French name at first but it soon caught on after a few people asked for seconds.'

'Can I have some?'

I passed her a dish and she ladled hot soup into it before sitting at the table. Babs dashed in with a new order, keeping her eyes down as usual as she plonked it on the bench.

'That's the last one tonight.' She blurted the words taking in the feeling of camaraderie between the women in front of her.

I put the order on plates and pinged the bell Lancelot had fixed up between the kitchen and the pub. Babs swanned in, pouted then took the plates and left.

We laughed.

'Gosh Rose, she is so transparent. She does not like you being in charge while Lance is away, does she?' If only it was just that, I thought.

I opened the drawer in the table and took out the note I had written earlier.

'Here is the address and phone number of Violetta's family.' Even this simple task put a catch in my voice. 'I told Melonie that Violetta's doctor may want to call, did I do right?'

Carol took the paper and looked at it. 'Oh that is the good side of York. I have a friend who lives there, I will combine the visits.'

'But you won't say…'

'No, of course not. It is only you, me and Melonie who will ever know what happened.'

'And Lancelot.' I said.

'He will never tell a soul either. He is a good man, I am sure you have realised this by now. Did he tell you why he has gone to Florence?'

I looked hard at her then. 'No. Why has he gone?'

She was reading my emotions and I hoped she could not see desperation.

'He didn't tell me either.' She laughed. 'It will be to see Cleona though, you do realise that Rose, don't you?'

'Of course.' I said clearing away the dishes. I tried to act as if I did not care one jot that he had gone so far to see a beautiful young woman with no children, a good education and not a guilty thing to run from. I do not think I succeeded.

Carol stayed until the sound of Babs' dad's car faded away. I fed and checked on the children and came down to share a pot of tea with Carol. She told me of a lovely old lady with a broken hip she had visited today and then of an old dog with the same problem.

'But I am only allowing one of them to be put down!' she smiled as she rubbed at Freddie's ears. 'Is he missing Lance much?'

'Ah yes, he is out working all day but when he is dropped off here he follows Sarah or me around. Even Servant can't cheer him up.'

'When his dad returns we will take him to the sea again.' She looked up to me. 'And you are bringing the children, we will have fun.'

She noticed my change in demeanour.

'Tell me Rose, why won't you go to the seaside? I already know you did not have a good marriage and it will do you good to share with a professional.' She pulled a chair closer to mine and held my hand. She was a woman, a doctor and sympathetic and my burden was heavy, so I talked.

'When Sarah was only 14 months and Ben six weeks, my
husband's cousin offered us the use of her house in
Scarborough for a week whilst they had a holiday in
Cornwall. He borrowed a van from a mate at work and we
set off to somewhere I had never been.' My words were
slow at first as they struggled past the pain heaped on top
of them. 'It was a hot week in August. On the first day
we took Sarah to the beach. It was almost midday and too
hot for us all. I spread out two towels on the soft sand and
we sat down. Almost immediately Ed stood up saying it
was too hot so he was going for a pint. I had nothing as
the plan was to get fish and chips and a pot of tea. Sarah
adored the sand and I managed a little paddle in the cold
water with her holding one hand and my other supporting
the baby. It grew hotter and hotter. I grew thirsty and so
did Sarah. Ben was fine as he was breast feeding, but he
was too hot. We had no money. I scanned the throngs of
people looking for Ed, maybe he couldn't find us. Maybe
he had returned to the wrong beach. We were getting
sunburned. I dared not move as I knew he would be angry
if he returned to where he left me and I was not there. I
tried to shade us with one of the towels but Sarah grew
fractious and we were hungry. People started to look at us
and one lady brought over a little cup of water for Sarah. I
was so embarrassed and swore we were all right. At four
pm, I was feeling quite ill. The people on the beach had
changed, some going off for food and new people came
full of vigour, putting up deck chairs then sharing picnics.
I tried to keep us cool in the sea but Sarah wanted to drink

it. There was still no sign of Ed. I feared the worst, he had been in a car crash. My nose was burnt by the sun and I was weak with hunger when at six thirty Ed stumbled down the beach and pulled Ben out of my arms and started to walk towards the road. Hurriedly we followed him, our feet plodding into the hot sand. He pushed us into the van. He was drunk. I told him we were worried about him and he should have come back sooner as we were hungry and thirsty. He ordered me to shut up. It was his holiday too and if he wanted a drink he had the right without moaning women and kids spoiling his fun. I was terrified he would kill us, driving like a drunken maniac. We hit one parked car and mounted a pavement. The children were thrown around like rag dolls. When we got back to the house he hit me for complaining. I tried to hydrate us all and ate the only food in the house, pickled onions and Cream Crackers. He wouldn't eat it and stormed off to eat at the pub. He did not come back until 2am. He locked us in the house the next day, said he could not stand our whining. It was OK as we had to recover. We ate the rest of the crackers and I found some Camomile lotion in the bathroom cupboard. I covered up our sunburn in an effort to cool and sooth us. He brought cold chips back for us at 4pm, they were greasy and limp but we gobbled them up.'

Carol looked stunned. I had hardly noticed her sitting there, so lost was I in my pain. I felt unhinged by unhappiness, hardly able to believe what I had just recounted.

When she spoke Carol's voice was thick. 'I had no idea
Rose. At first I had supposed you had a good marriage
looking at your beautiful children. How long ago did your
husband die?'

The question glued my eyes to the floor. I tried to drag a
voice from deep inside me where the truth lay festering in
fear.

'Not long.' I croaked.

Then, '…you won't say anything to Lancelot will you?' I
could not bear to have him know anything about my
previous life. He would look at me differently. Pity would
mix with curiosity.

Carol pulled me to her. 'Doctor's confidentiality. I know
you are not my patient but I always abide by that.' I did
not answer, my throat had thickened and my eyes bulged
with tears.

'Oh poor you. I would have taken my children and run
away.'

That simple statement had the effect of making me feel
less alone. She understood, maybe more women would.

'Was he cruel to the children Rose?'

I felt my face blanch, I had smothered so much that I
could not bear it.

'Please tell me he wasn't.'

'Well he never hit or strangled them.'

'Is that what he did to you Rose? It might be why your throat hurts and you have that cough.'

I felt tears well up. 'When Ben was born, my dad went to our house to look after Sarah so Ed could come in his work's van to pick me and the new born baby up from the hospital. My next door neighbour was there and two friends I had made at work. They were all excited and had laid on a lovely home baked tea.'

'That sounds nice.' Carol said.

'Well it would have been, only when Ed arrived at the hospital he smelled of beer. I was worried about him driving and when I said this he turned into a pub car park. He slammed the van door and left me and my five day old baby for two hours whilst he drank.'

'Oh Rose.'

'Somehow we managed to get home safely but my friends had not been able to wait and the tea was spoiled. Dad told me he was frantic with worry. I was so stressed and exhausted and parched.'

'Oh I cannot imagine how awful that must have been. Was he like this when your first baby was born?'

'Well I went to give birth by bus. He would not take me. The day after Sarah was born he stumbled into the ward with a gash on his forehead. It seems that he spent the night I was giving birth at a rugby club dance and had propositioned another man's wife. He got into a fight.'

Somehow, all this seemed to have happened to a different me. The one before I had picked up that heavy pan.

Carol was right. I did feel some relief in being able to tell just a small part of my awful life to someone. I slept well but woke early as I could not get images of what Lancelot might be doing out of my mind.

I started to fuss as the day of Lancelot's return grew near. I was desperate to see him but dreaded that he might not be alone. That night I had to cook for the police station party.

I had prepared as much as I could with the food when Babs arrived done up to the nines in expensive new shoes and dress. The earrings glittering on her lobes looked almost real. Woolworths were getting even better at costume jewellery. Diamonds were not a speciality of mine so what did I know? I don't know who she intended to impress and said so when I saw her preening herself in the mirror behind the bar.

She turned with a sarcastic glare.

'Do you think I would be after some middle aged policeman when I have Lancelot to look forward to.'

I stuttered out breath in surprise. 'Lancelot has gone to see his long term girlfriend you idiot!'

I should not have said that but she seemed not to take in what I said. 'You jealous cow, you are making that up. You will do anything to steal him off me.' She turned back to the mirror and smeared even more lipstick on her pouting mouth.

'I love him. And when he comes back I will propose to him. I'm not old fashioned in that way. He just needs a little push.'

'You don't love him. You love the idea of him Babs.'

Her lips curled as she got ready to spit out venom but she was halted by the door opening and the first group of off duty policemen spilling in for a great night out.

She pulled on the flirty smile, hoisted up her boobs and said. 'Get stuffed Rose, you know nothing.'

The raucous sound came right through to the pub kitchen and I was worried the children would wake but each time I ran up the stairs in between batches of home-made chips they were flat out. Babs was playing her taunting game and not responding to the bell that asked her to come in to pick up the food so I was forced to dash out with plates of gammon. The high spirits and playfulness made my progress slow. It made me angry to see Babs surrounded by a group of men and drinking scotch as she recounted her dad's building site jokes. I made a point of keeping my eyes down and never making eye contact with any-one who might have seen a photo of a missing woman. A wanted woman.

I thought I was clear when I finally took off my apron and hoped I could trust Babs to lock up properly. My breasts were heavy with milk and the babies would be needing me. The door flung open and a red faced Tony steered in a beaming man with short hair and a stiff stance.

''Ere she is…the best cook in the Dales.'

I tried to look welcoming through my tiredness.

'This is my super…Superintendent Knott to you Rose.'

The man shook my hand as if I had made a banquet for Buckingham Palace. He looked me clear in the eye and smiled. 'Hey, I have seen you somewhere before…never forget a pretty face. Where on earth…?'

There was a peeping sound outside. 'Ah!' he yelled louder than was necessary. 'That'll be my wife picking me up. Very distinctive horn the Rover has you know, don't usually let her drive it. Thanks for a lovely supper. Must come with my wife one night. You can show her how to cook, never got the knack for it, even after 20 years of marriage, haha.'

They were gone. That was all I needed, threats of recognition turning up at the pub. It all added to my aching head and dragging desire to have Lancelot back home. I slept on and off all night so that I was exhausted in the morning when Violetta woke me with hungry cries.

We all sat around the breakfast table. Ben in the highchair I had bought in a sale in town and Violetta in my arms. Freddie had been picked up at 7am and so I was surprised to hear him barking excitedly only two hours later. Sarah stopped shovelling Ready Brek into Ben's mouth, 'What a matter with Freddie mammy?'

'I don't know.' I said getting up and heading for the door but Freddie bound in with Lancelot beaming behind him.

'Ah what a lovely sight! I thought I would surprise you by coming home a day early. I could not stand that heat.'

I was unable control my face and had no idea what it showed. Good or bad.

'Is there any real Yorkshire tea for me? You should see what they serve in Italy…hot water in a glass with a tea bag on the side.' He went to each of the children and touched their cheek or chin in fond hello. Sarah was not happy with that and threw herself into his arms.

I took a cup and saucer from the dresser and plopped milk and poured tea. Could he see my hand shaking? He placed my beaming girl onto the floor, kissing her head.

'I have a surprise for you all waiting in the hall. Can I bring it in?'

I had to open my mouth to pull in enough air to keep me upright. How was I going to bear him loving another woman? I wished I had brushed my hair and washed the sleep from my eyes, maybe put on a clean ironed shirt but it was too late now.

Chapter Ten

Lance sipped some tea. 'Stay there all of you, and close your eyes.' Sarah giggled and obeyed excitedly but Ben and Violetta had no clue what was going on.

'Rose! Tight shut!' he said moving towards the door. 'I have been waiting for three years, now I am thrilled to have brought something of real beauty back with me.'

I heard rustling and footsteps and then the door closed again. In those few seconds my hopes clattered and my secrets flashed through my brain.

'Right, you can open your eyes.'

We both looked and I felt my breath leave my body. Lancelot was beaming from ear to ear.

'Here it is, I think this house will be greatly enhanced by this.'

He was holding a painting. It was of him with a puppy, who was clearly Freddie, tucked under his arm as he leaned against a dry stone wall. The hills spread out behind him dotted with sheep and lambs. It was his land and his beaming face which spoke loudly of intimate love felt by the hand that had held the brush.

Sarah clapped her hands, she had never seen a portrait before. 'Freddie, baby tiny Freddie.'

'Very good.' I managed to choke out the words. 'It captures you exactly.'

'I love it because it is history. Whoever lives in this house long after we have departed for the next life will have a sense of who worked and loved here before them.'

This could not be all…surely the artist must be waiting in the hall ready to be called out to have praise heaped upon her for her exquisite art.

'How come you brought this from Italy Lancelot?'

'It was started here, then the rest done from photographs taken at the same time.'

I stood up to take a closer look and saw the brush strokes and highlighting that made the painting so very alive. I looked at the signature. 'Cleona.'

'Who is the artist? They are very talented.'

'You are right there. A very close friend of mine...well more than that.' He looked embarrassed and said no more. I crushed my dreams underfoot, trying to trample them into nothing.

There was a rat-tat-tat on the door made by some-one who meant business. 'Come in!' Lancelot shouted then noticed my frightened look. 'Hey, it is only old Alfie, he always knocks like that, deaf as a post and thinks every-one else is.'

Into the kitchen bundled a well fed and well winter-reddened man exactly half as tall as Lancelot. He had straw bale twine tied around his waist keeping an old jacket, torn at the shoulder almost together around his bulging waist.

'Ah come for me money for t' tup you bought off me last fortnight lad.' He bellowed the words then looked at me, decided I was not worth much then looked at the teapot. 'Any brew going? Been out since five.'

Sarah clung to me and whispered, 'Is he a scarecrow mammy?' I shook my head as I said loudly. 'I'll pour you some. It's a bit strong mind. Milk?'

'Aye, Stronger the better lass.'

Lancelot turned towards the hallway. 'I'll just get your money Alfie,' he called before I heard his feet taking the stairs two at a time. Freddie clattered behind him.

The tea was guzzled noisily before a gnarled and bent hand wiped Alfie's mouth. His eyes turned to the portrait. 'Ah, that is a fine Swaledale scene and a pup I bred from the finest sheep dog bitch a man ever 'ad. Aye; Rosie were the kindest breeder and best mother pups could hope for.'

He looked at me as if it had just entered his head that he had never seen me before. 'Who are you then?'

'I am the pub cook, my name is Rose.'

A smile cracked his reddened face to show two teeth missing and toast crumbs hanging from the corners. 'Ha…same name as my girl eh? Well I hope you are half the mother she was.' He looked around at various eyes on him and frowned when he saw Violetta. 'Well I'll be damned.' His eyes sped to me. 'Looks like you are a good breeder too.'

He obviously meant that as a compliment so I tried not to show my surprise.

He peered at the picture again. 'What does that signature say? Spell it out for me lass, I din't bring me glasses out to work wi' me.'

Painfully I spelled out the name I had come to dread.

'Ah, that'll be Lance's Irish lass. She were a right beauty, and clever. Had 'is 'ead in a spin I can tell you. But didn't she go off to Spain or France or some such foreign place. Broke 'is 'eart. She back then? Could do wi' 'er beauty beaming about the Dales in winter I can tell you.'

It seemed like he could tell me lots and had no idea how his thoughts were stabbing me in the heart.

'Italy, Florence. She went there to paint I think.' It struck me then that I did not know anything.

'Oh, sounds 'ot and old, does Florence. Do they 'ave sheep there. Wouldn't like a place where sheep didn't thrive.'

'I don't know, it is a city I think, full of history and old buildings.'

Lancelot burst into the room then but he did not look as pleased as when he had left.

'Alfie, can I drop your money off at your farmhouse later. Haven't had time to go to the bank yet. Thought I had enough but…' he looked at me, his eyes hooded and devoid of all emotions I could recognise.

Alfie drained his mug then clunked it onto the table before dragging his hand across his mouth again. 'Aye that'll do lad. If I'm not in put money under me old mother's black clock on the mantel piece. You know the one.'

He turned at the door. 'Bye now all you young pups.'

The room seemed calmer when he left, Lancelot said nothing but turned to fill the kettle again now that his tea had gone cold.

The mood had changed and I did not know why.

'I'm off to get changed. Need to take the Dales back into my veins.' He said heading for the stairs. He did not look at me.

He did not come back for his tea but I heard the Landy start up then rattle off over the gravel.

Chapter Eleven

I was cutting up steaming steak and kidney pies for the pub when Lancelot came back in.

'Everything OK with the pub.' He asked sampling the gravy in a big pan.

'Yes, it all went well.'

He turned to go out as quickly as he'd come in and I remembered I had to ask him about ordering new meat. I followed him into the house kitchen, saw him pick up the portrait and take it upstairs. I had no idea why he was so cool…unless.

I returned to the food and Sarah spooning butter into soft lumps to mash into the potatoes. The babies were safe in their playpen and all should have been lovely but my mood was so dragged down by Lancelot's attitude towards me. I thought it must be to make sure I was clear about my position here when Cleona arrived with her paints and her love. I had to stop my thoughts from rambling about a man who was clearly taken and even had a second back up in his barmaid.

Later, I went through the pub to replace the menu card in the outside glass case and when I swung into the bar again Lancelot was counting the spirit bottles. Babs rushed in behind me, pushed past and flung herself at Lancelot.

'I heard you were back early!' She kissed him on the cheek and snuggled in to his chest. I had to follow the pungent wake of half a bottle of that expensive perfume, I held my breath until I got to the bar.

'I see my Saint Christopher kept you safe then. Did you wear it every day?'

He avoided the question but said. 'Is that Chanel Number Five you smell of Babs?'

'Yes, I knew you would like it.' She beamed.

'I saw it in the duty free shop, it is very expensive.' She dropped her arms from his neck and said.

'Yes, we are worth it though. Sheep and dog smells are not for every-one.'

He looked at me then and I could see his many emotions keeping his face closed. Babs did not seem capable of such perceptions because she asked. 'You can tell me all about your trip when you take me home tonight eh?'

I went into the kitchen to check on the food and children. It was a relief to get into the relatively soft smell of suppers.

All that week I was still feeling down. I had something else to depress me apart from Lancelot's coolness.

I was having trouble sleeping as so much whizzed about my head and flung my eyes open. I heard the owls hooting to each other, Servant yowling at some unknown intruder into his territory and the occasional footsteps passing my door as Lancelot padded downstairs for tea. I could just hear the kettle begin to whistle on the Aga when he must have lifted it off so that the babies would not wake to the loud screechy whistle below.

Carol turned up one breakfast time and made herself some toast which she brought to the table where I sat with Sarah and Ben. She smiled at Violetta who lay on the sofa in deep, milk filled sleep. 'Well she will be all right and that is for certain.'

My head jerked up in questioning but she had just taken a big crunch of toast and marmalade into her mouth. When she could, she laughed.

'Your face Rose! It is good news. I went to York yesterday and called on Violetta's blood family.'

'…and?' I willed her not to take another bite.

'They are a nice family, the father is a bit stern but I suppose his job as headmaster needs that. They live in a leafy suburb with a garden and a medium sized clean house.'

Pleased with my relief she allowed herself to finish her toast. 'I actually like Melonie and she took it on the chin when I told her that she could be facing a very different future if you had not been the wonderful mother that you are or we had gone to the police.'

'So, when will they collect their baby?' It hurt me to say those words.

'Well, Melonie said they would ring you on Monday at ten in the morning to arrange the pick-up.'

She looked at me and saw my face drop. 'So soon?'

'Don't look so glum. Violetta will have a lovely Granny who has already filled the house with baby stuff.'

This impending wrench of my heart lay heavily in my thoughts day and night.

Three days later when the children were in bed, I noticed Lancelot was still out as he seemed busier than usual lately, or maybe just trying to stay away from me. I went to my pan of mushroom and nutmeg soup to stir it but when I lifted the lid it bubbled up and spat brown soup onto my shirt. I rubbed it vigorously cursing that I had left my apron upstairs when I'd fed the babies. I was not keen on going to retrieve it as I might disturb the sleeping beauties but it was the only clean apron I had. I had to feel my way around in the dark room but had an idea I had tossed it on the bottom of the bed. Silently I lifted the blue and white stripes to my chest and eased the door shut after me. That waft of perfume entered my nostrils and I followed it to the top of the stairs. I saw, halfway down, Babs in new knee high boots and a bright red coat. Puzzled, I quickened my step but she stopped suddenly as Lancelot appeared at the bottom.

His eyes flicked from her to me, he saw the apron in my hand and then said.

'Babs, what are you doing in my house?'

She turned and for the first time saw me. She was obviously flustered but managed to blurt out. 'Rose asked me to help her find her apron.'

His eyes drifted from her to me and back again. She clutched at her bag then tried to pass Lancelot who grabbed her arm.

'Have you been in my room Babs?'

'No! I told you! Get off!' She wrenched her arm from his grip and flounced off. I came down to Lancelot, his eyes locked mine. 'Is that true, did you ask her to help?'

I shook my head and he sighed deeply as if he had been holding his breath for days.

At ten pm, when Babs brought in the last of the empty dishes from the pub she did not toss them carelessly beside the dishwasher as usual but began rinsing them.

'Rose.' She said with her back to me. 'We are all girls together here aren't we?'

'You won't say will you? That I wasn't helping you find your apron.'

I was silent, she swung round. 'Well he has to spend it all before decimalisation comes in next February doesn't he?'

'What?'

'His money. So what if I take a little to make myself nice for him?'

'He does have to spend it…him…not you Babs.'

'Well it will all be mine when we are married.'

'Married?'

'It is only a matter of time. I know how to hook a man and he is almost there. If you spoil it by telling on me I will get my own back on you in a way you will regret for the rest of your life.'

She stomped off back to the bar leaving me reeling with what she had said. How could she steal from the man who gave her her very living and she said she loved? I could never…it was then that the realisation of why Lancelot was being cool with me lit up my brain.

The next day Lancelot had a safe installed in his room. Of course he should have done this ages ago when he opened the pub but a little embarrassment that he had to lock his money away from me, hurt. When he came into my presence he lingered as if wanting to say something but could not form the words. I doubted that things could ever get back to normal.

It was Friday evening when I had settled the children and was back in the pub kitchen pouring the quiche filling into the pastry cases I had cooked earlier. The door swung open and Lancelot came over, picked bits of fried bacon from the plate on the table then watched as I finished all four tarts with nutmeg and black pepper. As I turned from putting the tray into the oven he took a step towards me.

'Rose, I need to apologise to you for my attitude since I came back from Florence.'

He was close and I could see that his green eyes which seemed to take on more of other colours depending on his mood had more hazel in them. I was really enjoying this eye contact and wondered if he could read me as well as I could read him.

'I was really struggling with where my money had gone. You were the only person in this house and you had been in my desk drawers when you got the writing paper. It tortured me to think that it was you who had taken it.'

'But I never would. I am not used to having any money. My pay packet is enough, especially as I have no rent or food bills. I would never ever steal. Especially from some-one who has been so kind to me, especially some-one I ...'

I managed to stop myself saying the words which were desperate to escape from my heart.

He looked me clear in the eye, I felt I was feeding off what he was sending me and yet I could not identify it.

'Well Babs will have to go. I won't go to the police but I will talk to her father. No doubt he will be storming in here with whatever lies she tells him about why I had to sack her. I won't confront her until Sunday night. We have heavy bookings for Saturday night and I cannot disappoint them by having to close.'

'I always thought that you and Babs…well…you know.'

He looked surprised. 'Babs? Babs? She is inelegant, obvious and holds absolutely no appeal for me. I like women of substance, caring and creativity. She doesn't even like animals for heaven's sake!'

Warmth crept into his face and softened it. He pulled me towards him in an apologetic hug and although it was a touch I so longed for and that burned into my very lonely soul I pulled away. He looked hurt but I knew I was saving him and myself from guilt. When Cleona arrived I would not be able to look her in the eye.

'I have something to tell you.' I blurted out.

'Oh,' he looked worried. 'You aren't going to leave are you? A pub with no barmaid and then no cook!'

'No, I am not leaving…not yet anyway. But Violetta is.' He noticed the catch in my voice that I had every time I had to say her name.

'What? No. But we love her so much.'

It was a treat for my ears hearing him say that. 'That is exactly why I have to let her go.'

'I don't understand?'

'I have found her real mother.'

His brows came down in query so I told him the whole story.

There was a lull as he took it all in. 'Well if Carol has checked her out and she is responsible I am sure it is for the best. But you will be bereft.' He looked like he wanted to draw me near again and it took all my strength not to encourage it.

'What did you mean when you said you were not leaving… yet?'

'When your fiancée gets here you won't want me around.'

'My what? How do you?...Oh Carol!'

He started laughing then and I smiled. His face lit up and all his cares slipped away.

'Rose I do not have a fiancée. No-one is coming here.'

'But I thought that was why you went to Florence and you came back with your portrait painted by her.'

'Well yes. I did travel to see her as I thought it was not fair to tell her what I had to say in a letter. And, I wanted the portrait very much.'

'Oh…'

'I had a wonderful romance with Cleona at uni in York, we grew into adults together and loved each other. But things change. When I saw her in Italy I could see she had grown away from me too and there was an Italian art dealer who seemed to turn up where ever we were eating.'

'Cleona started this painting of me when she was here two summers ago, she took lots of photos in order to finish it and her letters were full of how it was progressing and how lovely it was. She seemed to have run out of steam however and had to finish it in a rush, the paint was hardly dry when I got there.' He laughed again.

'No the only thing of her here will be the painting. She does not want to live in the cold Yorkshire Dales with a sheep farmer. Who can blame her?'

She must be mad, I thought. I would love to do exactly that for the rest of my life. New thoughts clattered into my brain, a great wall of possibilities I could never be at peace enough to contemplate but he stopped them all by saying.

'So, when will Violetta go?'

'In the morning.' I tried not to betray my sadness but my voice seemed hoarse.

It was a warm night, after I settled the children I ran a bath, keen to try the new herbal essence I had bought in Darlington. As the water ran I looked out of the window to the summer beauty beyond the house. The dry stone walls and the shepherd barns to match, all the sheep and summer green trees. The shadows slid like melting wax down the Dales. I was safe in this room, my children were secure in this beautiful place I didn't even know existed a few months ago. If only it could always be like this. But it couldn't. The water was too hot when I stuck my foot in so I wafted and splashed cold water up and down the bath enjoying the sound. Warm water relaxed my tired limbs, it felt luxurious just lying there soaking.

With my guard down, thoughts began to creep in. Stray murmurs echoed around the tiled walls and my throat began to tickle, I coughed repeatedly. This brought the feel of harsh hands around my neck and images of mad eyes and vicious words. I had created a false life for us here, one pretence had begotten another. These kind people who surrounded me knew nothing of my secret grief. Inside my head and heart was the only record of my life until something propelled me here. The awful movie played on and I felt it dragging at my sanity. I had to clear my head so I got out, pulling the thick towel around my body.

I dried myself noticing that some of my thinness was rounding out so I did not appear so angular. I ran the comb through my hair, it was fairer now, lightened by the summer sun just as it did when I spent all the school holidays outside. I had bought a Revlon body lotion fragranced with Intimate. The smell swathed me as I softened every inch of my body. This was a small luxury I could never have had before and I wallowed in it. I reached for the cream to dab on my face and realised I had left it in the bedroom. I gripped the towel around me. The babies slept peacefully as I quietly opened the new jar of Ponds and dabbed some on my cheeks and forehead. It was too dark to see so I closed the door on my way out to the bathroom. I was almost there when Lancelot bounded up the stairs two at a time, Freddie at his heels. His mouth spread in amusement as he took in my glowing red face with blobs of white cream.

'You look...erm...well, clean. Is this some new female thing us poor men know nothing about.'

I felt embarrassed that he had seen me like this, suddenly the towel seemed too small.

'Oh I thought you'd be ages yet. Have you locked up?'

'No, Babs has her dad in for a free drink before he drives her home. She said she would do it. Did you fall asleep in the bath?'

'No...I ...'

He ordered Freddie to his bed, now outside his bedroom door since the dog had developed a loud canine snore. 'Good boy.' He said before turning back to me. As always, he dazzled me...but there was something new. Some secret he expected me to share in, it came from his very being. I dropped my eyes from his.

He moved nearer making my heart pound into my ears. He must be able to hear such banging.

'Let me help you.' He murmured putting his hand to my cheek and smoothing in the cream, languidly. I did not know a man's touch could be so gentle. It felt divine but it made me freeze with terror at the thoughts flooding my mind and escaping into my body.

We both glanced at the window as we saw the car lights drive away, but it could not take us from the united cocoon of burning fascination for each other.

'You smell lovely.' He said softly as his hand went to the small of my back pulling me towards him. He smoothed the cream gently into my whole face, sliding over my scarred lip. It was lovely, like silk on petals. His touch had so much strength behind it and yet was light and sensual. He gently moved his fingers down to my throat and just as they moved towards my breasts he lifted them away.

Softly, he pulled me to him and I leaned in helplessly, shaking with need and fear.

'That makes me so happy.' He whispered putting his hands under my damp hair and stroking behind my ears. He eased my face closer to his.

His mouth was at my ear. Breath so close. He was drawing in air huskily, his face relaxed as if he had lost control of his senses. He could not be mine and yet I wanted him so much I was ready to fall from my ship into his warm, beautiful sea, to be covered and calmed by the deepest of waters as long as I could cling to him forever like this. My hands moved deep in the softness of his hair. His eyes rested on my mouth.

'I want to be the reason for your happiness Rose.' He lifted his eyes to bore into mine. The golden specks in his green eyes seemed to dance seductively.

Something shifted in that moment.

My eyes flashed to his, did he mean this? Was this really happening? I looked at his lovely mouth and all I could think was that I wanted it on mine.

'You look so lovely Rose.' He took my hand, kissing the fingertips so gently.

'Are the babies all right? Can you come to my room…would you like to?'

I did not know what to do. I had never been treated like this in my life. Should I turn and run on my weak, shaking legs? Maybe slap his beautiful, beseeching face? In the end I just went with my deep longing and smiled over a slight nod.

The cool sheets set my body tingling as he laid me down. The towel fell open. I was quivering with pleasure and need. My body began to flutter as he peeled off his clothes, never taking his eyes from mine. How long could I bear it before we began to unlock our hunger?

His fingertips floated onto me. The space between his skin and mine crackled with need. I reached up to his muddled hair I could now miraculously touch. His mouth ghosted over me. Loving me…wanting me.

He gazed into my eyes so much that we seemed to become one being. I could never get close enough to him to slake the way I felt. Quivering with pleasure and need, he dissolved me in shared desire. I was quaking, glowing. His face, soaked in intensity, was so near. We were skin to skin. Heartbeat, wonder and joy bashed in my ears. I felt his palm print on the back of my neck. His very touch sent me soaring to an agonising perfection of joint need. Gasps of wonder left his lovely mouth. My body spasmed. I felt blood flush beneath my teased and glowing skin. My heart was going like mad. I did not know who I really was until this moment. And now I knew us both. He was a big man and the feel of him made me realise how often I had wondered just how he was in his rawest of moments. I never knew how it felt to be held so ravenously.

His voice was just a breathy whisper.

'These breasts are so brave, so noble and so lovely. I have wanted to hold them as much as I have wanted to hold you.'

He breathed and kissed all the way down my body and I adored it. I never thought there could be such sweetness in life. Of everything I loved, my babies, nature the animals…here was something new, something so precious that I was afraid to have it.

He looked at me…deeper than anyone had ever seen before and his soul touched mine making me his forever. 'Shall we do this….shall we make each other belong?'

I could only nod, wanting him to move quickly and yet oh so very slowly. Which is what he did. His delicious body came to mine, shocking me with vibrations of delicate ecstasy. The shock of the contact I had longed for sent me into hopeless stupor. His beauty was magnified now, every muscle and length was mine to touch.

We seemed to know each other so well as we wrapped each other in splendour. It was clear with every soft touch that he had wanted me as much as I had longed for him. He was strong and gentle, as he gave into our exquisite joint needs and loved me until we knew we could love like this forever. I never knew you could be as one with a man. Now I never wanted to be anything but in his arms. Our groans of appreciation and satisfaction seared themselves into the walls of his room long after we had uttered them.

When we had exhausted every need, gentle and fierce he laid down sleepily beside me.

'I now know what bliss is.' He whispered gently into my neck as he pushed my hair back lovingly. We were both locked into the narcotic bliss of early love.

I breathed out long and pulled him closer to gaze drugged, into his eyes. There was no need to say 'Me too'. He knew what the smile in my eyes meant so he pulled me close and put his lips to mine with such gentle intensity. With that glorious kiss oozing into our minds, into everything, bonding us for ever, we slept.

We woke at the shock of the hall door being cracked open. Freddie growled. Lancelot ordered him back. There was noise on the stairs.

Lancelot pulled on his jeans, I was scrabbling for my towel. It was still dark. Freddie was barking now and he meant business. The door opened. A man in a hooded anorak was standing with a knife gripped in anger. It was Ed. It was obvious what we had been doing.

Everything fell away then. All that breathless writhing, deep connections of being, wild passion. It was all corrupted by the scowling man before us. He took in our sweat streaked hair. The crumpled linen. An invisible blade of panic sliced through me.

Our eyes met, there was such coldness in them. His hard eyes bulged there was such rage streaked through them.

'You whore. I knew you had left me for another man.' His face contorted with hate.

'So this was the fancy-man you had been going behind my back with. Got together and planned the whole thing did you?' He yanked the towel from my grip so that I stood naked in all my shame.

Lancelot stood between us, his brain scrabbling with the confusion.

'Where are my children? No one takes another man's son.' He was jabbing the knife at me but I bent to retrieve my towel, wrapping it around me, tucking it tight across my breasts. Suddenly he turned.

He crossed the landing and flung open the children's door. We followed, it was all in a flash.

Sarah was lying spread out on the bed she shared with me, Ben, with his arms up either side of his head was lying crossways beside her. He went over to them. That was when he saw the drawer with my beautiful Violetta sleeping peacefully.

'Well, well, well. You are even worse than I thought.' His eyes fixed on me as if the sheer intensity of his gaze could break me. There was a disturbing glimmer in his hard eyes. He was capable of anything.

Sarah woke then and screamed. 'Mammy! The nasty daddy is here! Mammy!'

'I knew there had to be an awful secret why you left me.' You filthy whore. How many men had you? How many did you offer yourself to when I was at work slaving away to keep my family in luxury? So you had this in your belly when you were nagging me stupid about having a little drink. No wonder you ran way. Couldn't blame this one on me obviously.'

His wiry grip closed across my wrist in a horror I had prayed I would never feel again. My thoughts scrambled back to terrible memories. Feeble light shone on his teeth and eyes but they lit nothing of his blackness. His eyebrows, pulled down and contorted with fury, were a forest of unkempt hairs. Freddie growled, Lancelot ordered him to go behind him.

'The only one I can be sure is mine is Ben. I am taking him with me.' He started to go over to the bed but I ran, putting myself between Ed and Ben. Lancelot was on high alert but he did not know what was going on. The full force of Ed's blue lit anger shot at me.

'Get out of my way woman!' he pointed the knife right at my face so that I stepped back. His face looked shrivelled with drink, smoking and hatred. I could hardly bear to look at it.

Lancelot, puzzled, looked at me. 'Is this your husband?'

'Too bloody right I am. But as she has so obviously fooled you too you can keep the filthy cow, she is rubbish.'

He picked up Ben who wriggled in the awkwardness of how he was grabbed. Sarah, scared by the shouting, started to shake

'Don't worry Sarah. I don't want you, I always doubted you belonged to me. Too many men sniffing about at that solicitor's office your mother worked in. She started to suck Humph's ear. Ed wrenched the bear from her. 'I put this filthy toy in the bin! When I put something in the bin it stays there.' He threw it across the room where it thumped onto the wall then slid defeated to the floor.

I could see that Lancelot was struggling to assess the situation, ready to defend us but not knowing why.

I tried to grab Ben. 'He needs breast feeding. Leave him alone!'

Ed pushed me to the floor in a way I should have expected, I had suffered this so many times. Only now I would not have his hands around my neck squeezing me into submission. I heard a crack as Lancelot's fist broke Ed's nose. He fell with Ben screaming on top of him.

Lancelot helped me up, I grabbed at Ben holding his red screaming body to me, and then he pulled Ed to his feet, blood dripping onto his anorak. I kicked the knife under the bed. I put Ben down beside Sarah, 'Look after him!' Violetta started crying then but I had to follow Lancelot, he did not know what Ed was capable of.

Ed was pushed down the stairs so quickly that his feet clattered. Lancelot was behind him as he ran into the pub, the door was open.

'Get out of my place now! Or I will have you locked up for breaking and entering.'

Ed turned then, glaring at me in disgust. 'You won't always have your fancy man to save you slut. You will never be free. You won't even see me coming.'

Lancelot moved towards Ed who dashed to the table where Babs had left the top off a bottle of Grouse beside her dirty scotch and pint glasses. He smashed a glass and held it in front of him jabbing it towards Lancelot. He projected such terror in his white rimmed eyes.

'You thought you could run away from me? You know I never give up although I was near to it when I met a willing widow from the Co-op. She made me forget you for a while but then I broke into your dad's house and found the letter.' He snarled at us his eyes streaked with rage.

I was confused. 'I had to write to my dad, let him know I was all right but I did not say where I was.'

'I never saw any letter from you.' He snarled. 'It was a letter from a 'concerned friend', she put you to shame by telling your dad everything about your rotten life, including this address. Said you were shacked up with some poor bloke who you were blackmailing into keeping you here. I met her last night. Tidy bit of stuff. Told me where you were hiding my kids. She kindly agreed to leave the door open for me.'

His mouth curled in hate as he left the words to swirl for a moment in the foul atmosphere he created.

Suddenly, he grabbed the bottle of Scotch and drank huge gulps from it through the blood running from his nose, then smashed it to the floor. Lancelot ran at him winding him with his head to his stomach but Ed quickly recovered, grabbed Lancelot in a headlock and held the broken glass right up to Lancelot's eyes. Freddie flew at Ed's leg where he was kicked with such force he flew into the air. I grabbed the dog's collar, holding him back. Ed glared at me. A white hot thump of rage pulled at the appalling fate that would link me to this awful man forever.

'Get me my bloody son or your fancy-man will never see your lying face again.' Panicking, I ran out as if to get Ben but I heard the fight start again so I dashed into the pub kitchen to grab the nearest thing I could.

I took the pan I had used to fry steaks in last night and swung it with all my might at my husband's leering head. This time there was no hesitation. No second thoughts for me, no calming down and returning the pan to its resting place. This time there was a crack, it resounded up my arm and Ed hit the ground.

Lancelot stood up, took the pan from me and looked at Ed. Freddie slunk close and was comforted by his master.

'Oh my God. I have killed him.'

Sarah had scuttled down the stairs and was wide eyed with fear.

'Is the nasty daddy dead mammy?'

She ran to me as Lancelot bent to examine Ed.

'No Sarah! He is just sleeping.' He said reassuringly to my daughter.

'Did he steal all our money mammy, then drinked it?'

'Yes darling. He just needs a good sleep, he will be all right.'

Lancelot looked at me with compassion mixed with things I had no energy left to decipher.

Sarah said, 'I don't want nasty daddy here mammy, this is nice house, no shouting, no crying for mammy here.'

'Shhh, he will not come again Sarah.' I tried to give reassurance I did not feel.

'He might put Humph in the bin again mammy.'

Lancelot stared at me with a sad understanding. His heart was breaking for us with the images this little girl had in her two year old head. He went over to her and scooped her into his arms. The wails from the babies pulled at me.

'Sarah, go back to bed with mammy now. I will take the nasty daddy home and put him to bed. He will never come back. Humph is safe, don't you worry about that.'

I lay wide eyed beside my comforted children listening to the pub door being closed. Then some scuffling, a car door slamming. I eased Sarah from my arms and went to the window just in time to see a white van pull away. As it passed the lit window I read the words 'Lawson's Joinery' and a Newcastle phone number. Ed had driven here in a works van. But now Lancelot was taking him away in it. My heart thumped was he alive or dead? What had I got this lovely caring man into? This is what I had feared all these months. What had he said about a letter?

Suddenly I was hit by a burst of blinding clarity.

I lay staring at the ceiling for what seemed like hours. Then I heard footsteps and Freddie barking at a rabbit.

I ran down to the pub just as Lancelot and his dog came in. He looked drawn and exhausted. Blood was turning brown on his clothes, it was Ed's blood. The physical stain more horrifying than the stain he made on my life. He had a red cut across his cheekbone. It was my fault. I had brought my terrible man into this lovely man's life.

'Is he...?'

Lancelot stood still just staring at me as if he had never seen me before. Now he knew I was a liar and he had just made love to a married woman.

'Your husband is not dead Rose. I put him in the Abbey cellars, I left his van outside, then threw the keys into the stream. He'll find them when his thirst hits.' His voice sounded different, thicker and with no love in it.

'I think we have some talking to do. Please make us some tea.'

With a heavy heart I went into the house kitchen and filled the kettle then put it onto the Aga. He obviously felt tricked and I felt like I was being crucified.

He came in and Freddie lay down at his feet. His gaze was intensely brutal.

'Rose, I can tell that you had a cruel and terrible marriage, but why the lies?' There was none of the closeness of earlier that night. He stared at me with a terrible wretchedness.

'Who are you Rose? Not the person I thought I knew and loved. Who are you?'

A weary shadow closed over his eyes. With sadness, I could sense that he was sealing shut doors within himself that he had only just opened.

His voice was not soft or loving. He was talking in a sad but determined manner. Ed had taken him away from me. It would never end. I felt like an elephant had trodden on my heart. Not for a moment did I betray my feelings.

I had no words to explain and anyway my brain would not form any sense. I just turned and left. I was lost once more.

I could not stay here now. This was the ugliest scar of all on my painful life. Lancelot did not deserve this. It was me who had stained his life much more than Ed's blood had stained his shirt. I would pass Violetta over to her real mother in the morning then I would be off. To where, I had no clue. I just knew I had no place here now. I counted the moths crashing against the window for hours before I put out the light.

I slept not one wink.

In the morning I heard Lancelot clatter away to his sheep before I fed Violetta for the very last time. I looked down at this beautiful face and cried. I would miss her so much.

It was a rose petal dawn but it failed to cheer me. I stepped out to see if the fresh air could clear my head. Swallows swooped and wheeled just above my head as they gathered flies to feed their chicks.

Sarah, was feeding a crumpled Humph on the kitchen floor. She had stuck a plaster onto his nose. She cooed to him softly, cuddling and kissing him with thoughts of last night fading like a bad dream. How I wish I could do the same. She had no idea that once again her nasty daddy had ruined our lives. I spooned oatmeal into Ben's mouth, he was irritable, stiffening up as I held him. He turned away from the food and yelled. He would have to go back to bed. The waking of last night had upset him. I tried to at least get some milk into him but he refused even this, stiffening his body and getting more and more fractious.

I lay beside him on the bed smoothing his soft baby hair, so like my mother's. I loved him so much that it hurt. If Ed had taken him last night I would have shrivelled up and died. I snuggled him close, patting his well-padded bottom and singing quietly and slowly. 'Sparkly babies are us....sparkly babies are us', to the tune of Happy Birthday. This song had started when Sarah had her first birthday and dad had given her a balloon filled with glitter. She bit into it and was covered in shiny glitter, but the bang made her scream and I made up those words to sing slowly and softly as I patted her bottom and held her close. It always worked its charm and did now as I watched his eyes droop and his breathing slow. Violetta gurgled in her drawer. When Ben had finally sunk into desperately needed sleep, I eased up and went to her. She beamed at me. I hoped she would give this same love to her real mother.

I had packed her clothes in a box yesterday, before I was thrust into this fug of fear and insecurity again. I picked her up and called down for Sarah to come for her bath. She came in just as the steam was rising and I was taking off Violetta's nappy. She tickled the baby's toes and kissed her.

'Sarah. Remember what I told you, Violetta's first mammy is coming today to take Violetta to live with her.'

A sad shadow passed over her face. 'Can we visit mammy? Me love my baby.'

'I am sure we can pet. She will be happier with her first family. It's where she belongs.' I tried to inject excitement into my voice but it was hard when I felt none.

When the water was right I lifted Sarah into the bath and she positioned herself to hold Violetta as she always did. She began soaping her baby with a soft sponge, a job she regarded as her duty. Usually Ben was splashing at the other end of the bath.

'Where Ben mammy?'

'He is still tired pet so I put him back to bed.'

She did not look up or stop washing the baby but she said. 'Did nasty daddy wake him?'

She had not forgotten. She continually surprised me with her ability to deal with things. I recognised then how much like my father she was.

'Yes darling but all is well now.' It broke my heart to lie like this but I could never tell her that I had to find a new way to hide us from the man who would never rest until he found us.

Chapter Twelve

I dressed Violetta in the white Babygro with the tiny rosebuds all over it. She looked beautiful and smelled like Johnson's baby powder. She felt soft yet firm and so cuddly that I wondered how I would ever hand her over in just one hour. As I breast fed her for what would be the last time I tried to imprint everything about her into my mind. Her tight curls, her wide nose and those eyes that locked onto mine as if to pull love from my very soul. I felt such an energy between us and yet I had to let her go.

Sarah, feeling such a sense of occasion, pulled on the delicate lawn dress we had both fallen for on our last trip to Northallerton when Carol had offered us a lift. She knew how pink suited her and handed me the hairbrush then turned her back so that I might brush her hair into the pulled back side bits she liked tied with ribbon. I put Violetta down on the bed beside me and looked at Ben who was still flat out. He was in a deeply restorative sleep.

I glanced at the clock. Only five minutes before ten o'clock when Melonie and her parents had said they would come for part of my heart.

Somehow, in spite of my thumping chest, I brushed my own hair and put on a light slick of my lipstick, pinching at my cheeks as I looked in the mirror. My head felt cotton-woolly with shock and lack of sleep. My life once again was poisoned by the pernicious being I had married out of fear and disgrace.

How did I ever think I had the chance of a decent life? The past few months had started to salve and plaster over the horrors and hurts of my life. Now that plaster had been viciously ripped off taking extra skin as it revealed the septic, putrid, maggot-writhing truth. I would always belong to Ed.

I heard a car crunch at stones in front of the pub.

This was it. The moment I had longed for and dreaded since that very first moment I had held Violetta to my breast. I held her close now as I followed the clattering footsteps of my excited daughter down the stairs. She stood at the door of the house looking back and up at me in an urging to quickly turn the sneck and see the new family of the baby she had called hers.

Three people stood nervously on the step. My eyes met Melonie's, the woman who had grown Violetta in her body and who now deserved to have her in her arms. Behind her was an anxious looking lady. She was of a butterball build, a kind woman who fed others and herself well. She held onto the arm of a tight lipped man with greying hair and a proud stance. All their eyes fell onto Violetta. The women to feast on the pleasure of a baby belonging to them and the man's to check if he could ever love this child whose existence had rocked his world. Did he know the father was white? Is this why his glare tore around us all as if to examine us all for the truth.

I stepped back to allow every one into the house kitchen. Sarah looked at Melonie and smiled. 'Are you my baby's first mammy?'

Melonie managed a smile but her words were slow as if she was only now realising how much we loved her baby.

'I am, I will love her as much as you do so not to worry. I have a new pram and lots of new clothes. Don't I mother?' She turned to the woman whose eyes had never left Violetta.

I then did something I did not want to do and it took every ounce of my strength. I held out Violetta and placed her into Melonie's arms. As she took her baby tears welled up and dropped onto the white sprigged Babygro. Her chest heaved as she blurted out months of a mother's agony without her child. She breathed in the smell and held her baby so tightly I was worried but I had to allow this outpouring to happen. Melonie's mother stepped forward and her arms went around her weeping daughter. Melonie eased back and placed Violetta into her arms and the look of wonder glowed from her. She seemed to have been sprinkled with the magic fairy dust of all Grandmothers. I felt a stab to know that my own mother had never experienced this and that Sarah and Ben would never know the pure love only a Granny can inject into a child's life.

'Mother, this is Violetta Rose, your granddaughter.'

Sarah clung to my legs so I lifted her so she could have the same view as I had.

The man took it all in but still stood back, tight lipped and straight backed.

'Time to go now,' His voice was a deep base and it brought reality into the room. He turned to go back out to the car. When we heard a door bang shut all three women shared a look.

'Do not worry Rose. My husband is a proud man who has been hurt by this new twist to his life, but he loved Melonie to distraction when she was born and still does. As soon as he takes Violetta into his arms he will feel that same family pull that I do. He is a good man struggling with his feelings. He will be a wonderful grandfather.'

Sarah had been taking it all in quietly. 'Can we visit my baby?'

Melonie's mother bent towards her. 'I can see what a great job you have made of looking after the baby we all share and you are welcome at our house anytime. We would be proud to have you there.' Her eyes turned to me and she pulled me close. 'Thanks for keeping this a secret Rose.' She whispered into my ear, I knew then that she realised the implications if I had gone to the police.

We all walked out to the car where Melonie's dad sat in the driver's seat staring straight ahead. He had opened the two back doors which allowed his family to carefully get in with Violetta snuggled into Melonie's arms. The beam from her told me it would be fine. I could not take my gaze from the baby I had nurtured for these past months and yet I had to let her go from my arms but she would stay in my heart always.

'Sarah. We have something for you.' Melonie said offering a box wrapped in bright paper.

My sad faced little girl took it and I bent into the car to give Violetta her last kiss and wish her all the things I could never have given her. My eyes met Melonie's and she mouthed words we both knew were inadequate. 'Thank you.' She handed me a card in a sealed envelope.

I shut the car door, took Sarah's hand and watched as the car turned and took away our precious baby into her new life.

The surprise parcel under Sarah's arm took second place to her stunned and sorrowful look.

'Let's get inside and see what the nice lady gave you.' She plodded in and put the box on the table. I could see she was as sad as I was.

'Shall I help you open it pet?' she nodded and I tore at the Sellotape to reveal a box. I held it up to show her the beautiful black baby doll wearing a nappy and sucking a dummy. Sarah did not put out her hands so I removed the doll from its box. It felt soft. I almost cried at the sensitivity and kindness of Melonie. I knew then for certain that Violetta would be well cared for. The card was adorned with simple roses and inside was written an address and telephone number, underneath was written; 'I have no words.'

Sarah did not react as I put the doll into her arms. Slowly, she walked to the sofa, climbed up and snuggled into the corner. Her face turned away from not only me but the world that had taken away her baby. I had to let her work it out.

It broke my heart. Her arms were full of the doll and mine now felt empty. I felt an overwhelming urge to fill them with baby chubbiness.

Wiping tears from my cheeks I ran up the stairs to check on Ben, hoping to get him bathed and ready so we could go for a brisk walk to blow away the cobwebs and sadness.

The bedroom door was ajar which puzzled me as I knew I had shut it to keep the noise out. I went past the bed to open the curtains then turned to get my son.

He was gone.

Chapter Thirteen

Had he rolled off onto the carpet? I checked frantically. Had he finally learned to crawl and gone into the bathroom? It was empty. Lancelot's room then? I flung open the door shouting his name. I ran down the stairs. Had he managed those? I tore around the house yelling 'Ben! Ben! Ben!' He was nowhere.

My soul retreated to other times. To beery breath and scrabbling for food. To the imprisonment of my very being.

The shock left me removed from reality, yet reality is what I had to act in. I tried desperately to focus my mind.

I dashed into the pub kitchen...then the pub. The door was swinging open. There was a strong smell of whiskey. I noticed the shelf where usually there stood three bottles, it was empty. One bottle was smashed against the bar. Shards of glass lying in pungent gold liquid. My heart caught on a fresh wave of pain.

There was only one person who could have done this.

The searing panic of a mother who had lost a child macerated my brain. I could not think. I could not breathe. Panic clawed at my stomach. I had to get my baby back. Ed was drunk and cruel. Vindictive and revengeful.

And he was driving.

A car pulled up and Carol got out. 'Have I missed the big event…' she took in my ravaged look and stopped. 'What is it?'

She put her hand out to my arm but I pushed it away.

'Look after Sarah for me please!' I called, already running in the direction I thought my baby might be. I do not know what terror pushed adrenalin into my muscles but I ran faster than I have ever run before. I dashed over rocks and grass, scrabbled over walls and tumbled down steep hills in a panic of fear. Desperate and ragged breath clawed inside my lungs. It was stupid but I had no control. I feared for the life of my baby. I had to save him.

I ran onto the moors where the wind whipped my hair into my face. I lost sight of the pub and any roads. I was frantic and out of control. Where was he? My precious baby in the care of a drunken violent man. I came to woodland lower down and I burst through trees, twigs and thorns tearing at my face and legs. I hurled myself on, my lungs straining for oxygen I hardly had time to take in.

Terrible and tangible memories threw themselves through my whirling mind. I know what he did to me. What could he do to a helpless baby?

I felt a strong arm clutch at my elbow and I flung around ready to attack with the last breath in my body.

'Stop! Stop!'

It was Lancelot. I threw myself into his arms.

'I came home for lunch and Carol told me you had run out like a demon. What is it?'

'Ed has taken Ben!'

'Right! I have the Landy up on the road. Come on. We will have a better chance in that.'

Freddie barked a welcome when he saw me but everything seemed outside of the dark lead coffin of my mind.

We sped over bumps and tussocks and big rocks as we left the road. 'This is the short cut to the Abbey.' Lancelot was concentrating on the mad driving. He was prodded by the same desperation as I was.

        'Where does Ed live?'

'What?' My brain would not function through the severe pain.

'I need to know so I can go in that direction!' He yelled above the rattle of the vehicle. My heart tore free of my chest in fear.

My voice came out wracked in desperation. He turned the Landrover around and sped on. We clattered over cattle grids searching over stone walls, sheep and hedges which blurred at the very edge of my dazed yet frantic mind. This could not be happening.

Lancelot floored the accelerator. 'Look to your left!' he yelled jerking the wheel round and throwing my shoulder against the metal door. My sore eyes stretched open to take in what we were heading for.

The van was in front of us. The Land Rover skidded to a dust raising stop. I could hear Ben wailing in hunger and fright. We ran to the doors and tried to yank one open but they were locked. I started to bang on the window but Ed just put two fingers up and Ben wailed louder.

Lancelot ran to the Landrover and opened the back door to lift out a jack. I knew he was going to smash the windows.

Ed must have seen him in the rear view mirror as he flung open the door, knocking me to the ground, then bent to grab Ben and ran towards the ravine. Ben shrieked. I ran after them but stopped dead when Ed reached the edge of the cliff and held my baby over as if to drop him into the rocky river below.

'For God's sake Ed, Ben is hungry and cold. Just pass him to me.'

The hood on his anorak was blowing around his face, he pushed Ben into his jacket then zipped it up as far as it would go.

'There, he will be warm beside his dad, and if you two buggar off I can get him to a shop and feed the noisy sod.'

He stepped back catching his heel on a rock and stumbled. I screamed but he caught a gnarled branch of an old hawthorn tree. Lancelot ran towards him stopping suddenly when he saw how near the edge Ed stood.

'Just give me the baby and you can go home.' He held out his arms, but this only angered Ed further. I saw fierce determination tighten his mouth.

All I could see of Ben was his red wailing face with the tiny teeth catching the light as his mouth opened and shut. His little arms were moving frantically inside the coat. He wanted me…I had to comfort my frightened son. I took two steps with my arms outstretched.

Ed took one step back and disappeared. My sense of dread suddenly turned into full blown alarm. Blood thumped in my ears

'Oh my God!' I screamed and dashed to the edge. At the bottom were jagged rocks and then the river…but no Ed or Ben. It was quiet. This silence was more terrifying than Ben's screaming.

Lancelot lay flat and looked down, I fell to my stomach and saw what he saw.

Chapter Fourteen

Ed was hanging down, caught on the roots of the hawthorn tree by his hood. He was choking and so was my baby.

I swivelled so that my feet were over the edge, I had to get my baby…my baby…my baby.

I felt Lancelot's arms grip me roughly and pull me up. 'Run to the Landy, get the rope Freddie uses as a bed. Quick!'

I have never run so fast over the few yards. Dog smell whooshed out to me as I yanked the back door open, the rope was heavy and covered in hairs but I pushed it over my shoulder and ran back. Freddie overtook me and ran to his master. Lancelot was at the base of the sturdy hawthorn tree pulling and pushing at it. He yanked the rope from me and tied one end to the gnarled trunk and the other under my arms. I was terrified but it was something I had to do.

'Rose, you won't be strong enough to pull me back up so you will have to go down to help them. OK'

I nodded and he wrapped the rope around his wrist and eased me over the edge, dangling and out of control until I shouted that I was there. The rope burned into my flesh but I thought only of Ben. He was growing blue in the face so tight was the zip around his throat. I put out my hands and even then...even when I was trying to save the life of my son, Ed kicked and flayed his fists at me.

'Stop it Ed. He is choking!'

He looked surprised then and I realised that as he couldn't see him he did not know that the zip was digging in and tight around the neck. The weight of them both was dragging them down.

'Let me ease the zip so he can breathe Ed.' I said the words gently as I could and put my hands out. I supported Ben's head so the pressure was taken off and pulled gently at the zip. I did not want him to fall out.

I gripped my baby with one hand summoning all the strength I had ever had in my entire life. It was all there, super human effort seemed to flow into my arms. I eased the zip down a few inches at a time until he was free. I held his limp baby body to my chest and it was then that Ed's anger flared as it always did and he yanked so hard to try to take Ben from me that the zip opened completely right to the bottom of his anorak. This took away any support he had from his coat hanging by the hood and he tipped forward, his weight was too much so that his arms shot out of the sleeves and he seemed to somersault down leaving the hood still caught on the pointed root. He crashed twice into jagged rock before he hit the bottom. I had to look. He lay awkwardly with his legs at impossible angles.

'Up Lancelot! Up.'

The rope tore into my flesh until my head was level with Lancelot's boots. He could not leave loose of the rope to take Ben from me so I had to scrabble with my one free arm until the tension was off. My baby never seemed heavier. I turned Ben in my arms as Lancelot loosened the knot. He was limp, his lips had a blue tinge but I could detect slight breathing. He was not conscious.

Leaving the rope and Ed we ran to the Landrover.

'I know where the hospital is in Harrogate, my mother died in there, I know it well.'

Over the bumps and rattles of the stony moors, I managed to keep Ben's little head upright and his body cushioned by my breasts. It seemed an age until we reached a smooth road and the traffic of the town. Lancelot drove through three red traffic lights and swerved around people crossing the road, nothing would stop him. At last he skidded into the emergency bay and ran out shouting for help. Two nurses and a doctor came running, took Ben from me and disappeared into a mass of corridors and smells I did not know. The loss of my baby from my arms jerked tears into my heart and I wailed.

I was pulled into a circle of masculine arms. They held up my shaking and weak body. 'He is in the best hands Rose.'

'But I want him, I should be with him.' I wailed.

A nurse appeared with a clipboard, she gave me one shot of empathy from her eyes then switched them to business.

'We need some details from you...'

'How is he,' I interrupted, 'where is he?'

'He is in surgery and I will take you to him as soon as I am able. Please wait here.' She opened a door to a private room with six chairs and an old magazine strewn Formica table. I was still in agonies of waiting when Lancelot came back from finding a public phone to ring Carol. He swung into the room and I stood up.

'Any news?'

I shook my head.

'Carol tells me that Sarah is fine, she is going to take her to her own house to distract her. She has an old Jack Russell there needing hugs.'

We sat down lost in our own private worries. The only sound was the moving of the second hand on the wall clock. Each tick sounded like life was ending. I froze into my deeply buried mind.

As the door burst open the same nurse would not allow her eyes to meet mine. 'You can see your son now.'

'How is he?' I asked but she walked her special nurse's shoes so fast I do not think she heard.

To see your baby with tubes up his nose and machines surrounding his still body is to have your heart sink to your feet. I rushed forward to stroke his brow but he did not react.

'He is resting. The best thing you can do is let him, you need to recover too. Come back in the morning.'

There was nothing that could make me leave my baby alone. We found the public phone again and I talked to Sarah who told me she was having a holiday with Carol and Boo who was old and grey around her lips and had to be lifted out into the garden. I told her how lucky she was and that Ben and I were fine. My hope was that she would never find out what her father had done and how ill Ben had been. I would think of some story to explain why we were away when I took Ben home. I thanked God for Carol.

Lancelot made sure I had enough pillows and a blanket to make my stay tolerable in the upright green chair beside Ben's bed. He left for a while and reappeared with sandwiches and crisps and a bottle of milk.

'Sorry, this is all I could get. I have to go back to sort stuff out.' he said smoothing my brow. 'Let me know when he wakes up.' I thought then that he meant his sheep and his pub. It wasn't until later that I knew just how much he was taking off my shoulders.

Ben did not wake up. His eyes, the eyes that brightened when he saw me or Sarah and reminded me so much of my mother stayed shut forever.

I wailed my agony of loss into the sky. I sounded like a wounded animal. There had never been a pain like that of a mother whose child had died. Never.

Naked distress distorted my face, my body lost its strength. I no longer wanted this life that injected such pain into my veins.

The doctors explained that it was only a machine that made my baby's tiny chest move up and down, that Ben, the essence that made him so alive, his very soul had already left his chubby, soft body. The hood had cut off his air supply.

He suffered from lack of oxygen...he was brain dead. I agreed to let the doctors turn off the machine which gave him false breath. I suffered strange sensations barrelling into me...crushing me. An ancient inconsolable despair that shredded me from my soul to my heart as it engulfed me. I was gaping with the agony of loss.

I spoke to the police without emotion, without anything, I was drained and utterly helpless. I had made and adored that beautiful boy. How could his existence be separated from mine?

I would never wrap my arms around my bouncing baby boy again, never have his weight on my hip, his sweet mouth at my breast. I had grown this little person in my own body. I had nurtured him. I was supposed to be able to save him. I tried. I couldn't; of that I was guilty. I was spiked on a meat-hook through my very being.

I wailed his name to the sky. 'Ben! Where are you? Ben! Ben! Ben!' It tore me to shreds. How could my baby be warm in my arms and then not even exist? Where was he? His tiny hold on life had snapped. He was gone...gone...gone.

I just wanted to loosen my grip on reality and follow him, I wanted to sail into death with him, my baby boy. Only the image of Sarah saved me. We buried him in the same churchyard as my mother and I hoped that somehow she would be looking after him in the same way she had looked after me. My father, saddened that I had not run to him with my troubles, asked me to move in with him. But I needed the peace and beauty of the Dales and he needed the love of the kind woman he loved in return.

As I left his house I turned, who was that with the red, swollen, grief devastated face in the mirror. My soul was gouged by an angry ocean of anguish, the waves of which were a thousand feet tall crashing relentlessly on my pain. My arms ached to hold my baby. My hip wanted that weight of my son sitting on it as he kicked his legs in pleasure. Gone were the tiny teeth and the funny question mark hair. Gone where?

Lancelot took me home. I could never find the way as I took no notice of what was outside myself and Sarah whose face seemed permanently crumpled. Everything was bleak and hollow, sounds filtered through the lead coffin of my grief. How could life go on when my baby was dead? How could the stones lie on the road? The branches blow in the wind as they always did? Did they not know that the world had ended? Why hadn't everything stopped? That kind and caring man put me to bed and I stayed there for three days. He took Sarah on the trips to show her what Freddie did with the sheep or left her with Carol so that I could weep.

Nothing could lift me from this deep pit I had slid into. It was as if my heart was beating outside my body. Sobbing uncontrollably, I was locked into some dark place my heart had never shown me. A new day crept in from the east and my baby was not here to see it.

Lancelot ran a bath and ordered me into it. He left Sarah and me until we were wrinkled and then shouted through the door that breakfast was on the kitchen table in five minutes. He took in our limp, damp bodies as we flopped into the chairs ignoring his creamy scrambled eggs and bacon. We managed a few half-hearted forkfuls and drank lots of tea.

'How are you feeling today Mr Humph?' he said sitting next to the bear on his cushioned chair. 'Oh too tired to speak, Sarah will tell me though won't you?' He fixed his warm eyes on my daughter, encouraging her to speak.

She lifted her eyes to him and said. 'Humph is sad and floppy same as us.'

She slid off her chair and threw herself at Lancelot who embraced her and let her cry big fat tears. We were both grey skinned and devoid of normality. My mind and body were frozen ridged.

Sarah could not understand why she'd had two babies and now she had none. I could not understand it either. How had my plan to free my children from the awful life I had birthed them into end in death? I should have stayed in my awful marriage. That way I would have still had my baby boy. If I had known it was a choice between misery and this bone aching grief, I would have stayed. I would have taken the beatings and fought to give my children a good life, made sure they never saw the abuse or the drinking, the self-obsession, the neglect. My arms would have been enough for them surely. Even as I thought this I knew it would never have been possible. But this...this?

I could never go to Lancelot's bed again yet he helped me in every way he could.

He closed the pub, without a barmaid or a cook it could not work and he said he was too busy with worming his flocks anyway but I knew he was doing it to take pressure off me.

He let me grieve with my daughter while he handled everything. I was fed his chicken vegetable soup, I ignored it at first but gradually ate a little and then enough to make me function. Mostly, I just lay in bed with Sarah and Humph whose ear was always wet as he lay in Sarah's tear wracked embrace. Every day I woke to find the precipice still yawning at my feet.

Babs was shamed and sacked. She had stolen money from Lancelot and my baby from me. Lancelot had driven her home when she had turned up for work, told her angry father exactly what she had done and told her he would not tell the police as long as she stayed away from us forever.

After a month, when I was at last able to drag myself a few steps, Lancelot asked if he could take me to see my dad and sort out my house sale.

The mornings mumbled themselves awake. At 8am after a sleepless night, Sarah and I climbed into the front seat of the Defender and listened as Freddie jumped into his ring of rope. The same rope that I had hung from to save my son's life. I was lost in the feeling of my empty arms with Sarah leaning into me sucking at Humph's ear. She did not want to go to our old house either. Lancelot fired up the engine then he looked at my raw and ragged self. My baby's death leaked into my life like a stain that could never be removed.

'What shall we do first Rose? Your flowers will wilt if left too long.'

I had gathered the last roses of autumn and arranged them with hydrangea heads and the parsley flowers for Ben. 'The...church please.' I could not bring myself to say the word grave in relation to my baby. As we trundled towards the road he looked at me.

'You mean the grave Rose. You must say the words, 'my son has died and we are going to his grave'. You cannot heal until you accept these truths. His words were arrows into my heart but I knew he was right.

He was wise and meaning to help but my mouth seemed welded shut.

On the journey of an hour and a half I did not speak. He pointed out interesting things to Sarah in an effort to lift her spirits and she reacted slightly to ponies in fields and rabbits in hedgerows.

Freddie leapt gleefully around the gravestones sniffing new and exciting smells of a place he had never been. How I envied him as my heart dragged on the path along with my shoes. Lancelot filled the vases he had brought with water at the tap near the gate and I divided the flowers into two bunches for the family I loved, buried only three graves apart. The churchyard spread down the hill with magnificent views of the Durham countryside climbing away and up from the valley. We could see the woods where I grew up and I scanned them thinking of how innocent I was then. I carefully avoided the little copse where my guilt was created along with my fear of being found out. As we neared the tiny grave I started to shake and Lancelot took my elbow steering me on. How could my little smiling, drooling baby be lying there in that cold ground? I cried with everything but tears.

The October wind whipped my hair around my face and Sarah clung to my leg. She helped place the flowers on the bare soil, it was the closest we could get to the one we wanted in our arms.

We left Sarah with my dad, the two were delighted to be together and I was heartened to see such mutual joy as we left for the task I wished I could avoid.

The estate agent was arriving at noon so I had an hour to pick up anything I might need. The police had given me the keys and as we drove up it seemed so incongruous to see Lancelot and Freddie in what had become my past. I was embarrassed to let them see the life I had run away from. The Landrover too looked out of place in the sooty terraced street.

'Are you all right?' Lancelot asked as I opened the door to plunge into my old pain. I managed a nod and then stepped out to smell the coal smoke and the crumbling bricks. The peeling paint on the full height door into the tiny yard creaked and I plodded in to see old newspapers and beer cans blowing about on the cracked concrete. The door was right in front of my face but my hands shook so much I could not get the key into the hole. The place would be how it was when Ed had left it not knowing he would never return.

My hand seemed to take over to turn the key and push the door open into my awful past.

Lancelot was right behind me and I thought of what he would think of how I had lived before he ever knew me. The bin was overflowing with fish and chip papers and beer cans. Drained lager bottles almost filled the work surfaces leading my eye to three empty whisky bottles in the sink. The old twin-tub washing machine, pulled out of its home beneath the bench stood lopsided and full of dirty water and Ed's work clothes. That loose caster had finally come off. I turned the switch but it only proved what I had thought, the machine had finally given up in its old age.

I turned to look at Lancelot but his eyes were not on the mess but on me, I think I saw understanding and compassion in his eyes. I pulled in a ragged breath of old feelings and stepped into the sitting room. Old newspapers scattered around the easy chairs and the floor with even more lager bottles. The fire had long gone out and smelled of old burned paper blown out of the grate by a strong downward wind. The photo I wish I had burned still sat on the mantelpiece covered in soot and dust, I hoped Lancelot would not notice it. The frame clattered as I turned it face down.

There was a rap on the door and Lancelot opened it thinking that it must be the estate agent who had come early. My heart lifted when I heard the voice of Jane from next door. A farm Landrover in a city street could only be a source of curiosity.

'EEE lass! Come here. You poor, poor bairn. What you had to go through and now this.' She pulled me to her and I breathed in that lovely old smell of her Lily of the Valley and home baked scones. 'Eee but there has been a scandal round here, I am so glad you were out of it. The Evening Chronicle splashed it all over, I thought I'd never see you again pet.'

This was the one person apart from my dad who had known and loved Ben, I loved her for this as well as other kindnesses she had shown me in my darkness. But she could never shine through what I was feeling now.

When I eased from her welcome embrace I said. 'This is Lancelot, I am the cook in his pub. We are meeting the estate agent soon.' She shook his hand politely.

Jane looked about. 'Right', she said rolling up her sleeves. 'Let's get this cleaned up. You'll never sell it in this tip.'

We took bin bags from beneath the kitchen sink and the two of them started clearing with much clanging and clinking. I had to face going upstairs but my feet were slow and heavy. My legs hardly held me up and I had to force my shaking hands to turn the handles. I opened the door to the children's room first with gulps of fear and pain. It was sad to see the little covers turned back exactly where I had left them six month ago. The drawers I had dragged open to yank out their few clothes still hung gaping and empty. I lifted the blue blankets and thin pillow from Ben's cot and buried my face into them. His smell was long gone but I found a tiny sock lost and alone. I started to bellow with grief and need.

I pushed the lone sock into my bra, near to my pulsating heart then steeled myself to go into the other bedroom. It smelled stale and the curtains were shut. I pulled them open and dust flew everywhere. I turned to see the bed, unmade and grubby. On the table beside it were cheap pearl earrings and hairbands sticking with black hairs. It no longer felt like my bed, some other woman had been here.

I steeled myself enough to go downstairs for a bin bag, only I would clear upstairs. I saw Jane and Lancelot whispering together and watched for a while with a lax enraptured face, he took in all she said. She was telling him of my life before him. They looked up when they heard me and got back to their tasks.

I pushed all the bedding from the double bed into bags and cleared everything lying about. Two pairs of Wrangler jeans and a jacket I had never seen before lay in a heap on the floor with a pair of knickers and a mismatched bra in a very large size.

I made the bed and cot in the children's room with a breaking heart.

 Next, I brought the stuffed bags downstairs and collected spray polish and dusters, this time they did not hear me as they were using the old Hoover dad had given me when he bought a new one. It was noisy and inefficient, I knew all the tricks to get it to work but wanted extra time upstairs. I polished all the furniture which was not much but I was only avoiding opening the wardrobe door until I had gathered strength.

Flinging open the door I saw, lopsidedly hanging there, the suit Ed got married in and wore at the children's Christenings, his few trousers and summer shirts, hung up but not ironed. Scrunched at the bottom was a bundle of the tatty clothes I had worn when I lived here along with the scarf I used to hide the friction burns on my neck. I pushed them all into the same rubbish bag. I dragged open all the drawers and pressed underwear and socks on top of everything else. I heard a rattle and put my hand into the back to find the tiny stub of that pale pink lipstick I had bought when I was working, the one he accused me of using to ensnare the 'fancy-man' of his imagination. I could not bear anything to be left. It was easy to clear the bathroom and clean everything in it but much harder to rid myself of the memories of bathing my two babies in that old white bath whilst sniffling back the hurt and tears from the bashing he had given seconds before. Two minutes before the agent came I had vacuumed the bedrooms and the stairs.

Jane was wiping the windowsills and Lancelot wiping out the last kitchen cupboard. I stared at the avocado coloured Formica and remembered when Ed had fitted it. He was a perfectionist in this. I had wanted cream units but he did not listen, in this as in everything else of his mean life, he did exactly as he pleased.

There was a knock on the door, Lancelot opened it with the last of the bags in his fists. 'I'll leave you to it, I need to take Freddie for a run.'

Jane followed him out saying she would put the kettle on next door. Thank goodness the agent was on time. I could never bear being alone in this horrible house. He was brief and efficient, he had seen lots of terraced houses just like this one. As I closed the door behind him my heart sank and my instincts were to follow him immediately. But there was one last thing. Only I could do it.

The warmth of Jane's kitchen soothed me a little. As I listened to the tinkling of cups and the slicing of bread she so deftly used to make cheese and pickle sandwiches, I let out a huge sigh. In this house, just a wall away from the awful life of the house next door, was normality. It sunk into my very being and soothed me.

'Where is Bobby this morning Jane?'

'Ah, he has been taken down his allotment by the young men along the street, well I say young, they are in their fifties but that is young to us. He'll be back with his tongue hanging out and a turnip and cabbage for supper.'

She placed three cups and plates around the lace covered table. 'Sit you down lass. It will all be over soon. I am glad he is dead and although you are too kind a soul to say so I bet you are too. He treated you badly, just remember that there was something wrong with him…not you. Good people do not go around destroying the lives of others.' She put both creased hands on the teapot and poured.

'Now then, before that handsome young man comes back tell me everything.'

I sipped hot tea and told her as much as I could without distressing her too much.

'And 'im…is he just your boss?'

She had a hopeful glint in her eye. I tried to ignore it but it was a light moment in all my sorrow.

'Hey you! Now what were you two whispering about when I came downstairs earlier? Eh?'

'Oh I was telling him what a terrible life that bugger had led you and how miserable you had been. Did I do wrong?' She looked so worried that I shook my head.

I was still in a fug of grief but I allowed a little of the comfort she offered to touch my heart. She had just poured me more tea when Lancelot walked in rapping his knuckles on the door as he did.

'Ah, sit down lad,' she said pushing a cup towards him. 'I made you a little sandwich.' I saw his eyes widen at the doorstep size bread before him but he took it in good humour.

We were all hungry, the sandwiches disappeared rapidly. Jane stood up to boil the kettle on the old stove. 'What did the agent say pet?'

'Oh, he took photos...said I should get about four thousand pounds for it. I'll have to repay the mortgage from that of course. I gave him all the keys, I never want to set foot in that place again.'

'Who can blame you lass? You just concentrate on that lovely girl of yours and getting your looks back.' She turned to Lancelot. 'She were a looker when she first came here, that bastard soon bashed it out of her, wore her down and drained her spirit.' Lancelot settled his eyes on me. 'I have seen it Jane, she was lovely just before this tragedy but it has taken its toll. I will make sure she gets her bloom back, don't you worry about that.' I saw something in his eyes then, something I would have welcomed a few weeks ago. But now? No, not now.

We were in the Landy again, weighed down with home-made scones and fairy cakes, after Freddie had bits of sausages fed to him in a farewell feast. Lancelot sighed as he pulled away, I noticed this even though I was waving madly to Jane. Something had changed between us.

Chapter Fifteen

I was thrilled to see how Maureen had entertained Sarah by helping her make a dressing up box of her old clothes and scarves. Even Humph was swathed in silk and wore two big gloves on his fat paws.

'Mammy! We are going to a dance.' Sarah yelled as soon as we entered. She was wearing a cream satin slip tied at the waist by a bright blue bow. Over her arm was a handbag which she opened to show me two old lipsticks and a powder compact. Maureen plopped a red beret onto Humph's head and we all laughed. It was a while since I had seen my daughter's face not streaked by tears.

'Thank you Maureen, I used to love playing dress up.'

'Oh no, she is so welcome, can you take this box of clothes back…you may have to? We cannot separate her from them.'

Sarah clonked about in black patent leather high-heel shoes with a gap at the back, wafting Maureen's Apple

Blossom scent as she went. It was the first time I had seen
her smile since she lost her brother and Violetta. I felt a
tugging at the corners of my own mouth. She was all I had
now and I would fight tooth and nail to make her happy.

Dad cuddled me fiercely as we prepared to leave,
Lancelot was helping Maureen put the clothes box into
the Landy. Then we watched them from the window as
they walked about the garden to let Freddie have a run.
'Maureen thinks it is too soon to tell you with…well you
know. But she is moving in tomorrow.' Some happiness
pierced my pain, he deserved a new life, 'I am thrilled
dad, she is so lovely.'

Lancelot walked in then and smiled at us hugging. 'You
must bring Maureen down to see us, it is only under two
hours and I am setting your daughter back to work just as
soon as she has worked out a winter menu.

'Aye son, you just keep her nose to the grindstone.' I
could see worry behind his eyes as he hugged me again
and came to watch us drive off. 'You take care of yourself
mind, not just that little lass of mine…you, my big lass.'

Sarah insisted on travelling in her finery and as she sat on
my knee she waved Humph's gloved paw wildly as her
Grandad blew kisses to us all.

Silence fell on us as we headed towards Yorkshire. I had
a lot to think about. The feeling of Ben's tiny sock safe in

my bra comforted me and distressed me in equal
measures. How could his sock be here and him not be?
How was he in a different place to me who had made him,
cared for him and loved him with all my heart?

I could not be sure of how the man beside me thought of
me now, he was re-opening the Lark and Lamb and I was
glad of it. I still had a job at least.

Lancelot only spoke when I asked him if we could stop at
the old abbey.

'Are you sure...that is where...' he said no more and I did
not know if he meant my trials when I was forced to
shelter there or that he had taken Ed there on that terrible
night. I did not know why I wanted to go...I just knew
that there was a healing force there that got me through
and I wanted to feel it again.

The journey was much quicker than the one I had trudged
on that wet night when I was lost and forlorn. As Lancelot
drove near he said to Sarah. 'Freddie has learned a new
work trick with the sheep. Would you like to see it?'

She beamed her pleasure. 'Mammy is going for a walk.'
He said turning off the engine. I planted her down in the
autumn sun in all her finery, she pushed Humph's gloves
further onto his paws and we turned to see the back door
of the Landrover open and Freddie leap from his new rope

bed which had a cushion donated by Jane pushed inside the coil. Lancelot gave me a concerned look then followed his dog and my daughter over the hill and I heard his commands when he must have seen sheep.

The October wind had not yet whipped the leaves from the trees down the hill where I had foraged for food. I could see the golden beech and yellow willow in front of the red maples. I had watched those leaves, bright green and unfurling, as we had gently swung on that branch. I could almost feel Ben in my arms…but only almost. They had changed and I had changed. These trees had seen life in vivid green and sunny skies and soon they would have bare branches and apparent death until the spring when it would all be the same for them.

For me, it would always be different. My baby would not be re-appearing fresh and new. He was gone. Like his father. I could only hope that he was not with him, the one who had taken his little life in selfish hate and spite.

I took the path to the ruins, this time my shoes did not let every stone hurt me. I was dry not wet and I had focused on hope instead of desperation. As my eyes adjusted to the gloom I saw my stones where I had lain the babies away from the rats. I knew Ed had been put here to recover from his drunkenness and his bang from my pan. That is the reason I had wanted to come. I'd had no input into his funeral, leaving that to his mother, the only one who cared. I had something to say to Ed and then I would forget about him and the pain he made me suffer for years along with this excruciating longing I would endure for the rest of my life.

I had to forgive him. The very word stuck in my throat. I wanted to hate him, to savage him with words he deserved but I knew it would be a life sentence for me unless I let it all go. I took my mind back to that first day I ever met him. I worked through that New Year's Eve party when he first asked me to dance to the Beatles 'I Wanna Hold Your Hand', right up to today. I could not let my heart be blackened by the clinging soot of his personality. I did not think that he ever thought he was a bad person. He did not seem to realise the pain he inflicted with his toxic mind and behaviour.

I tuned in to the energy I felt emanating from these stones that had once been holy to the people who had built an abbey and lived within its walls. There was healing here and I so desperately needed healing. I took out the tiny sock and pressed it to my lips, I would keep it with me forever. I closed my eyes and listened. It sounded different here now, no scrabbling rats and no howling wind. I imagined Ed on a chair on a stage. I was looking down and flicked a switch beside me which flooded him with a spotlight. He looked up but was blinded by the beam but I knew he could hear me as I said the three hardest words of my life. 'I forgive you.'

From my bag I took out the photo I had taken from the frame on the mantelpiece. I crinkled the paper I had hurriedly wrapped it in. I struck three matches before one lit. It burned brightly, melting first Ed's face then mine in my cheap wedding dress that I had had to sell when my babies were hungry. As the last red glow died, I stamped and spread the light ashes around with my foot.

He was gone. He was forgiven.

I let new feelings into my soul where I knew they would work slowly as long as I allowed it. Then, when I knew I would be healed I asked for the same for Ed where ever he was. With that I took my first steps to freedom.

Lancelot was a puzzle, he was kind and gave me tasks he hoped would eat through my grief enough to lift me. He set a date for the opening of the pub and asked me to prepare a winter menu. But I did not know how he felt about me. There was a need for him in my life but so much had happened that I did not know if it was love or something else. I often caught a sideways glance from him but he always shut it down as soon as I turned my face to see. At night Sarah cried and I cried when she slept. Violetta's drawer was just that now, a drawer, back in the chest were it belonged as if it had never been the cradle for another baby I had loved. My breast milk had long dried up with no babies to feed.

One night, after checking on my sleeping daughter, I looked in the mirror at a pale and gaunt face. It made the scar on my lip seem more vivid. I held my finger to my lips as I came out of the bathroom. Lancelot was just coming up the stairs.

He looked at me in concern. 'Is your scar hurting?'

He put his head to one side. 'You never did tell me how you got that. Was it an animal?'

I must have gone pale, I know my legs wobbled, because he led me downstairs to the sofa where he held me in his arms. He was warm and smelled so nice, clean and masculine. I wanted to stay there, sink into his caring but I couldn't. I pulled back and his eyes were so pleading as if he wanted to heal me but he did not know how. Suddenly I wanted to unburden myself of everything. He knew most of what trials I had clawed my way through but not that awful day when not only my face was scarred but my mind.

'When I was twelve, I used to run all day in the woods. I enjoyed nature and loved to pick wildflowers and care for any injured animal I came across. It had been a long winter. I had spent it in our cold house reading in bed. I remember the feel of one frozen hand holding the book out of the blankets and the slight relief of changing it for a warm one, until that too grew icy. At the first hint of sun that spring, when I was looking for new pussy willow to take home to dad who called it 'spring's promise,' I began finding sprung gin traps which had caught rabbits by the paws leaving them to die of hunger in terrible agony. I knew they had been made illegal a few years before as my father had been part of the loud voice against them. I tried releasing the strong metal teeth but I was too weak.'

He looked concerned. 'That is a terrible thing to see, who set those traps?'

'I didn't know. My father was the forester for those woods and I knew he would be angry as he was with all poachers. I ran home but when I entered our garden gate I remembered that he was away at a training course until the next evening. As soon as it was light I got up and dressed and ran out to where I had seen the traps. The stunning dawn chorus faded from my ears as I saw a line of six traps all set to catch badgers, foxes or rabbits, sometimes pheasants, who were innocently getting on with their lives. I took sticks and sprung each one, wincing at the loud snap as the ragged teeth grabbed the stick. All but one that is. The last one was near the broken bit of fence where the path led into the wood. I had the idea to gently pull that trap right to where the poacher would step as he entered the wood to check on his kills. I thought that a dose of his own medicine would teach him a lesson. I knew he would only come when it was dark.'

'So, what happened? Did you cut your lip then?'

'No, it was the next morning. Very early again, I had run to the woods to see what had happened. Dad was home but I never mentioned what I had done. An awful sight came before me. There was a man sitting on the ground with his right foot bleeding between the iron jaws of one of his own traps. He had a knife which he was using to try to open the trap but it did not work. He saw me staring at him and grunted to me to help. I bent down and made a stern look and told him it was his fault and that I hoped he would stop being so cruel now that he knew how it felt to be trapped.

He struck out at me with the knife and caught my lip. Shocked and in pain I ran home.

Later, Dad got him out. He ranted and raved, said he was going to the police. I spent months of sleepless nights waiting for them to drag me from my bed.'

'Of course he never went to the police. He was the criminal, the police would have arrested him. He would have known that.' Lancelot sounded angry on my behalf.

'And have you spent your life worrying about that?'

I nodded, feeling the childish guilt again and how Ed had used it to send me deeper into fear. Somehow, I slept that night.

Carol was kind and kept an eye on us, putting up with my unsmiling face and silence, on trips to Darlington and its shops.

One Monday she asked me if I liked the Lake District.

'I have never been, where is it?'

'Oh my dear, then you have missed one of life's greatest
pleasures, it's only an hour away from here.'

She downed her cup of breakfast tea and looked out of the
window. 'It is a bright November day and soon every leaf
will be blown from every branch but just now the lakes
and mountains will be joined with a spectacular display of
colour. Can you make us a sandwich and a flask of tea?'

As she made several phone calls. I made roast beef and
horseradish sandwiches and packed apples from the trees.
It was ten when we left and I had my eyes opened to
something I had never known existed. She took us first to
Ullswater where we drove around the lake, so near that I
thought we may fall in. The browns and reds of the trees
at the bottom of the hills across the lake reflected in the
water. Slowly, she drove us up Kirkstone Pass where
sheep were grazing really high up and on mountains so
steep Sarah asked if they were glued on. I had never seen
a mountain and was silent as we descended then turned
right onto a steep narrow road.

'This is The Struggle, a road named for obvious reasons.'
She smiled as we went downwards through a narrow gap
between rough stone walls bordering hills with browning
bracken and dying thistles.

The winding road lifted my spirits and to see Sarah struck
dumb with awe was in itself a revelation. Carol stopped
the car in a small pull off and we got out to look down on

a bit of another lake. She pointed to the silver sparkle between the trees.

'That is Windermere, the largest lake. When we have eaten we can drive down into Ambleside and look around the little town.'

We balanced our sandwiches on the dry stone wall as I took beauty into my soul. Carol was a good doctor to know how much this lifted me. Sarah sat Humph on the wall to offer him bread but she accidently knocked him backwards so he tumbled into the dry thistles standing in the well nibbled field. This was a very old wall and I could see it would dislodge if I scrambled over it so I had to walk down the Struggle until I came to a gate I could climb. I sneaked up behind the high wall and decided to give Sarah and Carol a fright by tossing the bear suddenly onto them. There were shrieks of laughter then Humph was propelled straight back to me, his one thin wet ear flapping before hitting me on the head made me laugh. Two faces peeped over the wall at me. I grabbed thistle seeds and blew them up at them but the breeze sent them right back at me so that I was covered in thistledown. This caused so much laughter that I stopped suddenly. Something had shifted, not all of my grief, just a little something like a door to the long journey of recovery. By the time Humph and I had walked back the giggling had subsided. The understanding look on Carol's face was just too much for me, I flung myself into her arms and wailed the sky down. Sarah hugged my legs and cried too. We all wanted Ben but we had to live on.

When we had gathered the strength to tidy away Carol drove us further down The Struggle to Ambleside then around Lake Windermere to the old town. The streets were narrow and quaint with butcher's shops selling real Cumberland sausage they had made that morning. Sarah insisted we took some home for Lancelot and Freddie. Carol bought us some Kendal Mint Cake which was more of a bar of sweet icing which we ate as we watched Sarah feed the ducks and swans with her crusts saved from her picnic. The over excited girl yawned as we got back into the car so we settled her in the back with two cushions and a thistle dotted Humph.

When Sarah fell asleep Carol drove off carefully and I became lost in trying to stop my arms feeling empty by admiring the beauty of the Lake District. There was a silence but I knew Carol was building up to something. She began to ask me questions which I was not sure how to answer, then she asked one I already knew the answer to but I kept quiet…I had been hiding that truth even from myself.

The next day was a busy one. I longed to look at Lancelot closely and for a long time but I could never lift my eyes to his as we worked together to get the Lark and Lamb open with a new menu and a new barmaid. He had a certain reserve about him as if he was keeping something back but we struggled on.

With no conniving Babs to interfere with the
advertisements around the little shops, surgery and
library, seven ladies applied for the job of fronting the
pub. We interviewed them together. Later as we discussed
which lady should have the job I noticed he easily
discarded the young and pretty girls in favour of a
pleasant mother of five who needed money so much that
he was sure she would work hard. Sheila had work-worn
hands, a beaming smile and as we later discovered an
inexhaustible stock of one-liners that had the customers
quipping and laughing all night in unsuccessful attempts
to outwit her. Her hair was brown and neat and her clothes
plain but she came in to collect the food as soon as I rang
the bell and never stole drinks. Her tip jar was always full
and she was never late. Lancelot could not believe how
much smoother everything was.

Despite this and the easy task of making, ahead of time,
big pans of bacon bone and leek broth which had become
the pub favourite, I was tired. One Sunday evening when I
had dashed up to check on a sleeping Sarah at nine pm it
was all I could do to stop myself plopping down beside
her for the night. But I still had apple crumbles to get out
of the oven and treacle tart to portion out.

I was in the middle of a big yawn when Lancelot and
Carol came into the pub kitchen together. 'Oh! Am I
working you too hard?' he smiled. I shook my head but
Carol fixed her eyes to mine then widened them, urging

me to be honest. I ignored her. I drew a big glass of water which I drank quickly.

'It is so hot in here and I was thirsty, that's all.' I said looking away from them both. 'Have you come in for pudding?'

'Yes please, what can we have?' Carol said.

'Please have the crumble, I have enough apples off those trees to feed an army. Every day Sarah and I go out we pick up tons. The leaves are falling now and they are covering the fruit.'

Lancelot laughed as he took two bowls from the cupboard. 'They have always been heavy fruiters, just take the best, the birds will be glad of the rest this winter. Freddie even gobbles them up if he gets the chance.'

'OK, there are some with pecks in and little hedgehog teeth too I think. The cookers are enormous and those Cox's Pippins are delicious, I am eating two a day...only another five hundred to go.'

'I'll take some!' said Carol. 'I can put them in my waiting room for the kids, try to get them off all those sherbet lemons and fruit gums they eat so many of.'

'You'd better, there are two boxes at the back door awaiting your pleasure.' I smiled loving the easy company we all had.

I received an offer on my old house the next week, it seemed quick but was probably because it was under-priced. I didn't care. I just wanted it out of my life. With the promise of my money I asked Lancelot if I could buy the old barn that looked down onto the pub and house. He looked surprised.

'Well if you want it. But you do not have to pay me, it is yours.'

'No. It has to be done properly. I need security and comfort and safety. I want to make a house of our own where no-one can enter.' I could not tell him the half formed plan I held in my sore brain. I had to work out details. My mind was on such a short tether that I felt I could not stretch out into real life. How could I carry out what was only a tiny light of an idea inside of me? I hardly had the fight to breathe. My mind was in a whirl of hope and dread. I had to do this. Would I ever have the strength?

His smile crashed but he said. 'Well you will need planning permission… are you thinking of leaving me here on my own?'

For the first time in weeks our eyes met and I saw something like dread.

'I don't know what I want Lancelot.' I mumbled, turning so that he could not see the truth I did not want him to realize.

'Why are you pushing me away?' He gently took my arm and turned me back. 'I realize that you want independence, but your work is here and you could not leave Sarah sleeping in a barn, however near, whilst you cooked.' His eyes searched mine so I closed them. He saw the tears I felt as they oozed out, he must have as he let go of my arm.

'Come on Rose, we have work to do.' I heard the door to the pub open and knew I was alone. No-one could reach me in the depths of my despair.

I worked. I cooked. I breathed. But all I cared about was Sarah. And my aching grief. How easy it had been to lose a child I had loved. Why not again. At any moment…for any reason.

I was only happy when my daughter was in my arms or at least my sight. My trips up the stairs to check on her became more and more frequent, frantic even. I tried to control how I felt but the clench of horror in my heart would never let me.

I was very tired. Lack of sleep showed on my face and lack of food on my body. I was cooking new and delicious food for the pub but it all turned my stomach, even tasting for seasoning, I had to steel myself just for this but I wretched into the sink with just a tiny taste on my tongue. I was frantically washing out the sink one evening when Lancelot swung into the pub kitchen. I saw him sniff the air at the rancid smell my body had heaved up but I just nodded when he asked me if I was alright.

Every night my daughter and I were wrapped in shared longing for the baby boy we missed so much. His tiny sock was in my bra all day and under my pillow all night. It was all I had of him as a tiny baby, that and the awful memory of how he had died by the selfish and cruel acts of his father. I was feeling sick with the grief of it but I would not tell Carol when she asked me how I was. She was wrong in her guessing...wasn't she?

Lancelot had a look on his face that I could not bear. It was pity, I think. He made me work but not too much. He put the pram away somewhere or maybe he gave it away. I could not bear to see it and now I could not bear not seeing it.

When Mrs Armitage came to do the cleaning I curled up on the bed with Sarah reading her stories from books brought by Carol. She became lost in other worlds, in tales of other lives until they mentioned babies or little boys, then I could not read on...and we had to take another book from a stack we had read before that I knew would not stab me through the heart.

It was cooler now, leaves were blowing around the garden gusting into piles in corners and edges. Servant pounced then disappeared into the crisp golden heaps then waited for Freddie to go by before leaping out at him to roll about and then run off to more autumn fun. We watched from the window as our thinning, miserable bodies could not take the falling temperatures. We were lost in indescribable sadness, on a miserable journey with no end or horizon. Carol turned up then bundled us into her car and drove us unseeing to the shops where she led us to warm coats and jolly scarves with matching gloves. I bought them to please her but we never went out.

I could vaguely see Lancelot talking in a lowered tone to his sister in law, then Carol would try to lift my spirits with suggested trips I would not take. I could hardly take it in as my brain had exploded and scattered like flapping birds.

'You have to join real life Rose. You have so much to give, work for the future…not just for you… for others.' How would I have energy for normal life when I had a leaching fire inside me which was being fed with bits of my broken heart?

'How could he do it? How could he take my child from me Carol, how?' Her arm went about me, 'You can lose your mind trying to understand some-one else's.' She held me until the wracking cries subsided and then tucked us up on the sofa with a blanket. 'There is nothing to do with grief but to go through it Rose. You have to be brave.'

Some good had to come out of everything my dad had told me often. What good could come out of this? I had an idea, a good idea but I did not have the strength to even start to carry it out. I asked Carol if she ever came across abused women, ones who needed help to escape. She told me of two cases she knew of. A tiny light turned on deep, deep in my pain.

Carol brought me a book on grief that I devoured and wept over. It was 'A Grief Observed,' by C S Lewis. Some things went into my head and some did not but it felt good and excruciating in equal measures when his words touched my grief as if he knew it well.

One afternoon, when the wind blew wailing noises around the house I sat with Sarah wrapped in that same blanket on the sofa pulled nearer the stove. Lancelot had gone for a hot bath as he was chilled through checking on his sheep. Freddie as usual had clattered up behind him.

I was smoothing my daughter's brow and singing to comfort her. Suddenly she let out a big wail on a breath she must have stored for ages.

'I want my babies mammy!' I could not stop her crying. My heart broke to know that she felt the same pain I did.

She wailed as if she would never be comforted. There was only one thing I could think of. It was now time to admit what I had been refusing to accept. I pulled her to my tummy, so that her ear was on my belly button.

'Shush now. Put your head here…can you hear anything?' The wailing ceased.

I knew it was too soon for what was in me to leap and box like the others had done.

'Squishing and gurgling mammy, did you eat fishies?'
She was so sweet as she sniffed away her tears. I dabbed
at her wet face then gently eased it back to my body.

'I am growing you a new baby Sarah, there just where
your ear was.' The words struggled through the ache of
longing for Ben.

Putting her ear harder to my tummy. 'Can he cry yet
mammy?'

Freddie flung himself into the room wide eyed and with
tongue lolling. I looked up to see Lancelot standing at the
door. He looked warm from the bath and wore a new blue
jumper, soft and cosy like his face. For the time it took to
take one breath between us we looked at each other, each
trying to dive deeper into the other's eyes. I saw him
glance at the bruise of fatigue beneath my eyes. Some
undeniable force kept our gazes locked together.

Sarah was still concentrating on hearing something deep
and hidden in my body. 'Will the baby have the lovely
daddy mammy? Not the nasty one?'

Understanding flowed between us like a welcome breeze.

He took the few steps to us and kissed her on the head, his
eyes never left mine as he spoke.

'Yes Sarah, the baby will have the lovely daddy. And so
will you, the new baby will belong to us all.'

I felt a flicker of love and hope and a shocking dose of light, like snowdrops pushing through the cold January earth. Was it in my grasp to be loved as I had always longed for? I was alive. All I had to do was keep breathing. Maybe my soul had not been murdered? I felt strength flow into me as Lancelot held my eyes with his. I knew for certain then who it was I had to help.

Ends

August Smith Copyright.

Printed in Great Britain
by Amazon